# MULTIVERSES

## AN ANTHOLOGY OF ALTERNATE REALITIES

ALSO BY PRESTON GRASSMANN
AND AVAILABLE FROM TITAN BOOKS

*Out of the Ruins*

# MULTIVERSES

## AN ANTHOLOGY OF ALTERNATE REALITIES

Edited by

**PRESTON GRASSMANN**

**TITAN** BOOKS

# MULTIVERSES

## AN ANTHOLOGY OF ALTERNATE REALITIES

Print edition ISBN: 9781803362328
E-book edition ISBN: 9781803362335

Published by Titan Books
A division of Titan Publishing Group Ltd
144 Southwark Street, London SE1 0UP
www.titanbooks.com

First edition: March 2023
10 9 8 7 6 5 4 3 2 1

A CIP catalogue record for this title is available from the British Library.

Printed and bound by CPI Group (UK) Ltd, Croydon, CR0 4YY.

"The Duchess . . . was resolved to make a world of her own invention, and this world was composed of sensitive and rational self-moving matter."
**Margaret Cavendish**, *The Blazing World*

"Imagining a world creates it, if it isn't already there."
**N.K. Jemisin**, *The City We Became*

# TABLE OF CONTENTS

# WORLDS IN WAITING:
## AN INTRODUCTION

### PRESTON GRASSMANN

**Even within** our beloved genre of science fiction, so accepting of new ideas and perspectives, there are those who prefer to set limits and guidelines, as if to protect their sacred temples from the vines of strangler trees. Fortunately, there are many more of us who turn to the genre for its inclusiveness, to celebrate the kind of diversity that foreshadows and calls into being a world of heterogeneous complexity. Nowhere is this more apparent than in our celebration of the "multiverse," where divergence and difference are its raison d'être, and whether it's books like *Kindred* by Octavia Butler, the MCU, or the diamond glare of Moorcock's myriad suns, there is something in it for everyone.

Long before the "multiverse" became the pop-culture buzzword of modern science fiction, the notion of other universes and worlds existing in parallel with our own is as old as science itself. A third-century BCE philosopher named Chrysippus made the claim that our world was in a state of eternal regeneration, prefiguring the concept of many universes existing over time. It was part of Ancient Greek atomism, which proposed that colliding atoms could bring about an infinity of parallel worlds. However, it wasn't until 1873 that the word itself made its first appearance in an issue of *Scientific*

*American*, in which William Donovan referred to it in a debate about planetary motion and God: "The Great Mechanic presides over a universe, and not merely a cohering multiverse." Thirty years later, the word reappeared in a lecture by the philosopher-psychologist William James, who referred to the indifference of nature as "a moral multiverse… and not a moral universe." But as with many endeavors in science, the idea of parallel worlds began in early examples of science fiction (or proto-science fiction). In *The Blazing World* (1666), for example, Margaret Cavendish refers to a utopian world that exists parallel to our own. In *Men Like Gods* (1923), H.G. Wells writes about an alternate Earth in a far-future utopia. Despite the abundance of examples in the genre, it wasn't until the publication of Michael Moorcock's *The Blood Red Game* and *Sundered Worlds* that the "multiverse" became a literary phenomenon. From that point on, it took root and broke through the genre like the banyan trees striving for World Tree status, extending into every part of science fiction. Although it appeared in early hard science fiction, like Isaac Asimov's *End of Eternity* and Greg Egan's *Diaspora*, it opened into the alternate histories of Philip K. Dick's *The Man in the High Castle* and Kingsley Amis's *The Alteration*. It emerges in the fantasy of the Chrestomanci series by Diana Wynne Jones and The Dark is Rising sequence by Susan Cooper. It extends outwards, giving rise to new subgenres with works like Paul Di Filippo's The Steampunk Trilogy and William Gibson and Bruce Sterling's *The Difference Engine*. Thankfully, the multiverse is *worlds*-wide, as broad-ranging and all-inclusive as the word itself implies.

At the very core of all science fiction is the question "what if?" What if surgical operations could be performed between one universe and another, as we see in "Banish" by Alastair Reynolds? What if we could view different versions of ourselves in others, as in "Cracks" by Chana Porter? What if a transpacific tunnel had been built after

World War I, connecting the US and Japan, as in Ken Liu's "A Brief History of the Trans-Pacific Tunnel"? The question can be asked of both the past and the future, or a present that offers a multiplicity of choices, of worlds unlike ours. It can be seen in the dream-logic reality of Yukimi Ogawa's "Amber Too Red, Like Ember," and Alix E. Harrow's world of witch-librarians in "A Witch's Guide to Escape: A Practical Compendium of Portal Fantasies." In some form, the question is at the heart of every story in this book, and the myriad answers on offer are never short of compelling. What better way to celebrate the wide-ranging, kick-ass diversity of our genre than with an anthology of multiverse stories. If you yearn for original stories about other universes, alternate histories (and futures), and parallel worlds, then you've come to the right place.

If ever there was a time when we were in need of a multiverse, it's here and now, when all the future worlds of the past have collapsed into some other timeline that some of us would rather escape from. It is with that spirit in mind, with a scope as wide as its title implies, that I've included a broad range of stories here, from a diverse gathering of international voices. I hope you enjoy them as much as I have.

# PARALLEL WORLDS

"Ghosts are, as it were, shreds
and fragments of other worlds"

**Fyodor Dostoevsky,** *Crime and Punishment*

# BANISH

## ALASTAIR REYNOLDS

**The call** came in on a Monday afternoon, a little after three. Within half an hour I had reviewed my caseload for the rest of the week, spoken to my usual surgical team, bribed and arm-twisted colleagues, arranged workarounds where possible, and apologised to those patients whose procedures might need to wait until I returned. By four, I had confirmed my availability and travel arrangements were already falling into place.

I left the hospital, drove home and explained to Fabio that I had been summoned to Geneva.

Fabio watched, leaning against the doorframe, hand on hip as I threw things into a grubby plastic suitcase. I kept an overnight bag on standby but I expected to be away for at least the duration of the window.

"What's the case?"

"A tricky one. Tumour at the base of the brain, hard to reach, and in risky territory."

"Tiger country."

"Exactly." He had been living with me long enough to pick up the lingua franca of surgeons. "We need to get the tumour out without doing too much damage on the way, and make sure the margins are completely clean. Then there's some bone under the skull that doesn't look good on the scans, so that also needs to come out." I paused, dithering over exactly how many pairs of underwear I really needed. "The other side are printing up a ceramic scaffold, ready for when we go in."

Fabio nodded. "But you've done something similar, or they wouldn't bring you in?"

"Three similar ones. Two went pretty well."

"And the third?"

"A disaster." I looked up from my packing. "That still makes me and my team about the best possible hope for this patient."

"Isn't there a version of your team over there?"

"Evidently not, or they wouldn't go to this much trouble." I shoved a ski-patterned winter jumper into the case, then took it out again. It would be much colder in Geneva than Johannesburg, but I doubted that I'd be spending much time outdoors.

"How long do you have?"

"Overnight flight, arriving early morning Tuesday. From what they're telling us, our window stays open until somewhere between Thursday evening and Friday morning. Back by Saturday evening at the latest, I'd imagine." I drifted to my bedside table, thinking of taking something to read. As always there was a teetering pile of prose and technical literature. I picked up the small, orange-backed collection of Christina Aroyo poetry I had been working through lately, then put it back down again. Who was I kidding? What with the medical reading I needed to do, the planning and preparation ahead of the surgery, and then the small matter of the operation itself, I'd be wiped out by the time I got back to my bed.

"You're learning," Fabio said, smiling as he read my thought process.

"Slowly."

We kissed goodbye as a black Mercedes arrived outside. Bang on time. I slung my case in the back, got in, waved to Fabio as the car moved off. The driver nodded at me through the rear-view mirror, but said nothing through the glass of his Covid screen. It was a frictionless ride to the airport, traffic easy and the lights all green, allowing us to speed through intersections. Strings were being pulled at all levels, with nothing left to chance.

By the time I got to the terminal, just before six, Bruno and Fillipe were already there, bags at their feet. We greeted each other with the wariness of old friends summoned to battle, caught between the excitement of a challenge and the burden of expectation now placed upon us.

"We lose tonight travelling, and then tomorrow we have to coordinate with the local surgical teams," Bruno said, scratching his chin with a familiar complaining look. "That's a lot of lost time, when we're already up against it."

"It is not as bad as it seems," Fillipe said, always one to look on the bright side. "We cannot go in until the scaffold is printed, and that will not be until Wednesday morning."

I frowned. "What's keeping them?"

Bruno shouldered his Adidas bag. "They're a few years behind us when it comes to 3-D printing. On the plus side, we're handling the computer design work, so that part can be done quickly."

"You're better briefed than me."

He shrugged. "I read on the ride in. But don't worry. Plenty of time to catch up on the flight."

Half an hour later we were wheels up, all of us sitting together in a window row. As soon as the seat-belt light went off, I folded down my tray-table and powered up my Chromebook. I connected to the Swissair Wi-Fi and delved into my email. Bunching up at the top, in and around the usual admin messages, were a set of patient files, medical images and secure hyperlinks, all of them originating from a dedicated World Health Organization account.

The plane banked, golden glare from the setting sun cutting across my screen. I leaned over Bruno and tugged down the plastic window shield.

"Basal meningioma," I said, beginning to skim through the patient notes again now that the immediate rush was over. "Man in his sixties, in otherwise good health. It's a displacing rather than infiltrating tumour, so that'll help with the suction. Margins should be obvious. We shouldn't have to remove too much healthy tissue."

"The bone is a mess," Fillipe commented.

"Yes. Looks mushy. But there's plenty of good bone around the bad, for anchoring the scaffold." I used the tracker pad to zoom in on one of the scans, where a gridded pattern indicated the intended placement of the printed implant. "Do you think we might want to be a little more conservative with those margins?"

"We'll talk it through with the other side," Bruno said unconcernedly.

I browsed through the documents, piecing together a gradually clearer picture of the work ahead of us. I was already visualising surprises, pitfalls and the possible dodges we might use to get out of them.

"You know, this is tricky," I said, "but I'm surprised they bounced it all the way up to World Health. It's flattering to us that they want our expertise, but I'm surprised they felt their own teams weren't up to the job."

Bruno tore into a packet of salted peanuts. "Maybe they're as behind on neurosurgery as they are on 3-D printing."

I nodded half-heartedly, but deep down I knew it was unlikely. The worlds where we had already done remote surgery tended to be at a similar level to our own across a range of scientific, medical and engineering disciplines, rarely being more than five to ten years out of step in any one area. That was how it needed to be: what the quantum engineers called a "multiversal self-selection effect". There were countless worlds out there with vastly different histories to our own, but unless they had been doing very similar experiments in quantum computation, with similar technical set-ups, the odds were against a window opening up between us and them in the first place.

I read for four hours, then spent the rest of the eleven-hour flight trying to get some sleep ahead of a full day's work. By the time we touched down in Zurich I was in that brittle, jangling state of semi-alertness, red-eyed and overdosed on lukewarm coffee. A small executive plane took us to Geneva, where a smiling, relieved WHO delegation met us with a black limousine and a full police escort. It was mid morning on Tuesday, cold and foggy, a contrast to the last time I had been here, in the full bloom of spring. I barely had time to blink before we were driving into the sleek, glass-fronted WHO complex. There was just time to check in to our allocated rooms, have a quick shower and freshen up before we were ushered into a windowless, wood-panelled teleconferencing suite.

Coffee arrived while technicians fussed over the link to the other side. The signal was good, but it needed constant nursing. On a previous visit I'd asked if we could see the quantum computer down in the basement, the one that was whispering to its counterpart in the other version of the WHO. I was gently discouraged; apparently it looked just like any other room full of gently humming, LED-blinking cabinets, and the technicians got itchy whenever someone got too close to their baby.

Up in the conference room, on clean-scrubbed screens, surgical staff and administrators were filing into a room not dissimilar to our own, in their counterpart to the WHO. Sometimes it was called the WHO, sometimes something else, but the basics never changed. It was nearly always located in Geneva.

Introductions were made, names and faces noted, friendly professional banter exchanged. They looked just like us, down to their tired but guardedly hopeful expressions. But they were not us, nor were any of their names known to us, other than my opposite number, Beckmann. It was quite likely that they had counterparts over here who were still in medicine but who had been pulled into different disciplines, far from neurosurgery. The same would apply to our counterparts in their worldline.

"It is good of you to come at such short notice," Beckmann told me through the screen. "We can all imagine the disruption it must cause to your schedules, as well as the time away from families."

"If we can save a life, then it's worth any amount of inconvenience," I replied.

"Your expertise in this type of procedure will be invaluable."

"It's just luck, if you can call it that, that we're a little further ahead of the curve in this area," I answered diplomatically. "I'm sure, if we had time, we would find that there are many surgical approaches where you have the lead on us."

"Time is the one thing not on our side," Beckmann answered regretfully. "I gather you have had a chance to review our plan for the bone scaffold?"

"Yes, and it looks good." I glanced at the WHO dossier in front of me, containing hard-copy summaries of much of the information that had already come through on my laptop, as well as a few overnight additions. "Your side kindly shared your 3-D printer software compatibility protocols with us. That allowed us to tweak the design a little on our side, just strengthening a few things here and there, and lightening where we don't need as much density, so we can speed up the print."

"I gather you had some concern over the margins?"

"Nothing major," I allowed, pausing to sip at the coffee. "I always want to make sure we removed all the diseased bone, but until we're actually in there, looking at it, we can't be totally confident about the margins."

"Would you like to abandon the current print, and go with a revised design, to cover a wider margin?"

I glanced at my team. The obvious answer was "yes", because then we would be covering ourselves against any nasty surprises once we had the skull open. But restarting the design and print process now would push the actual surgery even further back. "I think we continue…" I said, mouthing a silent "for now", just to cover myself.

"Very well then. Perhaps now we might review the remote surgical set-up?"

"No better time," I agreed.

We abandoned our drinks and biscuits and adjourned from the conference suite into the adjoining remote surgical theatre. Screens and cameras dotted around the room meant that we could carry on the dialogue with our colleagues on the other side as they moved into their own operating theatre, the one where the actual surgery would take place. At the moment there was just a dummy on the table, but in all other respects the set-up was just as it would be on the day of the procedure, with all the necessary equipment wheeled in and all staff gowned and scrubbed in appropriately.

"If all goes well," I said, "our only involvement will be through your screens, offering guidance when you need it."

"But we must be ready for more than that," Beckmann said.

So we were. If my team needed to get physical, there were two levels of engagement. The first and simplest was through robotic surgical devices that could be operated via cameras and hand controls. These hulking devices, shrouded in sterile plastic wrapping, were familiar to us all, even if there were slight differences in manufacture and function between the robots on their side and ours. Those differences were easily smoothed out by software, so that if I operated the robot in our theatre, the one in the counterpart would respond accordingly, seamlessly transferring my intentions from one worldline to the next.

If that proved insufficient – the surgery needing the precision and finesse of a surgeon's hands – then we would go up a level, donning haptic feedback suits with full virtual-reality immersion. These would allow us to operate human-like mannequins with arms, hands and fingers. That was very much a last resort, though, because it would mean cutting Beckmann's team entirely out of the loop, and no one wanted that. Although we would never deal with these people again after the window closed, we had a strong sense of professional empathy. I could imagine how humiliating it would feel for me if I was on the end of the same treatment.

These machines – the robots and the haptic rigs – were the reason my team had needed to fly to Geneva, rather than doing it all remotely from Joburg. The quantum computers handling the cross-talk between the two worldlines already introduced a degree of latency into the information flow. Any additional timelag on top of that built-in latency would have made the surgery far harder and far riskier. Nothing could be done about the gradual degradation in the signal, though, nor the inevitable point when the link became swamped in noise.

Chatting amiably to the other side, we completed a thorough check-out of the robots and haptics. Donning the VR goggles, each of us got the chance to feel momentarily embedded in that other worldline, just as if we had been born in it. I wondered if I was alone in feeling an urge to escape out into that curious counterpart to Geneva, to wander its streets, taste its airs and begin to gain some understanding of the altered world beyond it. Somewhere out there was almost certainly another me, another Fabio. Perhaps we had even met and fallen in love, although there was no guarantee of that.

With the theatres covered, we moved back into the conference room. There were just a few small details to be attended to. Each of us now had a separate browser running in a sandbox on our laptop. These were linked through to the WHO server connected to the basement, allowing access to the parallel internet on the other side. The purpose of this link was strictly professional: it allowed both teams to access medical databases and literature in the alternate worldline, enabling a fruitful cross-fertilisation of knowledge. There were no restrictions on the use of the browsers – the WHO treated us like adults, not children – but we were strongly discouraged from surfing the wider web. We did not need to know about the history of the other worldline, just that there was a man needing our help.

One of us had never been much good at taking encouragement, though.

••• 

Late in the afternoon, after the third meeting of the day, I found I needed some urgent fresh air. I grabbed a coffee from a machine and found my way out onto a balcony, looking out over a grey cityscape already settling into dusk. The darkening ground dropped away in leafy terraces toward the lake, for the moment mist-shrouded. Lights were coming on, inviting against the gloom. I took in invigorating breaths, pushing away the drowsiness that would probably dog me all the way back to Johannesburg.

The meetings might have been gruelling, but I could feel my confidence building. The tumour was in a difficult place, but gradually we – my team and Beckmann's – had converged on a strategy we all liked, one that minimised the chances of wreaking too much havoc on the way. Once the tumour had been excised and pressure relieved on surrounding structures, the worst of the patient's symptoms should start to ease. I could do nothing about post-operative complications, the long road to recovery or the chances of the cancer returning. Of the ultimate outcome, with the window long closed, we would be forever ignorant. But with the work we would do in the operating theatre, at least I could guarantee the patient the best possible odds of success.

The door slid open behind me. Bruno joined me on the balcony, elbows on the railing, saying nothing.

I waited a few moments then started to speak, about to make some observation about anaesthetic levels.

Bruno said, "It's Banish."

I looked at him properly. He was visibly shaken, his pallor clammy, a man in shock.

"It's what?" I asked.

"The patient is Banish," he stated again, speaking slowly and clearly. "He's alive in Beckmann's worldline."

I shook my head slowly, wondering what had got into him. "I saw the name. I can't even remember it now. Edward something. Edvard, maybe. It hardly matters given that we won't be speaking to him before or after the operation. But it wasn't Banish."

"Banish was not his birthname. It's a name he adopted, a *nom de guerre*. The real name, the one almost no one knows – except his victims and war-crimes prosecutors – that's the one belonging to our patient." He paused, rattled but beginning to recover his usual composure. "In Beckmann's worldline, they don't know about Banish. Or the war." His eyes widened with amazement. "It just didn't happen. Switzerland stays the same, of course – it always does. But the rest of Europe – it's totally different. I didn't even recognise half the names of the countries!"

I nodded slowly, believing everything he said. "There's a reason we're not supposed to look this stuff up. What made you do it in the first place?"

"I just wanted to know a bit more about the man we were going to save. What his life was like, what kind of person he was." He looked down, abashed. "I shouldn't have done it. That was mistake number one, although don't tell me you've never done it. Number two was telling you. Look, I'm sorry."

I watched city traffic for a few moments. "Maybe it's not so bad. We all make different life choices. You say there was no war in his worldline. That means he can't be a war criminal."

"He isn't," Bruno said falteringly.

"Good."

"But he's not much better. He's a politician. Populist, hardline anti-immigration, anti-democratic, you name it. Corrupt to the eyeballs, too. He's almost as bad as the real Banish. He just didn't get the chance to become an all-out murdering warlord."

"Well, now at least we know why they bumped this up the chain. VIP treatment for our bad boy."

"It's not a joke."

"And the crimes of his counterpart also aren't his responsibility – or ours."

"But he's the same man!" Bruno pleaded. "It's just that his life played out differently, because of other factors in his worldline."

I tightened my fingers on the cold grey metal of the balcony railing, imagining it as a gun barrel. "We don't get to judge him, Bruno. History's already done that, in our worldline. That's why Banish hanged himself, before he could go before the International Criminal Court."

"It just seems wrong," Bruno said. "Think of his victims, the dead and the displaced. The ones he disappeared on his rise to power. The artists and the critics he put in the ground. Did they have the benefit of a hugely expensive surgical team, beaming in from another dimension?"

"That's the WHO's call, not ours."

His lips moved nearly silently. "It stinks."

"And sometime between Thursday and Friday, we'll lose the link with his worldline. Whatever happens in there, we'll never hear from them again and vice versa. That box of tricks, down in the basement? The odds against it achieving another resonant lock with the same worldline are so huge, there aren't enough zeros in the universe to calculate it. He'll be gone, forgotten – and you and I will be knee-deep in another list of surgical cases."

"You say it doesn't matter?"

"I'm saying… out of sight, out of mind."

Bruno pondered my answer. "It's not good enough for me. I worry about what he'll do after we take out that tumour. He's not so old, for a politician. I used the sandbox browser to access some articles about the rise in popularity of his pro-nationalist party…" I groaned, but he carried on doggedly. "What's to say he doesn't start a war in his worldline in a year or two, just as bad as the one we had? Or worse?"

"Or maybe he renounces his ways and becomes a nice, caring human being." I shrugged. "We can't know, Bruno, and that's why there's no sense in worrying about it." Before he could doubt my moral compass, I added: "I don't like it either. There are a million people I'd sooner be treating than Banish's slightly less evil shadow. But we've agreed to help Beckmann's team with their patient, and that's all that matters."

He brooded. "Fillipe won't like it."

I thought about what I knew about Fillipe's family, and how the war had touched them. "No, he wouldn't. Which is as good a reason as any not to tell him."

Bruno said nothing. To the east, even as the city fell into the night, the fog was beginning to lift from the steely shimmer of Lake Geneva.

• • •

Half an hour later I was just about keeping a lid on all-out mutiny in my surgical team. We were in my room, the three of us. I was leaning against the window, trying to keep my cool. Fillipe was practically foaming at the mouth, standing at the foot of my bed, phone clutched in his hand, looking like he was close to bludgeoning someone with it. Bruno sat on the bed, his face a mask of dejection, just about ready to crawl under the sheets.

"Just keep it down!" I implored as Fillipe's voice broke into a shout. "We're professionals – and sounds carry through these walls!"

"I am not lifting a finger to help that bastard. Not after what he did!"

"That's precisely the point! The man we're meant to be treating didn't do any of those things!" I had to fight not to start shouting just as loudly as Fillipe. "We have to separate our thoughts about Banish from the man Beckmann has asked us to treat. They aren't the same!"

"He has the same name, he was born in the same town, he went to the same school, he married the same woman! How much closer do you want it?"

"I am sorry," Bruno said pitifully, for about the twentieth time. "I shouldn't have looked."

"I am very glad you did look!" Fillipe snapped back, also not for the first time. "Now I do not get to have to have the stain of saving him on my conscience!"

"Let's be clear," I said. "We have an obligation. We have agreed to do this surgery. The moment we accepted the challenge, there was no going back. If we back out now – for whatever spurious reason – we will be embarrassing our superiors, letting down Beckmann, bringing disgrace to our profession and more than likely signing that man's death warrant."

"He matters so much to them, let Beckmann have a go!"

"They'll screw it up. They know it, and so do we. That's why they came to us. Because they're good doctors and they've got the humility to know when to ask for help."

"If they were good doctors, they would not want to save a monster," Fillipe snarled, as angry with himself as he was with the situation. "All right, so they are probably good doctors," he allowed, some of his fury beginning to break. "But they do not know! Maybe if they did…"

"For all we know," I said steadily, "they've been doing some browsing of their own, via our internet. And Beckmann might be busy trying to stamp out a very similar rebellion over on their side. But like it or not, it all comes down to the same thing. They'll have committed to this surgery. It's far, far too late to back out."

"It is abstract for you," Fillipe said. "It is personal for me. You both know that. What he did… it can never be forgiven. Not here, not in Beckmann's worldline." Resignedly – he could never stay angry for long – he sat down next to Bruno. "I am sorry, my friends. You are both dear to me, and I know this will open a rift between us. But I cannot be part of this. Not while that man lives, free of justice, never even knowing of the blood on his soul."

"You can't leave," I said.

"I will." He waggled the phone at me, showing the Swissair app he already had open. "Go ahead with the surgery. You will not need me."

Bruno breathed heavily, his whole belly moving. I could tell that he was digging deep, trying to find something – anything – that might placate Fillipe. "What if we left a message for him, to be passed on to him after he regains consciousness? A letter, that we can entrust to Beckmann."

Fillipe looked scornful. "A letter, to balance what he did?"

"Just to let him know – we know what you were capable of, but still we operated." Bruno shrugged heavily. "It's just a suggestion. I don't want you to leave, Fillipe. But I understand your reasons."

"I am not cross with you," Fillipe said, eyeing me once to let me know I was included in this calculus. "Just this situation."

"It needn't be a letter," I said quietly.

Fillipe looked at me with a faint guarded curiosity.

●●●

It was Wednesday morning. The mutiny had blown over. We were due to scrub in and start operating in a couple of hours.

"I'd like to delay," I told the opposing team, bracing myself for the inevitable response.

"The link is already showing measurable deterioration!" Beckmann protested.

"It is," I agreed. "But it's a long way from breaking down completely. At the moment – and for the next twenty-four hours or so – we won't notice any worsening latency. The best estimate is that we still have until Friday – and late Thursday evening at the very worst. I'd like to propose that we go in early tomorrow, when we have twelve to eighteen hours of useful surgical time ahead of us."

"But we are ready!"

"It's the implant," I admitted. "I had my doubts about the bone margins, as you knew. I'm afraid the scans we took yesterday have dented my confidence in the existing design. We'll need to take out more bone, and for that reason we need a larger scaffold." I paused. "But the good news is that we can still make this work, provided we agree immediately. We have the design already worked up and ready to be shot through to your printer. I understand we've even managed to tweak your deposition software a little, to speed up the print time."

Beckmann's team consulted. They went off-mike. They did not like this last-minute change of plan, and their frustration was all too evident in the video feed. Practically speaking, though, they had no choice but to bow to my proposal, and I knew it. After going all the way up to WHO, and calling in our expertise, they were all but obliged to do my bidding.

"What if there is a problem with the print?"

"There won't be, but if there is, you still have the first scaffold. If pushed, we'll use it – but you may have to deal with the consequences down the line."

"What if the link degrades ahead of prediction?"

"Same answer," I said smugly, and then instantly hated myself for it. "We'll be ready to go in at any point. I just think it makes tremendous clinical sense to wait for the second scaffold, if we are to give…" I stumbled, for I had nearly said his name, his *nom de guerre*. "If we are to give this man the best outcome." I looked around at my team, as well as theirs. "And I think we can agree that we all want that?"

"Very well," came the eventual reply.

• • •

I unpacked, tossing things out of my suitcase onto the bed. I was tired after the flight, but it was good to be home.

Fabio picked up the Christina Aroyo book, frowning slightly. "You took this in the end? I could have sworn…" But then he glanced back at the stack of books on the bedside table. "So now we have two copies?"

"I picked that one up in Geneva."

"Because you couldn't stand to be away from it for a few days?" He was smiling, gently sceptical. "It's taken you months to get half-way through the first copy."

"There was a line in one of her war poems," I offered. "It was bugging me, because I couldn't quite remember it. I suppose I could have tried looking it up, but it seemed easier just to buy a second copy." I continued with my unpacking. "Do you think she'd have forgiven Banish, if she'd lived?"

He mused on my words for a moment.

"You're thinking of that one about letting go of hate."

"Yes – I keep circling back to that one. It's a really beautiful statement."

"Written about a month before they disappeared her. I wonder if she'd have changed her views, knowing what was about to happen."

"I think she was strong enough to hold to her convictions," I said. "But, of course, I can't know. I just prefer to think she was better than her enemies."

"Theoretical." He looked at me shrewdly. "Or did you bump into her on the other side? Did she take a side-career into medicine?"

It was an awkward conversation and we both knew it. I suppose the clever thing would have been to just find the poem online, or at the very least leave the second copy of the book back in Geneva, for someone else to enjoy. That way I wouldn't have had to explain myself. But the truth was that I wanted some testament, something tangible to connect me to the events of the last few days. The window was closed; no information about Banish or his fate could ever reach me now. I was confident that we had done the best possible job.

Fillipe and I had worked quickly, shaping a larger implant using the usual medical-proprietary CAD program. I brought in Bruno, of course, but only because I thought it important that he knew and approved, that he was fully in on the act: our responsibility equal.

I showed him the CAD image of the implant before we emailed it through the WHO server. A fine, mesh-like structure, soon to be a physical object.

"It won't last," I told him. "Normal bone growth eventually supplants and absorbs the scaffold. But by then its work is done."

"The mesh is opaque," Bruno said, dabbing his finger at an area of the image where the CAD looked scruffy, imperfectly resolved.

"It's not," I answered, zooming in with the mouse. "It's just a slight thickening of the nanopore mesh along some of the x and y axes. It'll print properly, and there won't be any surgical ramifications."

"What have you done?" He stared and stared, seeing and not seeing.

"It is just a line," Fillipe said. "There's no reason at all for Beckmann's team to notice it. Even if they do, they will just assume it is an artefact of the printing process."

"It's the message you suggested," I told Bruno. "But we don't leave a letter. Or anything that Beckmann will ever pass on to Banish. In fact, the only people who'll ever know about this are us."

"Whose line?" But Bruno dipped his eyes to the copy of the book I had next to the computer.

"'Embers on snow, melting into nothing,'" I said. "From the Christina Aroyo poem 'In a Time of Ashes'."

He was silent, his breathing the only sound above the whisper of the computer's fan.

"We are doing this?"

"If you consent," I answered. "There's another file, without her words. We can send either one through, and they'll take the same time to print."

"Her words," he said slowly, as if the idea were unfolding before him, delicious and dangerous. "In his head. Literally *in his head*?"

"Under his brain. Written there. Until the bone growth supplants them."

He turned to Fillipe. "This is enough?"

"It is not. Nothing would ever be enough. But it is… sufficient." He smiled tightly. "I will remain. We will complete the work."

Bruno's eyes widened as the ramifications of our plan worked their way through his mind.

"Maybe it's sufficient. But is this… right?"

"I don't know," I admitted. "Very probably it isn't. Very probably we'd be struck off if anyone ever found about this. Maybe put in prison. But what I do know is this: we're doing no harm to him, and I was sincere about those extra bone margins. They will help, and I'd never have lied about that. But this…" I gestured at the words. "This is something. It's not restitution, it's not justice, but it's still something. They're her words."

"Her words," Bruno echoed.

"Her words," Fillipe agreed.

After a silence, Bruno laid his hand on mine. Fillipe followed, the three of us bound together, saying nothing, but our hearts and minds fully set.

# CRACKS

## CHANA PORTER

**So, I'm** at Whole Foods doing some late-night shopping, reaching for a bunch of organic bananas, when I accidentally touch fingers with a woman who looks exactly like me. I don't mean this woman and I resemble each other, like we could be cousins or even sisters, or have the same color hair or body type. I mean she looks exactly the same as me—my face, my collarbone, my neck. The birthmark on my right cheek. She is me. Only her posture is better and she's a little thinner. I assume her teeth would be whiter than mine, if she smiled. I'm certain if someone called out "Jean Yee!" she would turn around. She's wearing high-quality jeans and a T-shirt that looks effortlessly expensive. A flat, perfect stomach. I hate her. This surprises me. She's all I strive to become. So why don't I love her a little, just for proving it's possible?

I like to say that, in an alternate timeline, if I wasn't an architect I'd be a nutritionist. Over the years I've become a health nut. It gives me a sense of control in a chaotic world. Social media has cemented my hobby into an obsession. I style my acai bowls for Instagram, get paid in likes and follows. I ferment my own pickles. I could write you a treatise on gut health. My body is my temple, though as I approach my late thirties I have trouble keeping the belly fat off, no matter how many hot yoga classes I take. It's genetic, or so I thought until I saw myself wearing a size 26 waist in raw dark-blue denim.

I like shopping late at night. My fellow night owls make some weird choices, mostly drug or alcohol induced, but there are far fewer problems to analyze. It's a numbers game. At night I don't feel as crushed by our collective toxic relationship to food and cooking, not to mention GMOs, Big Agriculture, and single-use plastic. Lately a lot of the things I do to avoid getting depressed aren't working. B-12. Fatty acids. Vitamin D. The astonishing power of a good night's sleep. I find the only thing that works consistently is imagining I'm on a space station, a million miles away, watching our beautiful blue-green planet from above. Up in space it's very quiet and very lonely. I feel numb and that brings a kind of peace. When I am numb for long enough, I let my mind return to Earth. I realize how much I missed the Earth—its noise, its chaos, how immediate and all-consuming every tragedy feels. Then I am grateful again to walk around on solid ground. Green plants are tiny miracles, giving us air to breathe. The world is simple again.

The first thing I notice about my twin is that she's buying a lot of things I would never buy, including wine. I see her put a family-size box of Honey Nut Cheerios into her cart, followed by a package of fruit-flavored individual yogurt cups with cartoon animals on the packaging. This knowledge hits me like a freight train: she has children. I vacillate between anger and pity. She must really have her life together. Also, why is she shopping at night? Shouldn't she be putting her children to bed?

I like shopping at night because I'm trying to limit my screen time to a two-hour window in the late afternoon; then I'm cut off. I imagined without my laptop bathing me in blue light I'd be someone who takes Epsom salt baths, someone who reads great literature, but I find I am neither. The pathways of my brain have been pruned to prefer 150 characters or less. Sitting in the bathtub makes me think about the water crisis and I find that instead of unwinding I'm having a soggy panic attack.

I begin to see glimpses of myself among her groceries. Wild-caught salmon fillets. Endive. A bag of mixed baby greens called Powerhouse Blend next to the supplies for kids' lunches: turkey slices, whole-wheat bread, yellow mustard. A bottle of vinaigrette, which I find sad (it's so easy to make). There's a big round grapefruit next to a blood orange. A bag of shelled pistachios, salted. Then, I realize, I know this dinner. This is a date-night dinner in my rotation, so easy to prepare but it looks fancy—salmon encrusted in chopped pistachios, with roasted slices of blood orange, served on a bed of wilted greens. If I'm cooking for a man, I might roast some new potatoes. I see them then, in their little mesh bag—the tricolor, tiny potatoes, each no bigger than the first phalanx of my thumb. Red, white, and purple. They will be delicious blistered with olive oil and sea salt. I think about this woman and her husband, with their whole-food diets while her children eat sugar and gluten and processed wheat. Maybe they do a sort of "date night" meal after the kids are put to sleep. He's a feminist. He puts the children to bed while she has her "me" time—Pilates class, grocery shopping, a hot bath. Maybe she puts on a dress even though they're just staying home, and he cleans the kitchen really well. He lights a candle. She puts on lip gloss. He thinks about changing clothes then he doesn't, because he would just be putting on a different black T-shirt. She plates dinner. He decants the wine. They share one good bottle and no more, because they have a healthy relationship with alcohol.

I'm angry now, in a wild, vulnerable kind of way that I recognize too well. Here we go again: the most sullen, bitterest version of myself rears her head. My least favorite. But she takes over, and you know what? She does make some good points. Why haven't I gotten a hello, or even a nod? Doesn't this other self see me, know me, for who I am? We've been shopping together for a good twenty minutes! Who does she think she is?

How about this: I follow her to her parking spot. Bash her head in with a brick. I strangle her with the strap of one of her reusable shopping bags. She struggles but makes very little sound. We're evenly matched. She's maybe a bit stronger than I am upper-body-wise, probably from lifting toddlers up and down all day. *Mama, up! Mama, want up!*

But I have the element of surprise. This is a dream, she thinks; this is a nightmare. She is losing oxygen. Then she's limp in my arms. I dump her body, almost identical to my own, in the Gowanus. I get into her SUV and press Home on the GPS. I fumble to find my house keys in front of a posh brownstone in Park Slope. My husband hugs me hello, asks me why I've parked in the street instead of in "the spot." I tell him I'm not feeling well, I need a shower, to lie down. He says go relax, he'll move the car, he'll put the groceries away. I take a shower under the waterfall faucet, wash the blood off my neck, dry my hair with her fluffy towels. Her bedsheets are so soft. Like getting into a bowl of creamy yogurt. Organic, 100% bamboo, probably $400. Her husband—my husband—comes in and fucks me in the dark. I put my face down in the sheets and I feel like I'm swimming. I bet Oprah loves these sheets. He moves his fingers in a winning combination, I cum because he knows how to make me cum, he's an expert in my pussy, then climaxes right after me. Efficient, passionate, polite. We go to sleep on silk pillowcases. In the middle of the night, a little child looks at me from my side of the bed. His voice is high and clear.

"Who are you?" he asks. "Where is Mom?"

• • •

"Excuse me," I say as she's opening cartons of eggs to check for cracks. There's plenty of room for me by the eggs, but she politely moves aside. I take her place in front of the free-range extra-large browns and watch as she moves on toward the dairy case.

Lactose isn't our friend but we can manage fine on a raw goat's milk or even sheep, for special occasions. Is she celebrating? Entertaining? Is the wine for a cheese-plate pairing, not for her own consumption? Is she so well adjusted she can buy alcohol for friends and not drink it herself?

"Hey," I say loudly. She turns to look at me directly for the first time.

Her face is blank. She's looking a little tired, actually, around the eyes, and this punctures my bitterness. I get more sleep than she does, or at least a deeper REM cycle. "I'm sorry," she says. "Do I know you?" She's holding a round of brie in one hand and a slab of hard cheddar in the other. I'm not close enough to tell what kind of milk they're made from.

"No, I'm sorry," I say. My bitterness is replaced by self-consciousness. "It's my mistake."

"Maybe just from the grocery store," she says graciously. This easy kindness makes me love her a little.

"I like shopping at night," I say.

"Oh, me too," she says. "It's so quiet." She peers into my basket. "Are those dried blueberries?"

I nod. "I'm making chia pudding." I pause, but she's still with me, so I keep going. "And a high-energy trail mix."

She nods and considers her own cart. "I'm actually a nutritionist," she says. "I thought I'd be that kind of parent, chia pudding for breakfast, trail mixes instead of chips. It's always a battle. You compromise where you have to." We stroll towards the canned goods together like old friends.

"We grew up on margarine and diet soda," I say, placing a can of chickpeas in my basket. "Pop tarts. We turned out okay, didn't we?" She cocks her head as if she's listening to something far away. And then she shrugs, smiles at me with her very white teeth, and goes about her way. I don't turn to see her at the checkout line, to discover if she's remembered the reusable bags or if she left them in the trunk of her SUV. I bless her silently, and let her go.

• • •

I see myself again a couple of weeks later at the coffee shop. I'm a barista now, with dyed red hair and a nose ring. A smattering of tattoos up and down my arms. I always thought I'd look good with a nose ring but I was too timid to get one. I do look good, I think, as I watch myself steam milk. The nose ring catches the light.

This me is chubbier, with big, heavy breasts. I felt so jealous of my thin twin from the grocery store, but there's no denying it—this weight suits me. Her face—that is, my face—looks round and happy. Her shoulders are relaxed; her eyes are bright. She seems rested. It might be the caffeine she's been sucking down all morning. I sit there for hours but I can't seem to think of what to say to her. I even order a bagel with cream cheese, in some kind of solidarity, and of course I don't eat it, but it gives me permission to stay longer. I watch her stealthily text on her phone when there aren't any customers. I watch her brew tea and stir lemonade. I watch her ice lattes and froth milk. Almond. Soy. Oat. I have never tried to work at a coffee shop. I have never had a job that wasn't a stepping stone in my career—an internship at a gallery, a gig as a museum guide. I worked so hard to get to where I am, and now I can't leave. Because of all the years I spent climbing. Because of debt. I'm not saying being a barista is easy. A slow barista can make you miss the train, make you late for work, ruin your morning, ruin your life. The stakes feel too high for minimum wage plus tips. She does it well, though, juggling the demands of a constant stream of people. She makes eye contact. She chats with regulars, but keeps the line moving. By the end of her shift, I will think of how to break the ice. I could start a conversation about which non-dairy milk is the easiest to froth. But maybe she's actually one of those people who aren't that interested in talking about their jobs. Maybe we can take a walk, or sit in a park together and people watch. I would like to be her friend.

Or how about this: I seduce myself and we end up going back to her apartment. We have the sex I have always wanted but was too timid to ask for. I don't have to ask. We just know. She gags me with my own panties. Fingers my pussy and ass like she's carrying a bowling ball. I make her wait for me, kneeling on the bathroom floor, mouth open, tongue out like a dog, while I slowly shower. After she's shaking with anticipation I sit on her chubby little face. Penetrate each other with raw sweet potato (organic and washed, of course). As we take turns topping each other, I'm not worried about how my body looks while I'm fucking or if the noises I'm making sound arousing or annoying. I'm not performing. And maybe, now that I've had authentic sex, now that I know what it feels like, to be inside my own experience, instead of on the ceiling, wondering if my belly looks flabby, then perhaps I can do it again. With a different person—with someone who is not myself.

I have finally thought of my opening line ("Hey, can I buy you a coffee?") when she emerges from the bathroom. She's looking fresh and pretty, without her apron and wearing a different shirt. I stand up. It's now or never. But as I'm walking towards her, I see her eyes light up, not at me, but at someone walking through the door. It's a tough-looking woman, sexy, holding two black full-face helmets. The woman slings an arm around my shoulder and I put my hand in her back pocket. I watch myself leave with the woman, who is presumably my girlfriend. They roar off together on their motorcycle, into the not-quite sunset.

This guts me in a way I couldn't anticipate. I imagine they share an apartment in Queens. They either have two cats or two dogs, and certainly a CSA share. I stare at the door, afraid to blink or I'll cry in the coffee shop in the middle of the afternoon, alone, with my stale bagel. I pick up the bagel and take a bite. Discover it's not stale at all, still tender, with the wonderful boiled outside, just slightly chewy. The feeling of full-fat cream cheese on my tongue. I haven't eaten something that wasn't a health-food version of itself in many years, only the occasional sprouted gluten-free bagel, weirdly crumbly, with the too-sweet, oily tofu cream cheese. A mouthful of dirt. This happy woman and her too-cool girlfriend, who loves her. Someone who holds her every night.

I'm feeling pretty wobbly so I decide to go to a meeting. I feel a little better as soon as I enter the church basement. The smell of drip coffee. The folding chairs. This is the real church to me. Sometimes I feel like God loves failures and weakness more than she loves forward-marching perfection. That's why instead of only a world of angels and animals, she invented humans. Personally, I always grow the most through pain. But I am looking forward to growth without crisis, I think, just as my therapist taught me to, because I am carving neural pathways toward positivity.

I think about sharing my story first, but a man is already walking towards the podium. He's all eyebrows, Jewish maybe, or Cuban (or both). I settle in and drink my coffee. He's wearing a business suit, not terribly expensive, not super cheap. Ordinary. He looks like an office manager, or someone who works at a bank. When he speaks, his low soft voice makes me think of the sea.

I listen as he tells the story of my addiction, of how I hit bottom. There are small differences but overwhelmingly it's the same, down to when we crashed our car into the Wendy's drive-through on a solo road trip through West Virginia. He talks about how we had to show up in court in a different state multiple times, the warrants out for our arrest. How we went a year without telling anyone, not even a friend, about our legal troubles. How we finally got sober because the lying, the double life, the stress, and the fear was eating us alive. How the world is so much harder and so much easier now that we're showing up for it.

As he finishes I find myself wiping away tears, feeling purged, clean. I thank him for his story along with everyone else but say no more, and decline to speak for the rest of the night. What more could I say? He looks at my face a little longer than the others, directly into my eyes. Perhaps he recognizes me, in the way the two other women did not. I realize I've been going about my search for myself all wrong. It's just like me to get stuck on the packaging, and miss the contents.

Leaving the church, I wonder if all of my selves are addicts. Maybe the me in the supermarket can enjoy a glass or two at night without her world crashing down around her. Or maybe she's just kidding herself. I hope she's doing well. She did look like she needed some rest.

After the meeting I walk through the West Village. I think about catching the subway but it's a nice night. I feel proud of myself. It's been a rough few weeks (years, if I'm honest) and I am still sober. Walking down the road one day at a time. I cross the street to enter my building and I see myself yet again, driving a city bus. I turn to see myself in the alley, sleeping out on the street on a stack of flattened boxes. I see myself as a child sitting on a stoop in happy, dreamy boredom, aching to grow up because then I'd know all the answers. I see myself at a busy intersection, dancing in the middle of the street. My shirt off, my muscles ropy and glistening, my nipples hard. I say the Serenity Prayer under my breath. I watch, awestruck, as my hands move like birds, my arms outstretched and spinning. I am dancing with a purity of motion I've never known, dancing like I'm in the footlights, dancing like I'm on the head of a pin. The prayer becomes a jumble of my own making—asking for kindness when I can't be wise, asking for the wisdom to know when I'm not being kind.

• • •

My euphoria doesn't last. So I do what I do when I feel unstable. I call Francesca, my best friend. She's a screenwriter in LA. No matter what time it is on the West Coast, Franny never fails to pick up.

"I don't know what I'm doing," I whisper into the phone. "I want to quit my job. I want to quit my life. I keep seeing myself as other people, as other women. I imagine killing this other self, replacing her, or fucking her, seducing her, falling in love."

Franny laughs, and something in me relaxes. "That's the most twisted version of Fuck, Marry, Kill I've ever heard."

"Remember that night in college, with the sombrero? Those guys were such assholes!"

The line goes silent. Lately, when I talk about the old days she says nothing, or changes the subject. She doesn't reply with "Chubby bunny" when I say "Skinny rabbit," or any of our ancient stupid jokes. I wonder if she's depressed.

"I sometimes feel like I've killed another version of myself, or I've replaced her," Franny says slowly. "Like I'm a clone." She's been talking about leaving her husband. I don't know why such bitterness came. They had seemed so happy. But I guess we can't promise our future selves to anyone, even if we vowed to be there in sickness and in health.

"Maybe everything is like that," I sigh. I wish phones still had cords. "Maybe that's what living is, murdering your old self with your new ideas." A cord I could twist in my hand, like in middle school. Feel the stretch, the limitation.

• • •

I've spent a long time telling you the things I am not. I used my architecture degree to go into exhibition design. Now I work at a famous museum. My job is rather important. I do not get paid enough.

I meet with artists who have rough concepts and I have to figure out how to realize them—engineer, design, and oversee construction. Here I could tell you a story about a woman who charged me with building a series of winding tubes for spiders to hatch and multiply, and the chaos that followed, but I don't want to get sued. You get the idea. Sometimes I enjoy these Herculean tasks because that's where I can truly create. But at the end of the day, no matter how successful my design, their name is on the wall, not mine.

I have been looking for other jobs. My issue is that I'm often paralyzed by choice, so I end up doing the same thing, for far too long.

I go into work for a meeting with an up-and-coming artist to discuss her first solo show. I meet her in the west gallery, standing in front of Agnes Martin's "Loving Love." Immediately, I notice her posture, her straight black hair, her familiar rounded shoulders.

We sit and look at her book together on a low bench. Her paintings are big canvases of large circles, minimalistic. I can see the Martin influence. Mostly white space, accented by pastel— light orange, lemon yellow, an occasional soft pink. I like them. I point to one in particular, entitled "Two Doors of a Single Object."

"Can you tell me more about this one?"

She turns to look directly into my eyes.

"Starting from when I was eleven or so, I would spend hours and hours looking in the mirror," she says. "I could never get enough of my own face, and yet I didn't quite understand what I looked like.

If you asked me to pick myself out of a lineup, I would have had difficulty doing so. And I never, ever felt beautiful.

"This went on for years. Then one day, when I was around sixteen, I saw a girl that I couldn't stop looking at. We were in a crowded mall. I saw her in the food court. I wanted to drink in the sight of her like water. It was as if the whole world blurred away and there was only her. I told my friends I'd meet them later, and followed her for almost an hour. Finally, standing next to the shiny escalator, I saw our two images side by side. We were identical.

"After that, I started seeing other girls who looked like me. Girls with different haircuts, from different families. Rich girls, poor girls. It went on like this for many years. All through art school, into my adulthood. We got older. I saw different versions of myself wherever I went. For a while, I thought I was going mad."

She leans in close. I can see the sticky surface of her lip gloss. I resist the urge to reach out and touch her mouth as it moves. "But as you know, I was perfectly sane. I was seeing the cracks—windows into different realities. Like this. This crack won't stay open forever. Soon I have to go." The other Jean Yee took something small out of her pocket, and pressed it into my hand—a thumb drive. "This is a low-budget sci-fi movie called *Slipping*. It's a little silly, but it does a good job explaining the concept. All of the information you need is there."

There is a question I've carried around in my heart since I was eleven, sneaking the pink box wine from my parents' fridge after school. Chasing that warm feeling—the certainty, the ease. "Are you an alcoholic?" I ask my other self.

She frowns, tilting her head sympathetically. "No."

I squeeze my eyes shut. I want a drink. I want to crawl into bed and never leave. I open my eyes. "What happened to the girl at the mall?"

She leans in closer still. To a passerby, we might appear to be kissing. "We decided to trade." Her eyes burn bright, steady. "She took my life, and I took hers." Her voice is barely a whisper. "Is that what you want? Would you like to be me?"

I pull away from myself, pick up my purse. Make an excuse about running back to my office. She doesn't try to follow me. There is no fight, no grand climax. As I walk down the many stairs, out the front of the museum and into the sunshine, I wonder how many lives she's leap-frogged over to be where she is—successful, beautiful. A person of substance, with a Wikipedia page and a solo show at thirty-five.

But she did give me something—something real, something bigger than a sci-fi movie that claims to hold all my answers. As soon as I get home, I tender my resignation to the museum. I've always liked that turn of phrase. Tender my resignation. There's such a sweetness to it.

Then, I call Franny.

"You should make a movie," I say. "Called *Slipping*. About traveling between parallel realities."

"Yeah," she says, chuckling darkly into the phone. "A woman decides to leave her cheating husband, but then she slides into a different reality where he didn't cheat on her. So now she's really fucked!"

"Yeah!" I wander into the bathroom, begin drawing a bath. Pretend I'm twisting a phone cord between my fingers. "She has to figure out where to put those feelings of betrayal. Like, what even makes a person? Is it the sum total of events of our lives? A kind of experience abacus? Or is it something ineffable?" I look in my bathroom mirror, reach out and touch the girl in the glass. Her dark eyebrows, her full mouth. "I am not my face. Maybe I'm not even my memories?"

"Yeah," replies Franny, voice flat, drained of all its familiar warmth. "Like maybe her best friend from college has noticed something is wrong, but she can't quite put her finger on it. Because she can't laugh at any of the old stories. She doesn't remember any of their inside jokes."

I turn off the bath water, sit down on the closed toilet. "Yeah," I say slowly, but now the word feels odd, inert in my mouth. "Because that was a different person."

"The one you love has been replaced by another."

I look down at my hand. So pale, so small. For a melodramatic moment, it seems unlikely I will ever speak again.

"Jeannie," she says softly. "I want you to know—I love it when you call. I never had a friend like you before."

"Hold on." I test the water temperature. Strip off my clothes. "Sorry. So, who is your best friend from college, if it wasn't me?"

"A woman named Alice. She runs a rice-pudding shop in Minnesota. We've been drifting apart for years."

I climb into the tub, carefully place the phone on the soap dish. "Rice pudding?" I wrinkle my nose. "Is that even a thing?"

"I know—it seems like the worst possible kind of dessert. But I can't tell her that."

I sink lower into the warm water. "Franny, tell me something about you. About when you were young."

She's silent for a long moment. "Once, when I was a little girl, my parents took me and my sister hiking with our godmother—a big woman named Rose."

"Isn't that your mother's name?"

"Yeah—they would joke that this was the foundation of their friendship, two Roses in a garden. All-girls Catholic school in Chicago, little Roses in matching uniforms—can you even imagine?"

I smile. "I can see it."

"So we made it to the top of the mountain no problem. But as we walked along the flat cliffs to find a nice spot to eat our picnic lunch, my godmother Rose slipped and lost her balance, falling off the rock into the chasm below."

"Oh God!"

"My parents instantly grabbed her from the edge of the cliff, one on each arm, and hauled her to safety. It was instantaneous—the loss, the retrieval. She had no time to call out, or make any kind of sound. Then, as we sat down to eat, my father said something to me very quietly—something that I've never forgotten.

"He said, 'Somewhere, we are having a very different day.' I was the only one who could hear him."

We stay on the line until long after the water gets cold. Not talking, just listening to our breath moving within our fragile, miraculous lungs.

# A THRESHOLD HYPOTHESIS

## JAYAPRAKASH SATYAMURTHY

*Threshold: Gateway*
**The hack:**

"To us, you are one. To you, we are many. We are coming."

I wake up shivering. But.

It's never a dream. That becomes obvious quite soon.

It starts in a bar. It could start anywhere, but this is my story, and I'll start it in a bar. It was a place I didn't know very well. My regular drinking place had closed down and I was scouting for a replacement.

It was one of the older pubs in town and it was just around the corner from my flat. I'd never been there because I usually went drinking near my office. It was called the Sherlock, and it was built back when people who started pubs in Bangalore were still trying to emulate the traditional British pub. There was some wood panelling in the main room on the ground floor, and a few silhouettes of the sleuth were framed behind the bar counter, but there the attempt at carrying the theme ceased. For the most part it was an average Bangalore pub: nondescript furniture, a few plastic chairs replacing the wooden ones that the place had started out with as and when they wore out, some drab prints on the walls (flowers, landscapes, all murky and disheartened), waiters in black waistcoats, that sort of thing. The draught beer was okay, the plate of fries was disappointing. The music was a mix tape of mainstream rock hits, starting with "Hotel California" and "Black Magic Woman" and working its way all the way up to "Alive" and "Creep". Music sure became cheerless in the '90s. There's probably more upbeat stuff today, but neither the Sherlock nor I knew or cared about it.

I tried to get a couple of my friends from the old place to join me there, but it was too far off for them, one reason why I never made it my regular. The second time I plonked down there, I sat upstairs in a small balcony area where they'd put out some chairs and tables. I ordered the roasted groundnuts – I wasn't going to try the sodden, discouraged fries in that place again – and a pint. After a while, my order arrived. Close on its heels, a middle-aged man came and sat down at the table next to mine. After a while, he turned to me. "Not trying the fries, are you?" He sniggered. He had a salt and pepper beard, thinning hair, mostly still black, slightly hawkish features – sharp nose, keen eyes – wore a denim shirt, white jeans, rubber slippers. "Hah!" I chortled back, a little half-heartedly. I didn't mind making pub acquaintances, but I wasn't so sure about this fellow – he looked like he might be a bit of a bore, a bit of a crank.

Sure enough, a while later he was inducing a deep sense of stultification in me with a long, rambling account of faceless ghosts some old school pal of his had seen near Naga Theatre back in his long-fled youth. Finally, securing my continued attention by ordering a pitcher for us to share, he moved into the chair across my table and glanced about furtively. *Here it comes*, I thought to myself. *The come-on, the con, the big put-on.*

"It isn't just seeing things, you know? Sometimes you can go somewhere else. Parts of Bangalore aren't in Bangalore at all."

He was breathing heavily and continuing to glance about him in a nervous manner. He repeated, in a sibilant whisper, "Parts of Bangalore aren't in Bangalore at all."

I laughed nervously, turned the topic to cricket, which he followed enthusiastically, and politics, which we argued about extensively. When the waiter came around for the last call, I ordered us a tap each to wind up. We parted outside the pub, each stumbling back to his own home. I only saw him again once, before the end.

A few weeks later, I decided the Sherlock wasn't cutting it and I started going to Guzzler's on Rest House Road, where a few of my old gang were to be found. Guzzler's used to have a cowboy theme when it was first built and it still had a few old paintings some local artist had made, based on those British-published cowboy comics we all used to read back in the '80s. Guzzler's is a cheerful place, well-lit, comfortable seats, hard liquor as well as beer, good food and snacks. The music was a slightly wider selection of rock hits, including some classic metal and hard rock like Uriah Heep, Iron Maiden, Rainbow, things like that. Afterwards, we went down to a dark corner down the street and shared a joint. Now there are two corners in this area that have a plaque on them – one's on the corner of MG Road and Brigade Road and it says *Ismail Sait's Corner*. That one's on the wall of a fancy clothing store and it's kept shiny and clean. At this other corner, there is a crumbling colonial bungalow and a plaque that reads *Johnny Sait's Corner*. I'd seen it lots of times, and I decided to tell my friends about it. So I launched into the whole story of the plaques and my theories about the brothers Sait when Vik told me to shut up. Vik is a software programmer with Wolverine sideburns, by the way. He wears thick glasses and looks a bit like a brown-skinned Ray Manzarek. "Shut up," he said. "I don't see any Johnny Sait's Corner. You're fucking spaced, man."

"You shut up," I replied, turning around to point out the evidence.

*Fuck me.*

It wasn't there. The bungalow was, although it didn't look as decrepit as I remembered, someone had slapped a lick of paint on it and fixed the broken windows. There was even a small flower garden. Had I dreamed the whole thing up? It seemed unlikely, but one time I'd dreamed of a friend's death and it had felt so final and real that I called his house in the morning to offer my condolences, only to have him answer the phone himself, quite alive.

So I laughed it off, took a few more drags and then headed home.

Three days later, I'd gone down to the corner with another friend for a quick tipper, and it was there again. The crumbling bungalow and Johnny Sait's plaque. I rushed back to Guzzler's and pulled Vik out. He came along, grumbling about "wasted wankers", then he saw it.

"Fuck me."

"Indeed."

"That is so weird. That is the weirdest thing."

I nodded in agreement. Our other friend, Anit, who'd recently moved to town from Calcutta, said he couldn't see anything. That, of course, added to our general befuddlement. We stood there staring for a while, then we heard a police whistle from the distance and headed back to Guzzler's to pay up and head out. We were drinking after closing time and the Bangalore cops like to bust people for that from time to time, probably because it's easy to coax bribes out of them.

Okay, both these stories have kind of fallen into a pattern and you're thinking I'm some weirdo who keeps going out to drink, has weird things happen to him, then goes home. Probably drinking too much, and all that pot can't be healthy.

So here's another place where it begins.

I work in an advertising agency. There was a time when I loved this. There was a time when I hated it. These days, I honestly can't be bothered either way. I know what I have to do and I do it. A few times a year I do a job that I even like a bit and it goes in my portfolio. Once in a while I do a scam ad for award submissions. Once a year I trundle down to Goa Fest and party with the rest of the suckers in the biz.

But I was coming to a point. The part about working in advertising that you simply can't get too blasé about is meeting clients. It's just too much of an annoyance. Yes, I know that's such a snooty backroom crew thing to say, but I hate meetings anyway and when it's a meeting with a paying client, there's this added power dynamic that really suffocates me. I usually try to sulk in a corner doodling in my notepad, but it's harder now that I am supposed to be the Copy Supervisor for my team. Copy Sup. Copy Soup. Served up hot and steaming to cure what ails your marketing plan. Did I mention I work in an advertising agency?

This one, I had to go on my own and meet the rest of the office lot there – the account exec, the design head and a newbie whom we were dragging along on the principle that misery hates company but gets it anyway. I had an earlier meeting with another client to wrap up, which was how I wound up in the second client's massive campus on Sarjapur Road, wearing a visitor's pass with a very unflattering photo of me taken at the check-in on a webcam, wandering between identical buildings, quite lost.

Finally, I came to a small shack built next to the perimeter wall, way in the back of the building. A few rural-looking characters lounged about outside, sipping tea from small glasses. There was some construction going on elsewhere on the campus, so I figured this must be some temporary canteen for the workers. I stepped into a small, smoky room where a fat, sweaty, bare-chested man laboured over churning out hot dosas and a skinny waiter poured out steaming cups of tea from a battered tin kettle. I ordered a tea and then sat down on a low bench, blowing on it to cool it off. I looked around me. The room was really quite dark, but my eyes had finally adjusted. The men around me were all small-built, very thin, and dressed in rough-hewn dhotis and shirts. Some of them had scars on the visible parts of their bodies, long, dull, raised patches of flesh, like age-old whip marks. Several of them wore amulets tied around their upper arms. Some of them smoked beedis, one took a cigarette out of a red carton, unfamiliar but somehow also familiar. A man held a small, old-fashioned radio to his ears. Some old film song played. I tried to call my colleagues, but I couldn't get a signal. I finished my tea, left some coins on the counter and stepped out. Once I was around a corner from the shack, I got a signal. My colleagues got someone from the client's team to work out where I was and come fetch me.

I never wound up in that shack at that particular time of the week again but I did see some of those men again. I started going for morning walks in Coles Park, and on Tuesdays I saw a cluster of men in dhotis sitting around on their haunches, smoking. One of them had a red cigarette carton peeping out of his shirt pocket. One day, talking to my father on the phone, I remembered where I'd seen that carton before. When I was a boy, my father used to smoke a brand of cigarettes called Regent. Regent cigarettes came in red packs of ten with yellow lettering and an insignia of a crown. Later on, the packets had become a glossy champagne colour with gold lettering. By the time I was in high school, the brand had been discontinued. That was why the packet had seemed simultaneously familiar and obscure. I asked my father if they'd started selling Regent cigarettes again. They hadn't, he told me, and remarked on what a weird thing it was for me to wonder about suddenly.

The next Tuesday, I thought about talking to those men. When

I walked towards them, the sound of the traffic, soft at this time of the day but never completely absent, shut off. The weather felt different, too: colder, with wisps of mist in the air. Looking back, I can see that it was quite odd for me to forget why I'd stepped in their direction and resumed my walk at that point. At the time, it seemed quite natural and it was only later that I remembered about the men, their obsolete cigarettes and their archaic climate.

*There are places in Bangalore that are not Bangalore.* I thought about that man's words from time to time. I wasn't sure what they meant. My own working theory – there are other encounters I'm not telling you about because you'd think all I do in life is see weird things and my story will seem even less credible than it already is – was that these places were in fact Bangalore, but that they were glimpses of the past. Astral recordings, which was how some of the Victorian spiritualists explained hauntings, the ones who wanted to cling to a semblance of rationality in their credulity. Or like in that movie, *The Stone Tape*. It seemed to me that the city was like an old videotape which has been recorded over too many times on a crummy old VCR, and sometimes the old picture shows through. These were echoes of people and things from long ago. It was just ethereal playback, that was all.

I knew a few of the regulars in the park. One of the muscle men who hangs around the vertical bars and monkey gyms in the kiddy section – not to lure children, you understand, but to perform complicated body-building exercises using the vertical bars and so on – him and me, we'd stopped some truants throwing stones at one of the dogs in the park. There was an old man who fed pigeons that I'd sometimes spoken to. So I asked them about the archaic men.

The old man shook his head. He was a little old fellow with a small, round, brown head, dome-shaped cranium shining between long wisps of completely white hair. He wore a long grey kurta and a white dhoti. In fact, he looked a bit like some pre-independence Kannada poet. In reality, he was a retired professor of Eng. lit. Anyway, he shook his head and told me not to think too much about it.

"How long have you lived in Bangalore?" he asked me, just as I thought he had decided not to say any more.

"Um…" I calculated. "About twenty-five years."

He nodded. "That's it then. The city's in your bones now and you can see under its skin."

I tried to get more out of him, but he just repeated his initial admonition not to think too much about it, shouldered his bag of pigeon feed, hitched his dhoti up and walked away.

I spoke to the muscle man. He was dark, with slightly red eyes beaming out of his head, short-cropped curly hair, flat, broad features, very handsome in a very southern way. He was wearing some bi-coloured vest and a pair of red tracks. He'd never seen the men. On a sudden whim, I asked him how long he'd lived in Bangalore. "Only since I moved here for college. That was eight years back," he replied. We spoke a bit about the park dogs and the regular food deliveries we'd organized for them and then I carried on with my morning walk.

So there was a threshold. You'd see these things if you'd been in Bangalore long enough, if the city had become enough a part of you, you enough a part of the city to see its hidden faces. I still thought of these glimpses as echoes from the past, but it troubled me that I had drunk a very substantial glass of tea in that shack in my clients' campus. That meant there was something more than a mechanistic replay taking place. It meant reality was not what I had been taught it was.

As the days went by, I saw the small, dark men in many places. But I also saw things that could not be from any past I knew – men in SS uniforms travelling by rickshaw, whipping the rickshaw-pullers, men and women in gorgeous robes being driven in elegant limousines, strange gods and just *things*, shifty, chimeric things that slipped in through obscure portals and wreaked silent havoc in lost spaces of the night.

• • •

### Threshold
### The Prof:

One of my students once tried to make me read some of the science fiction novels he loved. He was convinced they were as much literature as the canonical texts I was employed to teach him and his classmates about. Sadly, a lot of them weren't really very good. There was a man named Heinlein who seemed to lack in basic human insight, another called Gibson who seemed to overestimate how machines could shape human nature. I liked some of the books though; there was a lady named Le Guin who seemed to have a graceful style and things to say. A man named Delany was quite brilliant too and often very challenging. Best of all, I liked the books by a man called Dick. I never did return those books to my students, in fact, the first time this had happened (students have failed to return many of my books, but I never lend them anything I cannot replace). Anyway, this man Dick uses a phrase in one of his novels: *the empire never ended*. The ensuing explication is akin to some of the spurious "phantom time" theories I have read about: that the Roman Empire never faded away and that all time since 70AD was a kind of mental creation, a collective illusion.

It is implausible. Unfalsifiable and hence not to be seriously considered as a theory. But I do wonder. I was only a boy of sixteen when this nation gained its freedom, but I remember the old order, the creamy layer of ruddy-faced British men at the very top, the higher-caste toadies working their way up the civil services ladder, the menial staff running about at their masters' beck and call. I remember the feeling of being a second-rate individual in your own homeland. I have seen the dream of freedom become real and I have watched the political class lose the will to create a nation worth being proud of, while the people give up their dreams for convenient and expensive consumerist illusions.

I have seen the empire go away, and a new empire led by fanatics, demagogues, demigods and corporate captains – the papers like to call them "honchos" – take its place. I know that the empire never ended, that empire will never end, it will only change its face and shape to fool us into believing in the illusion of change.

More than that, I know that reality is a part of their game. Dick's books, hamstrung as they are by his use of genre tropes and his obsession with Western esotericism, contain this truth. William S. Burroughs wrote this truth, but his books are too full of sex and drugs, and I could not teach them to my students. Reality is a part of their game and the best part, but also the worst, is that they are not very good at their game. Another of my student's favourite writers, Moorcock, linked all his disparate stories by saying they were all set in different parts of a multiverse. The idea of the multiverse is a key part of the creed of the religion of modern physics. The universe does not seem to make complete sense, so we imagine that there is some deep geometry which made its present face inevitable; or conversely that, somehow, every possible universe exists in a sort of foam of reality-bubbles, and hence so does ours. No great mystery, just the law of averages or something of that sort. I know the multiverse must be real, but it is not necessarily a cosmic foam with discrete realities separated by membranes. Instead, it is a superposition, a palimpsest, a video cassette (do you remember those? I remember when they were new) that has been recorded over too many times and starts to show traces of its old pictures. But that last metaphor is misleading, because all the pictures are new, all the pictures are now. Perhaps the coexistent realities are all staggered in some way, just enough out of sync with each other not to overlap. We've been tampering with the seals, and now things are starting to leak through. Realities are blending, in the corners where our dominant reality is weak, or somehow resonates best with other versions of itself.

These places where other dimensions break through are thresholds; we can walk into them and cross over. Sometimes, we can cross back, but I have known people who have never found their way back. The places are important, are the key, because things always happen around specific places and are only seen by those who know those places well. They are like the art experts who can spot a fake Mona Lisa across the room. Or maybe like the long-term intimates who can detect a tectonic shift in disposition from the mildest twitch of a cheek. In this way, too, thresholds are important: you need to have crossed a certain threshold of exposure to the city before you see the places where it shades into something else. Even then, you need some specific kind of mindset or brain chemistry; I have known people who have seen these things and then somehow rationalized or simply blocked them.

I have learned some of the stories of the people from these other worlds. The small, dark men in dhotis are night-soil workers, from a place that is congruent with our Bangalore's Grace Town. They belong to a particular sub-caste that was thought to be completely lost to forced conversions during the British era. In their world, social change slowed down to a near-stasis, and they are still cleaners of toilets and gutters, ostracised for their profession and doomed by this very ostracism to never aspire to any other. But they like their cigarettes, and their tea. Sometimes you can see them smoking beedis, or some brand of cigarette that is obsolete in our own reality. Twice I have even sipped tea in the rude stalls that they are allowed to run near the places where they work.

These men are harmless. They are deeply scarred and subdued by their lives and even when they crossover and rest in our version of the city for a while, they soon return, convinced that it is their karma to live the way they do.

Others are desperate. They come from other times, other circumstances. There is a world where India is part of the Glorious Third Reich and the Indian race – whatever that is – is being purified. They will always be Lesser Aryans, but still Aryans, of course, and by selective breeding their best traits will slowly be brought out. In the meantime, Indians with Negroid or Semitic features – that is to say, features that look like such to the golden-haired Master Race – are sterilized and put to work in the most gruelling, unsafe professions. The caste Hindus and fair-skinned northerners aid and abet the Master Race, initiating honour killings when the low-borns dally with their betters, confining them to slave pens and keeping them ignorant and brow-beaten. It is not this cowed majority that is desperate, though. They are merely desolate. It is, instead, the pampered lapdogs of the Master Race, the Lesser Aryans, who wish to come through. Some of them, at least. The ones who have received just enough education to understand what is wrong with their world. Their desperation seems to punch holes in reality, and often they may come through in a place that was not a threshold before. Once here, all they want to do is find a way to create a fake identity and blend into this world seamlessly. There is an underground network of fixers who will help them do this for a price, and that is yet another reason why so many are corrupt – they are forced into it by these touts in return for this new life.

Then there are the hunters. Some are British, some are German, some are Persian, Indian, Chinese, American. Some are not human at all. They are masters of India, or at least of Bangalore, in their own worlds and they come here to hunt humans. It is a thrill for them, apparently, to kill people in another world and leave behind unsolvable mysteries. Then there are the slavers; I probably do not need to explain them to you.

These are just some of the human interlopers. Animals cross the thresholds at will; they have always lived in more worlds than the one we can perceive. But there are also other things. Gods, strange gods who wander the worlds looking for devotees. Lost and lonely ghosts, simple-minded ones who can be thwarted with simple-minded admonitions to come another day. Less simple-minded and harmless things, strange god-creatures and growths that can be conjured by certain broken melodies. There are monsters, creatures that partake of variegated forms and have various, terrible appetites. It is hard for them to cross over, their realities are very different from ours and the overlap is very minimal, but a determined or lucky few make the crossing.

In the balance, it is definitely unsafe for us to cross over these thresholds, to step through these gates. The more activity there is at a threshold, the more persistent and permeable it becomes. The more fixed and substantial a threshold point becomes, the greater the likelihood that things we do not wish to encounter will come through. I think I have even seen signs that the threshold points can induce a larger leak-through, with sections of our reality changing, becoming pockets of alien life within our own city.

I do not know if this is happening in any other cities. You would think there would be reports if they are. But then again, I have read no reports of the things I personally know to have taken place in Bangalore. Whoever is playing the reality game, they do not want their errors publicized. Errors – or stages in their real plans? I do not know. All I know is that it does not do to think too much about the threshold points, to let yourself speculate for too long on what they imply, or to believe that you stand a chance of finding a better world on the other side. I have seen all the places; none of them are better. None of them, this one included, are any good. And there is worse to come.

• • •

### Faraway, Converging
### The swarm:

To us, you are one. To you, we are many, but we are one, too.

We come, keening on the high winds from where there is no space. We come, ululating, on tides from when there is no time. Are we fleeing something, some cosmic holocaust in some distant, wildly disparate dimension? Are we rushing headlong to some far-off and obscure fate, and your dimension is just a point that happens to be on the route, a rest stop along the way? Are you our goal, your flesh and bone and horn and nail, your tissues and sinews, your nerves and synapses, are you our prey, is this why we are converging upon your reality?

To tell the truth, or *a* truth, we do not know. We are multitudes and our motives are many; but this rush to the nexus where you happen to be is the prevailing trend. We are what our majority wills us to be, but the majority is one of direction, not necessarily purpose. In this we are truer to the rhythms of reality than you with your individual volition, your sapient choice-making.

So, yes. We are coming. Ripples spread in advance of us, loosening the ties of reality, weakening the walls between places that would never see each other otherwise. We are coming to this place, this one place amidst infinity, and then we will be gone and so will the place.

To us, you are one. To you, we are many. But we shall all be one. We shall all be none.

• • •

*Threshold: Nexus*
**The hack:**

This is not a nightmare. That became obvious pretty soon.

This story ends in a bar, too. It's my story, and I like bars. They are reassuring places, containing the basics of human nature: the need for oblivion and the instinct to exploit. So here I sit in this bar, drinking too much, talking to an older man, an older man with a salt-and-pepper beard, thinning hair, keen features like some anthropomorphic raptor, telling him that he was only partly correct. He leans in close and I hiss at him, trying not to be heard by anyone else, glancing around me nervously.

"Parts of Bangalore are not in Bangalore at all. Bangalore is not what we thought it was. It is a nexus. It is a target, and something is heading for it."

Outside, a night sky stretches out above the city. Dogs bark, cars honk and rumble. Songs echo from temples, from advertising jingles on a hundred thousand TV sets, shadows twist and writhe and loom over the shops and the slums and the office towers and the apartment blocks and the dying lakes and the litter-strewn parks and the people and all.

# CRUNCHABLES

## IAN MCDONALD

**I am** on the Moot at the bottom of the garden, observing the new type of aircraft, when Joyce calls from the backdoor that we're out of crunchables.

I'll explain. The previous owners of the house left a large concrete slab a metre square, thirty centimetres high. What it's for I have no notion, but Joyce calls it the Moot and the Moot is the best platform for observing what's new in aerial phenomena.

"We got pouches?" I ask.

"Elaine1 won't eat pouches," Joyce answers.

This vexes me. My role is to log and sketch new arrivals into this universe. I know you sneer at the Aerial Phenomena Observers Group, nosy old men with too much time on their hands, but ten years from now – maybe five years – you'll be glad someone was taking notes.

"She eats pouches when you give them to her."

"She only eats pouches when I put crunchables on top."

I finish my sketch of this thing in the sky: an aerial ribbon, I can best describe it as, very high and very long, because it is interrupted in places by clouds. Or maybe the sky, like some kind of bootlace weaving in and out of our reality.

"I suppose this means Ersin's."

"Ersin's."

"Is it still there? Have you checked?"

"You know I can't manage that loft ladder," Joyce says. Elaine1 does her want-feed miaow at the kitchen door. Why can't she be like Elaine2, who's happy to roll around on the Moot in the sun all day? It irks me that in another universe we had a patient, sweet-natured cat. At least we only got a cat. Some got dinosaurs. Or worse.

I unhook the loft door and pull down the Slingsby ladder. Careful over the joists: there're piles of tinned food, toilet paper and fuel for the generator up there, all happy to trip me up. We're responsible stockpilers. Two tins here, a packet of pasta there. I must put in proper light and flooring. Some day my luck will give out and through the ceiling I will go. I open the skylight, get up on the box and survey the skyline.

The aerial phenomenon I witnessed from the Moot is moving off to the northwest. Miles long and still no end to it. New zeppelins docked at Kennington airship tower. I like seeing zeppelins. Cloud over the summit of Quarter Mountain. On quiet nights when the wind blows right, I've heard the rumble of rockfalls from the two sheer sides where the Break tore it free from its home range and dropped it on top of Luton. East, the Wonderwall is vivid today. Some say it's like water. Some say a rippling rainbow heat-haze. Some a jellyfish stuffed with glitter. What nonsense! You can't stuff a jellyfish! All I know is that it goes right round Peckham and nothing gets out or in. What goes on behind it we do not know and we do not want to know.

It's not good to look at it for too long.

Those trees to the south, Dulwich way, they're new. Extraordinary great things. Rise straight up, they do, two or three kilometres, then in the final few hundred metres or so they open like huge red-green parasols. I'm not sure they have leaves –

these birding glasses really don't have the magnification for fine observations. The Dulwich mega-trees stand so close that their canopies – is that the term? – join and quite obscure Norwood. I see things flying. Large things, with more than two wings. I should make sketches but I have a mission. I hope the people got away. Funny that neither of us felt anything.

I note the location in my journal. It looks an admirable destination for an Adventure Club expedition. When I say Adventure Club, I mean of course the Men's Shed, since I'm in three organisations at the Shed: the Adventure Club, the Aerial Phenomena Observers Group and the South Camberwell Community Resilience Committee.

Everything has turned to adventure since the Break. Even a trip to the corner shop.

Three days and the smoke still goes up from across the river. At least the noise has stopped. *Wump-WUMP, wump-WUMP, wump-WUMP.* Day and night.

But Ersin's is the issue. If I go up on tiptoe and lean out over the roof tiles I can peer around the corner of Hope Street and check he's still there. Not only still there. He has the sign out for fuel. Never turn down an opportunity for fuel. If the Community Resilience Committee drives one point home, it's that. Always Be Fuelling.

"Fuel time," I tell Joyce on my way to the equipment room. She fetches the shopping trolley while I prep. The safety ropes. The Mace, in case of attack. Shotgun, in case of serious attack, by beast or – more likely – human. Twelve sovereigns sewn into the money belt. The old-fashioned compass. The most up-to-date map set. After a Break there's sometimes a way back, a long way round. If you're lucky and the landscapes line up, it may only take a few months. Matches. Water purification tablets. Water bottle. Decent knife. Solar phone charger, for when you make it back here again.

"Kiss for the bold explorer," I say at the front door.

"Kiss and Godspeed, bold explorer," Joyce says. I lean into my trolley. It's a hefty push. No one has filled in potholes since the Break. All infrastructure is in poor repair. The Festive Road Maintenance Committee tries to keep the gutters unblocked – we're prone to flooding – but to be honest, you never know one day to the next whether your drain is going to flow free or suddenly terminate in solid rock, or a mosaic wall, or cascade into some newly arrived underground catacomb. Still, you have to make an effort, don't you?

The madames Ong-Trett-Reloon hoe their beans in the front garden of Number 28.

"Good morning, Leighton." Yeterba Ong-Trett-Reloon says while Restingi Ong-Trett-Reloon says at the same time, "Going shopping?"

I respond with a "Good morning" and a simultaneous nod of the head. It takes practice to co-ordinate the gesture and the voice, especially if they contradict each other, but it would be height of bad manners to reply to only one of them. "Mellifret and Yotenda well?" I say. The Ong-Trett-Reloons came over in the initial Break, in their little car, along with a chunk of woodland and car park. The woodland still occupies the space where Numbers 27 and 29 were and the houses backing onto Festive Road. Yeterba/Restingi, Mellifret/Yotenda and their two sets of twins, Yalum/Dreynatfi and Clatori'inga/Yeterbeen. They'd been out for a countryside picnic when the Break hit. They come from a world where everyone is a twin. The Perrys, late of Number 28, were over visiting Keith and Margaret at Number 27 when the Break broke. They went with them, wherever that is. It's not always a straight swap from one universe to another. I've heard any God's amount of theories about the timing and location and meaning of the transitions: maps and leylines and number tricks and verses in the Bible and the Holy Koran. Fibonacci numbers. Kabala. Astrology. You name it. I tell you: there's no reason nor rhyme. No plan, no meaning. Reality is what happens.

But it happened sweetly for the Ong-Trett-Reloons, who moved straight into Number 28. We all pushed their car across the road into the drive. It hasn't moved since. Something to do with the shape of the charger plug. Tell you this: they're better neighbours than the Perrys ever were. And it's nice having what is effectively our own little private park on the road.

On the corner of Jubilee Gardens I hear airhorns. I stop at the junction. Three kids riding bopos come bowling on to Festive Road. Those bopos, they're quite a thing. Quills gleaming all colours of the rainbow. Claws bright like polished brass. Big teeth, like a beak divided in three, etched in fancy patterns with battery acid. One stops, rears on its four hind legs. It near throws its rider from her saddle. A bopo standing tall is the height of a second-floor window. That's a solid fall. No protective gear. Skittish, fretful creatures, bopos. I've learnt to keep well back from them. Why anyone would try to ride them, I don't know. Kids will ride anything. The rider waves to me and shouts a hello. I recognise her behind her dust mask: Rayleen from 112. She fires a blast from her warning airhorn, clicks her tongue and shakes the reins. Air whistles in the quills as the bopo dashes past. I watch them stalk and skip and shimmy and pounce up Festive Road, and they surely are a magnificent sight. Like heraldry come to life. And the riders keep the species alive. The rest of the fauna from bopo-universe got wiped out in traffic accidents within three months. And some were bigger than bopos.

Now I'm thinking of Letitia and James and the grandkids up in Edmonton. The mobile network was up most of last week so we could Zoom, but things change so fast. Worlds come and go every day. I think I'd feel something if they'd been caught – fingers crossed, whistle twice it doesn't happen – but we all believe magic stuff all the time since the Break. But every time we lose the network, those are long nights wondering if I'll ever hear from my girl again. And my boy Aaron in Thanet. That always was another universe.

I find Nazi Alert Advisories taped and cable-tied to everything that will hold one all over the junction with Kingsway. Usually I'd ignore them – I've never seen world-hopping Nazis, though the story is the multiverse is overrun with them. All those Hitler-wins universes, you know? Those Nazis are making solemn leagues and alliances to take over the rest of it. Urban legend, I say. But the Greater Kingsway Vigilance Group is guarding the junction in their folding chairs and picnic tables, and I know the kind of petty bastards they can be, so I just nod and say "Good morning" and turn left down by the zep port.

Derek calls me from the ticket office. Well, really it's a garden shed. And the zep port is an old 5G phone mast with a platform welded to the top and ladders lashed to the sides. You'll never get me up those things, like you'll never get me up in an airship. Zeps: handsome to look at, insanity to fly in. Parallel universes, it's always zeppelins.

"Shopping, Leighton?"

"Cat food, Deks," I answer. "Can't stop. Cat is hungry."

"Cats is always hungry," Derek says. "You see that weird shit in the sky?"

"Sky's nothing but weird shit, friend. You mean the thing looked like it was lacing up the sky?"

"That one. Want to hear my theory?"

I do not, but it would be the acme of bad manners to say that, so I click on the foot brake on my shopping trolley (fitted it myself with Amal's welding kit) and lean on the bar.

"This is my theory: what you say, my friend, is exactly the truth. In and out and in and out of our world. Sewing the multiverse back together. Someone out there doesn't like these damn worlds falling into each other. They've sent something to stitch up the tears and fix it."

"You think that, Deks? Folly! That doesn't fix nothing. Okay, maybe nothing new comes over, but what's here stays here. And what's there stays there. How's that a fix?"

I leave that pungent question with him. His brother, Sean, and his wife, Mercy, they got caught up in the South Kingsway Break. What came over was a square kilometre of desert with some ruins that looked ancient and modern at the same time. Where they've gone, not even God knows. The multiverse is big. The biggest you can imagine; the multiverse is bigger than that. Because if there's an infinity of things you can imagine, there's a bigger infinity of things you can't imagine. And the multiverse contains both of those. An infinite number of infinities.

That same damn vigilance group that put up the Nazi alert strung Do-Not-Cross tape all around that stretch of lone and level sands and hung radiation warnings like Christmas decorations. Nazis and radioactivity. Big scaries.

"Crunchables, Deks," I say. "And you have incoming." The shadow of a zep slides down the roofs and crosses the street. I could watch dockings all day but Derek will eat your afternoon so I flip off the foot brake and push. But I do glance up and there stands the pilot at the wheel with her peaked cap and huge epaulets, and there are the passengers in their wicker chairs behind the portholes. Some look down; some have already moved to the gangplank. Derek stirs his lazy ass to grab the mooring line, hook it to the winch and wind the airship in.

Ersin's stands on a little peninsula of our world jutting out into a zone of big grey tenements, block after block, street after street, straight and square and ugly. And grey. Sometimes when it Breaks, it Breaks clean and neat: rectangles, circles. Sometimes it's blobby and squiggly. There's a bit of Clapham that's like an octopus orgy. Grey City is like one of those cells you might have seen on old science shows: bits and blobs sticking out, sticking in. So Ersin's is tucked in the end of a little sock of our world among the grey tenements. What kind of world that is, I do not know. No bird of our world has ever perched on those roofs. No windows, only high slits just under the roof. At night, light beams from them in shafts. I've never been, but word from the Adventure Club says the walls are warm to the touch. And there's a high-pitched whining-whistle noise in your head like tinnitus that gets louder the further in you go. No one's ever made it past three streets. Well, maybe, but if they have they've never come back.

Ersin's was a fine Turkish corner store, but now it's a proper bazaar of wonders, with stuff on its shelves from all across the multiverse. Ersin caters to a diverse clientele.

I don't know what we'd do if Ersin's got taken. There's a Tesco Metro at Kendall Cross, but that's a sprint through the West Camberwell toxic rainforest or a long trek round Kennington Park and the crystal spires of the Elmington Estate.

Ersin's son Omer is on fuel duty.

"Maximum of three," he says. I take three – we never use more than two, but like I said, ABF: Always Be Fuelling. That ceiling's going to come down, Leighton, Joyce says. I shall be crushed in my bed; you wait and see. Omer helps me load the heavy plastic drums into my trolley. It's a heavy job, steering that cart around the tight turns between Ersin's aisles, but you got to get the fuel in early.

"Got new seeds," Ersin says. He is a small man with a big moustache and a proud bearing. "Borlotti beans, winter squash, beetroot. Rainbow chard."

Fancy stuff, but he takes what he can get. Sometimes I wonder if growing veg for seed might be a smart business proposition. But what's smart today could be stupid tomorrow. We don't know. That's the thing. Plan all you like but the multiverse has other ideas.

"Looking for cat food, Ersin."

"We've got Mews in. It's basically Whiskas in another universe."

"Is that pouches?"

"Cans."

"Like chopped meat in jelly or sometimes gravy?"

Ersin looks over his glasses to study a can.

"'Select cuts in a delicious casserole gravy.'"

"No. That will not do. I need crunchy stuff. In a big bag."

"Sorry, Leighton. Pouches is all we have."

I search the pet food top to bottom, front to back, for in a shop as comprehensive and ever-changing as Ersin's, stock can easily get mis-shelved, or pushed to the back. Customers shoot me hard looks. Some even grumble aloud as they squeeze past my trolley, but a man must be thorough. I don't want to come here more than I need. I find an empty cardboard display carton for Dreamies, which I would have bought as the absolute last resort, because I truly believe it is kitty-cocaine. Of Dreamies, there is none. I pay for the fuel and some milk, tea, Hobnobs – you can never have enough of those – and two Twirls. A reward for me and Joyce. The gold exchange rate has moved again. Never in the customer's favour, of course.

It's so much harder pushing that trolley loaded. The iffy wheel runs troublesome now and the dodgy steering sends it into every drain cover and pothole.

Bugger Nazi warnings. Look left, look right, look up and down – no sign of the vigilance group so I press straight on. Half-track patrols? No. Ornithopters with swastikas on their wings? Not one. Giant storm-trooper battle robots big as office blocks? Folly! But twenty steps past the end of Jubilee Road, the headache starts.

This is a particular kind of headache. I've only ever had it once before, but once is all you need. Imagine your brain turning inside out and all the new raw surfaces brushing against the inside of your skull. The slightest move of your head and everything goes swimming and catches fire. At the same time. And it's there all at once. Boom. Other headaches creep up: not this one. You get no warning. It is the warning.

There's a Break coming. A piece of our universe is about to come loose and fall into another. And a piece of another universe is about to take its place.

I know the drill. Head down, head on. Head fast. The headache comes first, then the wind that pushes away from the Break-line. Whatever caused the Break and keeps on causing it (I've heard theories from the Large Hadron Collider to 5G phone masts to the Book of Revelation), it's careful to keep people away from the cut line. People do not want to get caught there: that is one mean clean guillotine. The wind pushes me back toward Kingsway and away from Festive Road and Joyce. And my two Elaines. Head down. Head on. But the wind is stronger with every step and I am not a young man. And the drill is just the drill – paper learning – because the headache is as close as I've ever got to a Break.

I didn't look. The drill says it's best not to look.

But I have to look and *oh my days* I see why they tell you that now: it's like a wall of fire across the world, if fire was made of water and what might be faces. The gale blowing from it is a hurricane now. I fight for every step. I veer, I stagger. If I stumble, that wind will bowl me head-over-arse. And my head beats like a sound system. But it's not a wind. Does a wind have a voice? Voices? Wind is moving air. This is space itself moving.

The trolley. I have to let it go. Fuel, Hobnobs, tea, milk. And

Twirls. The wind catches the trolley and sends it sailing, turning as it rolls back to the inter-universal Nazis.

It's like walking into water. Roaring, shouting water that boils inside your head. In the flames are the faces, the faces between worlds. They turn. They look at me. At me.

I push forward, one last, everything push.

And I see what they see, all the time, forever. I am everything. I am everywhere. I touch everyone. I hear every voice in the multiverse shouting as one and yet each clear and distinct.

And I'm out. I'm through. And the wind that isn't a wind catches me and sends me reeling up past Jubilee Gardens. Sailing home to Festive Road. Almost bowls me over, it does, but Leighton Thomas always was light on his feet and I keep my balance and my bones intact and with every step the wind drops. I sit on the Ong-Trett-Reloonses' garden wall and they fluster and fuss – *are you all right can we make you some tea is there anything we can do with you* – but really I'm looking back down Festive Road, past Jubilee Gardens to a strip of scorched-looking savanna with what looks like a blue barrel with leaves coming out the top, only the size of a house. Half of a blue barrel with leaves coming out the top, I should say. It's been sliced clean and neat top to bottom.

That could have been me.

I never want to hear those everything-voices ever again. I don't want to feel those not-flames. They burn into the heart of everything.

There's a hollow in the centre of the barrel tree and in that hollow are squishy wriggling things about the size of my hand that start to spill out onto Festive Road. This is a job for the Men's Shed.

"I'm fine, thank you," I tell the Ong-Trett-Reloons. "Joyce will be worried."

"Of course, of course."

The strip of blue-barrel-land is narrow, about two houses' worth. I can see Jubilee Road right through it. Ersin's is likely still there. Won't know for sure until I get up into the attic. Maybe not today.

The boys at the Shed have a theory that the Break zones are getting smaller. Finer and finer slices. We'll all end up in a universe of our own.

"Joyce! I'm all right. I'm all right!"

She meets me at the front gate.

"Oh, Leighton, I was so worried. Oh, you're safe, you're safe."

She bustles me into the kitchen, sits me down, puts on the kettle.

"I got tea," I say. "But I lost it with the trolley."

Elaine rubs around my legs, tail up. Hungry-affectionate. Cats, I tell you – they are the worst creatures.

"Tea. Hobnobs. Three drums of fuel."

"We've plenty of fuel," Joyce says.

"Twirls."

Elaine1 stares at me, miaowing now.

"And crunchables for her."

"Crunchables?"

"They had some new stuff. Prime cuts in casserole. Like what I'd eat. No crunchables."

"Leighton, are you doting?" Joyce takes out a pouch and slides the contents into Elaine1's bowl. She is in like a beast. "Elaine only eats crunchables if there's meat on top."

# QUORUM'S EYE

## ALVARO ZINOS-AMARO

**The dread** started up in early fall and by winter it was Celosya Leus' constant companion. In a somatic, sweat-inducing way, the holidays made her sick. The barreling inevitability of what was to come, and with it the reminder of what had once been, flattened out her nervous system, left her with a dry mouth, and on the really lonely days, which was to say on regular days, pushed her to the edge of heaving. This year would go down just like the last three. She knew that with the same certainty she knew that her n-credits account always held a zero balance. When the final weeks of the year rolled around, Celosya's mom and brother would be swept up in the Interfaith Interface, becoming barely aware of her existence, and, alone in her room, she'd count down the days to the start of a meaningless new year.

Celosya knew that before quantum tunneling had been used to create the first Bridge to parallel realities, some seventy years ago, the festive season had been different. Back then every person was only that one person, and a group of these single selves would come together to celebrate. They made home-cooked meals and luxuriated in placid, pointless conversations. They drank. Sometimes they got in each other's faces over stupid shit. Some even caroled. Celosya's wandering mind fantasized about these scenarios. Her daydreaming brain would throw up tableaux of domestic contentment, perfected by their very imperfections. Unemployed, directionless, she had a lot of time on her hands to imagine these things. All she craved, as the year came to a close, was to spend a day or two off-chip with her mom and brother, so that they could experience the wonder of aloneness together. But she knew her family couldn't afford to pass up the Interfaith Interface, or I-Squared, as people called it. It was one of the biggest, and therefore one of the best-paying, multi-reality meta-data harvesting events of the year.

Thinking about this on an early November morning, hours before sunrise, Celosya felt the familiar nettle of self-blame sting her mood. She crept out from under the blankets, decided to skip breakfast, and headed out into the bracing cold. Four in the morning was the only time of day she liked to leave their apartment. The familiar rhythm of her brisk walk, the flush of cold air in her lungs, filled up the minutes with a kind of vitality that otherwise eluded her. The streets in her neighborhood were as empty as could be. She enjoyed avoiding people almost as much as they enjoyed avoiding themselves.

The few folks she passed were either on-chip or working Quorum. She couldn't blame them. People had to make a living. Of course her mom, Ailu, and her brother, Lum, would jump at the chance for I-Squared n-creds. They had to earn as much as possible to support Celosya's sorry self. If she'd had a job, any job, things might be different. But three years ago, barely seventeen, around the time Dad had died, she had dropped out of Quorum Prep, and with that decision forsaken any chance of a serious occupation. If you didn't neurally join the subset of parallel-reality selves who shared a certain kinship with you—your Quorum—you were just you. You could never hope to compete against other Quora, whole enclaves of selves merged in seamless trans-reality collaboration. For a while she worked low-wage jobs like customer-AI interface or nursing-home admin, but the gigs dried up fast, and there was always someone better qualified or Quorumed nipping at her heels.

On the return leg of her jaunt, Celosya saw her neighbor Nallide making her way towards their apartment complex. Celosya considered changing her route so as to avoid her, but her fingers were very cold, and she didn't mind Nallide as much as other people. When Celosya had been younger, the older woman had regaled her with stories of the pre-Bridge days. Only because of Nallide did Celosya know what the holidays used to be like, and it was Nallide who had given Celosya her first books on mathematics, print relics whose yellow-hued pages and distinctive musty odor made their initially indecipherable symbols that much more tantalizing.

"A mean cold today," Nallide said when Celosya was a few feet away.

"I don't mind it," Celosya said. She made every effort not to rub her hands together.

"I can see that," Nallide said unironically. The anticipation of daybreak danced in her black eyes.

"I should get back inside," Celosya said. "Before they wake up."

"Prove any good theorems lately?"

Celosya jerked her head. "That was a long time ago."

"Was it?" Nallide said. "Feels like yesterday."

When Celosya was a girl, every time she solved a problem or proved a theorem from one of the books Nallide had given her, Nallide would transfer n-creds to her account. Celosya had reflected, in the years since, that Nallide must be an exceptionally gullible person, because she took the young Celosya at her word whenever she told her about one of her math accomplishments. If Celosya had been raised differently, she might have taken advantage of the situation. She could, come to think of it, still take advantage of it now. But there was something about the depth of the creases on Nallide's face that discouraged such notions. Maybe it was because Nallide was so gullible—and too old to be Quorumed—that she hadn't gotten farther in life. She'd been performing the exact same tech maintenance job for twenty years, without promotions or rewards for loyalty. The world took her for granted. Which, Celosya considered, was one step up from her own ignoble level of non-existence.

On impulse Celosya asked, "Do you ever think about doing something else?"

Nallide's shoulders shifted in a peculiar way. She seemed to lean forward into time itself. "Inspecting and replacing Bridge drives is an important responsibility," she said. It sounded like she was reading from one of those ancient books.

"Right," Celosya said. "I meant... Well, I don't know. It's something I think about."

"What, gunning for my job?" Nallide laughed. "I should watch out then."

"No," Celosya said. "Just... things."

"What do you do when your mom and brother are working?" Nallide said.

In that moment, Celosya felt like the dawn might not arrive. Night would reign forever, and Celosya would be one of the few people on the planet that could cope with it. She couldn't blurt out that she idled the time away. "I keep myself busy," she said instead. "I still work on problems from the books you gave me. Sometimes new ones I look up on my own." That had happened once, exactly, two years before, but the memory burned bright, so Celosya followed the fuse.

"When I was your age," Nallide said, her voice tinged with wistfulness, "I dreamed of solving a Certified."

"I could if I wanted to," Celosya said quickly. "I know that for a fact. I just need to brush up on some things. It's boring but not hard."

Nallide's lips parted, revealing the tip of a smile. "I don't doubt that you could," she said. "Why don't you pick one, for kicks, and tell me about it when it's done?"

"Sure," Celosya said. She spoke faster than before, as though catching up to her own voice. "But why just one? I'll do five. Maybe ten. Otherwise it's not really worth putting in the effort."

"Whenever you crack that first one," Nallide said, "I'll give you some n-creds for old time's sake."

"You don't have to do that," Celosya said.

"True," Nallide replied. "But I'm sure you could find uses for them. You still work off-chip, don't you?"

"Of course," Celosya said. She didn't bother to hide her contempt. "Pen and paper. That's how some of the greatest problems were solved in the past. Before AIs, before the Bridge, before Quora. There was a man named Andrew Wiles who spent years writing things out in his office. Nobody even knew what he was doing. He worked totally alone. And he proved a beautiful theorem by Fermat, one that would be considered a triple Certified today."

"Really?"

"He didn't need to be part of a cluster of parallel selves," Celosya said. "He himself was enough."

"What does your mom say when you speak like this?"

"I've learned better," Celosya said. "But I know exactly what she'd say: 'Being part of a group doesn't stop making you an individual.'"

Nallide pretended to quote. She pursed her lips. "'We're all part of something greater.'" She seemed amused. "And what do you reply to that?"

"That an over-dependence on groups also makes us smaller."

"I've always known one thing about you," Nallide said. "Wherever you take yourself, others will follow—whether they're other yous or not."

"I'm going to be late," Celosya said, and IF'd her access code. The apartment door creaked open.

"I'll see you around," Nallide said, with unwelcome certainty.

• • •

Over the next few days, Celosya told herself that Nallide couldn't seriously expect her to solve a Certified problem, but a voice in the back of her head kept nagging at her. Celosya did everything she could to silence it. She spent her time looking out the window, listening to music, and reading anything but mathematics. One evening she received an alert of an n-credit transfer from Nallide. That was it, then. The old lady didn't actually expect her to do a full Certified. She was just using that as a front to be charitable. Otherwise she would have at least waited for Celosya to say something.

That night Celosya had trouble sleeping, and when 4 a.m. came around she couldn't muster the energy to roll out of bed. She lingered under the sheets until she heard her mother get up.

In the kitchen, Ailu said, "I hear you've taken on some kind of fiendishly difficult math problem others can't crack? Very impressive."

Celosya wanted to tell her that there had been a mistake, but her mouth danced to a different tune. "Maybe more than one," she said.

The words seemed to infuse her mom's frail body with vigor. Joy waxed crescent in Ailu's maroon eyes, breaking through the stained glass of a lifetime's labor. "I'm giving you something for your efforts," she said.

"Mom, don't worry about it," Celosya said. "Certified problems already have n-cred prizes attached."

"I get paid on Friday," her mother continued. "I'll see what I can do."

"Please, it's okay," Celosya said.

Ailu was still for a moment. "I'm so proud of you."

Celosya mumbled a thank you and retreated back to her room. She waited for Lum to start his on-chip shift flossing algorithms and then ventured outside. One of the girls she knew from Quorum Prep saw her on the building's front landing and smiled in her direction. Celosya received a retinal alert from her asking if she could help her sister with one of her math courses. With a blink she deleted it, then headed back inside and turned off all notifications. But a part of her dwelled on the request, not entirely displeased.

As the day passed, idle curiosity got the best of her, and she looked up the Certifieds she remembered. The problems looked intimidating and intractable. And if whole Quora couldn't conquer them, what made her think that her untrained, solitary self stood a chance? The third problem she spotted, though, sent her mind thinking about the convergence of harmonic series, and she wrote down some equations on a piece of paper, trying to tease out what they implied. Before she knew it, hours had passed and she'd filled out a dozen pages. A knock on the door told her Lum was on break. Before she had a chance to say she was busy, he opened the door a crack, saw her hunched over her notebook, and said, "Keep up the great work."

Celosya was about to tell him it was a misunderstanding, but before she uttered a sound he'd closed the door and left.

A week went by, and she managed to slip into the semblance of a routine. During her pre-dawn strolls she didn't see anyone she knew, and when she was back home she tinkered with her ideas regarding the convergence of infinite series. Most of the time she kept all alerts off and ignored incoming messages. It helped with her concentration and reduced her anxiety. One morning she was barely ten steps away from the apartment complex when Nallide seemed to step out of nowhere, a beatific smile sending ripples of wrinkles across the drooping folds of her cheeks.

"Look at you," Nallide said.

"Uh, hi," Celosya replied.

"You're so productive," the old woman said. "I never used to get up this early at your age. Now, of course, my schedule isn't my own…"

Her voice drifted off, and Celosya got the impression that Nallide hadn't slept in a long time, possibly days. Her eyes were festooned with ruptured blood vessels, and she held her right hand close to her side, trying to hide a slight tremor.

Celosya tried to picture the old woman when she had been Celosya's age, growing up with parents born into a completely different world. "Do you think that life was better," Celosya asked, "before the Bridge?"

Nallide didn't hesitate to respond. "Don't believe that for a minute. People used to agonize about whether we were alone in the universe. The Bridge showed us we're not—even if it's just more of us. I do wish I'd been younger when we developed the Quorum adaptation tech, though, so that I could have joined mine. What I wouldn't give for the pleasure of my own company…"

Celosya still had a couple of years to change her mind before her brain was too fully developed for the transformation. It was something she had become very good at not thinking about. "I don't need other *mes*," she said. "I've got enough with one."

A shadow of exhaustion fell across Nallide's face, the darkness sharpening the contours of her features. "Tell me about a problem you've worked out," she said.

"I'm partway through several," Celosya said. "I'll definitely let you know."

"That's my girl." Nallide appeared consumed by remembrance, and Celosya took advantage of the lapse in her attention to say goodbye and make a quick exit.

When she entered her apartment, she found Lum in the living room. She could tell from the trickling data-glimmers in the corners of his eyes that he was on-chip, but he retained enough active focus to have a conversation with her.

"Your name isn't attached to any Certifieds," he said. "Here, or elsewhere. My Quora checked."

Celosya paused. "That's because I haven't finished one yet," she said.

He stared straight at her. "Nallide seems to think otherwise, from the messages she's been sending Mom."

"How about you mind your own business?" Celosya said. "You, and however many hundred other versions of you I'm currently speaking with."

Lum said, "Me and my kinship selves have every right to be concerned. What are you really up to, Celosya? Stringing a senile neighbor along for n-creds? Lying to Mom so she won't kick you out?"

Celosya's pale face flushed. It was said that becoming connected to other yous across realities stabilized your mood and made you more resilient, that the Quorum provided a unique perspective stemming from the self but simultaneously outside of it. In this moment Celosya was especially thankful to be completely disconnected and independent, so she could experience everything as she truly felt it.

"I'm working on something important," she said, shaking her head.

"For who?"

"For me," she said.

"And who else?" he pressed.

"That's not my concern. The work is its own reward."

"No," Lum said, "your concern is you. That's the definition of selfish."

"Being myself doesn't make me selfish," she said, turning up her chin, "any more than being in your Quorum makes you selfless."

He sized her up. "Whatever else you are or aren't doing, one thing's for sure. You're leading people on."

Hearing those words, a deep feeling of forsakenness stabbed at Celosya, and no amount of mental prevarication allowed her to parry its blows. This wasn't the familiar forlornness she disliked but thought she must endure as the price of seeing herself clearly. It was an aloneness that hollowed her out, reducing what there was of her to see in the first place. She avoided Lum's gaze and walked off in silence.

Inside her room she opened her notebook in self-defiance, as though mocking her own efforts to clarify her ideas about series. What right did she have to complain about anyone else's choices, when she herself wasn't choosing more wisely but merely more solitarily? Lum was right, and his own choice to join his Quorum was proof that it wasn't the end of the world. Despite the new personality overlays, he was still the same old Lum. Being in quantum-tunneled communion with a set of parallel selves who shared a certain kinship with him hadn't rewritten his character, just added a few accents. And at least his work, though tedious, served a purpose. What was the point in her exploring ideas that no one else was interested in? If her other selves could see fit to join a Quorum, and they were versions of her, wasn't she just fooling herself by believing she was somehow different? She wasn't special. Pride before a fall—except you had to first rise in order to descend. She couldn't fall because she wasn't moving. Her pride, she thought, was the delusion that came from confusing *being lost* with *being*.

That night Celosya tumbled into an uneasy sleep and dreamed of numbers lined up like infinite steel bars in an endless jail.

• • •

The following few days she didn't leave the apartment. The I-Squared was only a week away now and memories of her dad assailed her, unbidden but dependable like clockwork. She lost her appetite. When her mom checked in on her, she told her she had a cold and just needed rest to recover. But eventually things became too suffocating in her room and she had to get out. She went for a walk on an overcast morning. After having been cooped up inside for so long, she found herself overcome by the desire to roam forever.

She turned on chip notifications and discovered several new requests for help with math items. There was also an additional n-cred transfer from Nallide, with a simple message attached: *One equation at a time.*

Without a conscious destination in mind, Celosya's legs ended up carrying her to her old neighborhood, where she'd lived when her parents had enrolled her in Quorum Prep. Their old apartment building was largely unchanged, except for a new dataglass finish to the main entrance, which did little to offset the surrounding grime. Eight blocks down the street was the building where she'd started her training to one day merge with her Quorum. The location had since been converted to a fulfillment center for local drone-based deliveries and she had no interest in revisiting it. But she remembered a pedestrian area nearby, finished with cobblestones and housing a small circular fountain comprising a flat marble base and two light-grey, wave-shaped pieces of granite. She remembered how after her first Quorum Prep classes she'd wandered off to the fountain and studied her shimmering reflection in the thin curtain of water flowing down those slate-colored slabs, pondering whether her other selves across the Bridge shared her same sense of inadequacy and despair. What was the point of being you, she had thought, if you were just one pigment in a collage? Every thought she'd harbored, every decision she'd made, was relativized by the circumstances of other realities, trivialized, all outcomes thrown into question, countless alternative possibilities birthed and validated. A defined vocabulary of experience could allow you to express something; a surfeit of such words turned all expressions into noise.

Feeling indulgent, she retraced her steps back to the cobblestone walkway, only to discover a new coffee shop on the corner of the street with outdoor seating and a parasol occupying the spot where the old water fountain had once been. Looking at the vapid expressions on the faces of the patrons sitting beneath the tyrannically large sunshade, she found it nearly impossible to conjure up an image of the fountain and superimpose it on the scene. As she was trying to do so, a new alert caught her attention. Apparently, Nallide had written to the Quorum Prep Institute, informing them of Celosya's recent mathematical work, and they were willing to re-test and potentially re-enroll her in the program.

If the fountain had still stood there, Celosya knew that her old doubts would have rematerialized, just as fresh as they had been three years ago, each debilitating consideration resurfacing in perfect tandem with the disappearance of the water rivulets into the crevices beneath the granite. But those weighty stones were gone, and the only circulation now was that of Celosya's own identity, flowing out into the multiverse and back into her being in an endless cycle of enigmatic, swirling self.

Perhaps, Celosya thought, she'd been approaching things the wrong way. What if the problem wasn't that a Quorum contained too many possibilities—but not enough? The group of kinship selves with which you connected neurally via chip could number in the hundreds, sometimes even thousands. But the multiverse contained *infinite* yous. It had always been assumed that certain kinship parameters were essential to the selection process of Quorum members in order to guarantee their fundamental compatibility. But what if that assumption was incorrect?

Celosya sat beneath the sunshade, ordered a cup of coffee, and opened up her notebook. All this time she'd been working on tricky series, sets of infinite numbers whose sums, despite all appearances to the contrary, somehow converged to finite results when she used the right techniques. Some of her methods, she knew, weren't strictly formally correct—but like Feynman's path integrals, they got the job done. What if her ideas could be modified to find the convergence of someone's infinite parallel selves, defining a new kind of supra-identity of self? What if varieties of individual expression were merely subcomponents of this larger, sum self?

At once, she wrote down symbols and began to sketch out her line of reasoning. Her wrist and fingers moved ever more rapidly in a frenzy of productivity, and for the first time since she'd started playing around with these notions she remained on-chip, plugged into society but undistracted by its clamor. The beauty and seeming inexorability of her calculations was all the buffer she needed. Despite her vigorous output, her entire body eased up, exuberant yet serene. For an instant, Celosya became woozy and feared that she might pass out. Then she understood that this was what it was like to be light, to truly dance with consciousness. She took a deep, steadying breath and resumed her work. Thinking of Nallide, she smiled. She proceeded, steady and unerring—one equation at a time. For what seemed like hours, the world remained quiet. But after a while, a lingering intrusion from the outside broke through, and Celosya found herself wondering how much Quorum Prep might have changed in three years.

# NINE HUNDRED GRANDMOTHERS

## PAUL DI FILIPPO

**The discovery** of the multiverse made it really hard to be a drug addict.

I knew this fact firsthand, since I was a drug addict myself. And a seasoned one, using and maintaining now for well over a decade. A guy who speaks with the voice of much sad experience. A survivor. Lucky, I guess you could call it—from one angle. Unlucky any other way. And while I didn't generally like to complain about my self-inflicted condition or throw a pity party, I really wished that we could go back to the old days, before anyone knew the universe continually duplicated itself infinitely, *mutatis mutandis*, during every instant of time.

In that lost era when all we experienced or expected was just a unique, singular universe, being a selfish junkie was much less work. Or, at least, so it seemed to me. There were fewer impediments to your chosen lifestyle. Although I appreciated this only in hindsight. For instance: all you had was one unique iteration of your social set, one collection of family, friends and fellow users to let down, disappoint and rip off. One set of random strangers to interact with casually or consequentially. Also, your fate and destiny were a single-track journey: one foot in front of the other, from innocence to perdition—or maybe, with luck, ending up at recovery and redemption. But whatever the destination, whatever sense of choice, there was an ignorance-is-bliss feeling that the trip was linear and relatively uncomplicated. A sense of fatedness. No branches or alternatives to consider, parallel worlds always in your face.

Also, there were only limited options for drugs, limited pushers, limited numbers of antagonistic authorities, cops and such, and limited quantities of do-gooders, social workers and society matrons.

But all of this simplicity—a simplicity we did not even realize we were enjoying, until presented with the endlessly recomplicated alternatives—existed only before Doctor Bryce Finney, PhD in Temporospatial Physics from the Rensselaer Polytechnic Institute, managed to open a portal to the nearest adjacent timeline to ours. And because he was accessing, without quite knowing what he was doing, the least divergent reality possible, he perforce opened his world-gate precisely onto his own laboratory, synced with his doppelganger or avatar, who was simultaneously opening a portal to our continuum. How the two Finneys, at first startled, then exultant, rejoiced and romped like mirrored twins at this earth-shattering moment, I leave it to you to imagine. Not that you have to actually use your imagination. The seminal moments are all on video, thanks to the lab surveillance cameras, with over one hundred billion YouTube views on my continuum alone. Curse Finney's genius soul!

And once Dr Finney had let Schrödinger's cat out of the bag, there was no putting it back in. The whole world had to adjust to the "reality of multiple realities," the phrase that all the media commentators used when witlessly referring to the discovery.

But luckily for the world—or worlds—the adjustment went pretty well, for a number of reasons. If you stop to consider how things could have gone—well, the revelation of parallel timelines and access thereto could have totally destroyed civilization, through any number of causes—war, disease, spiritual malaise, intellectual confusion, vast population shifts—but none of that bad stuff happened, for perfectly understandable and logical reasons, all things considered.

First off came expense and cost as a limiting factor. The machine that Finney had cobbled together bulked as large as a beach cottage, and there seemed to be solid theoretical limits on how much you could miniaturize it. Plus it used a boatload of power, siphoning off the entire output of the RPI's Walthousen Nuclear Research Reactor whenever it opened a portal. So there was not going to be any gadget worn on your wrist or belt that allowed an individual to jump blithely from one continuum to another whenever he or she had a whim.

Additionally, it turned out that the multiverse had a steep cosmic gradient. Establishing a connection to our least divergent neighbor used X amount of power, while moving further across the multiversal spectrum took more and more power as the divergence factor increased. It was as if the multiverse came with built-in barriers to discourage mingling. So the easiest continua to visit were the ones most like your starting point, and where was the allure in that? Going someplace practically identical to your origin, just to chat with your boring and predictable doppelganger? Shit, you could do that at home!

So after all the excitement and hullaballoo died down, people began to realize that the average citizen was never going to afford or make a crosstime jaunt, and that the easily reachable destinations were not that exciting.

It was true, however, that governments and big corporations and even smaller enterprises could manage to exploit the multiverse in a highly constrained fashion. Punching through directly to a greatly divergent timeline was soon deemed not cost-effective, except in the most dire emergencies or for the most grandiose rewards. But what you could do was mount a sequential expedition.

You sent your team to the next-door universe. Easy-peasy, relatively speaking. From there, using that timeline's equipment, your travelers jumped one universe further onward. From Universe Three, they moved to Universe Four, experiencing a slightly larger shift in consensus reality each time. After about a thousand jumps, you could hit some real weirdness full of interesting new stuff and people. And ideas were of course much more easily transportable than goods. But such travel took real time and physical exertion. And then you had to come back home the same laborious way.

So travel through the multiverse, regulated by a quickly established Crosstime Transit Bureau, quickly became something like the old Silk Road: a hard, dangerous, laborious trail to exotic destinations only dimly acknowledged or understood or even mundanely contemplated by the majority of stay-at-home folks. A route down which strange goods and notions might occasionally flow into your home, more often incrementally different rather than revolutionary.

Strange goods high in value, worthy of the efforts of securing them. Like drugs.

• • •

I'll pretend I'm introducing myself at some Narcotics Anonymous meeting, but I promise to keep it short and not bore you.

My name is Stafford Pinfold. Yes, of *those* Pinfolds, the family that got incredibly rich through a monopoly on practical nuclear fusion reactors. After nineteen years of respectable sobriety and general good behavior, I got hooked in my Ivy League college days. A sports injury led to an oxy habit, which was quickly followed by experimentation with, and addiction to, a large number of other illegal substances, ranging from ecstasy, heroin, and fentanyl to krokodil, basuco, and khat. Thankfully I only experimented lightly with the most heavily grievous stuff, and always returned to the vanilla drugs, which satisfied all my urges for escape from this prison called life.

My family—shocked and mourning, angry and sad—indulged me for a time, failing to cut off my allowance (easy money only led me to make more drug purchases), paying for my numerous rehab stints, staging heartfelt interventions, you know the drill. But ultimately, when I showed no signs of remorse or changing my ways, they went tough love and cut me off from all funds entirely. I was thrown right out onto the street. But even that failed to shame me or divert me from my addict's ways. I went down those all-too-familiar paths of utilitarian degradation to supply my habits, and finally became a low-level dealer, a "career" which allowed me to limp along as a maintenance case.

And then, as I hinted at the start of this sad tale, came the discovery of the multiverse.

I still recall my first experience with a trans-continuum drug. I was almost immediately seeking more out and so well on my path to ruination.

At that point in time, the dealer above me in the chain of supply was a tweaker gal whom everyone called "Mudball." She always dressed like some archetypical punk: big boots and flannels and chains and ripped pants. She exhibited all the typical ravages of a meth-head, and was meaner than ten junkyard dogs. But she knew her drugs and always had access to the best stuff.

I met Mudball one night in our usual rendezvous spot, an all-night diner named Terminal Lunch. Amidst the smell of stale hotdog water and uncleaned fryolator grease, she leaned in close, giving me way too intense a view of her ravaged complexion, and whispered, "I got something you're really gonna like. It's a ten-kay-divergence hit called extra-neosomaticum."

I was highly intrigued. A drug from ten thousand timelines distant. "Have you tried it yourself? What's it do?"

"Nah, it's not my thing. Plus it's too pricey. Here's the skinny. It gives you a ghost body."

"A ghost body? What's that?"

"From what my contacts tell me, you acquire a kind of invisible shell around yourself, shaped like yourself. You can sense this extra layer, whatever the fuck it's made of, and control it. It's totally malleable. Your consciousness expands into the shell. Plus, you get to see into extra dimensions."

"Sounds like pure fantasy."

"No way, it's a real phenom."

Well, I had never gone in for any of the psychedelics, even after having tried acid, psilocybin and many others, and despite Mudball's salesman protestations, this sounded like more of the same. "I don't know... It strikes me as a pretty useless high."

"What if I told you that Marfeo already tried it and was so blown away that he wanted me to sell it to him exclusively?"

Marfeo was another dealer at my level—a rival, I guess. He hated me because of my rich family, and I disliked him because of his ignorance and various loudly expressed prejudices. No way was I going to let him get a monopoly on this stuff, whatever it was.

"Okay, I'll try a hit. If it's any good, maybe I can push it to some of my more adventurous customers."

Mudball smiled, revealing her hideous meth-decayed teeth. She reached into her tattered, safety-pinned leather jacket and came out with a Ziploc bearing a single huge green pill stamped with the image of a Pac-Man ghost. It looked utterly innocuous. I paid her and we parted.

That night I took the pill and had one of the weirdest and most intense drug experiences of my whole veteran addict's life.

I was lying down on my couch when I felt the ectoplasmic shell begin to form about me. Soon I was encased toes to top in a wavery luminescent silhouette. I didn't know if anyone else could see it, but for me it shone with a pale green radiance. Then, without warning, my locus of consciousness changed. It seemed as if my brain was downloaded into the shell. And with that shift, I found I could manipulate my new form, extruding tentacles, swelling up like a balloon to fill the room. Next up, I gained something like Superman's microscopic, telescopic, X-ray vision. I could see through things and deep into sub-Planckian realms. The eleven hidden dimensions of our universe were revealed to me.

I sent one of my bodily probes through the wall and into my neighbor's apartment. A fat bus driver named, of all things, Ralph, my neighbor was sleeping. I used my pseudopod to grab a pack of his cigarettes and bring them back through the wide-open atoms of the wall. I had a smoke, and then proceeded to experiment with my new extra-corporeality.

After about three or four hours, during which I had lifted various items from my other neighbors and goosed awake the hard-working single mom four apartments away, I could feel the new abilities and sensations began to wane and, finally, disappear. I was left feeling fagged out and confused. The trip had been fun, but towards the end, I had already been starting to get bored. Nothing I personally wanted to repeat. The drug made me feel like a peeping tom, which troubled my residual conscience, believe it or not, and it reminded me too much of actual physical work. Still, I could see that several of my more adventurous customers would like to try it, and that it might develop into a steady product line. So the next day I contacted Mudball and arranged for a regular supply.

I had been selling the drug for only three weeks when the cops came for me. And not just the local boys or even the feds from my timeline. These were the enforcers from the Crosstime Transit Bureau. After this first encounter with the CTB goons, I learned that they were a kind of super SWAT team assembled from the worst badasses of various parallel worlds. They made my homegrown police look like a suburban housewives' book club.

You see now what I mean about the multiverse making everything worse and more complicated?

They busted in my door at 3 a.m., four big, heavily armed bruisers, one of whom had real fangs like a smilodon and green-tinged skin. Lord knows how many divergences separated his Earth from mine. Once I was awake, naked but able to respond somewhat intelligibly, the questioning started. Nothing physical, but they were relentless.

"Okay, kid, who sold you the X-neo?"

"I don't remember!"

"Do you know what that stuff's made from?"

"No…"

"The cerebral cortexes of Martian babies!"

"I don't believe you!"

Fang Guy laughed. "Well, you're smart not to. Harry's just jerking your chain. It's actually derived from element 125, an isotope high within the island of stability. You guys don't have it yet here. But it'll transfigure your neurons into itself if you use it long enough, and you'll end up permanently ghosted. You see why we can't let it loose on your timeline. Now, give with the names!"

I held out a little longer, but eventually caved. After all, it wasn't like Mudball and I were best friends or anything. She had palmed off heavily cut stuff on me often enough.

Amazingly, after I had ratted out Mudball, and the cops heard back from their peers that she had been successfully picked up—it was 7 a.m. by then—I was surprised to learn that I myself wasn't about to be arrested. "Nah, you're small fry. CTB just wants the higher-ups."

After they'd left, I sought to compose myself with a cup of coffee brewed with shaky hands and tried to figure out what came next in my life. Unfortunately, I couldn't come up with any plan other than continuing to deal drugs to supply my own habits, while hoping not to get caught again. And practically before I could even make any moves in that direction, Fate delivered the whole package to my door. Three days later, I got a text from an unknown number. The message simply said: *Come see me terminal lunch Friday midnight. Bonnaroo.*

Even though I had never met him, I knew Bonnaroo was Mudball's supplier, so I went.

He proved to be an immensely fat guy with a shaven head, dressed in some kind of weird one-piece suit made of a sparkly synthetic that revealed every possible roll and crevice you did not desire to see. I had a sense he wasn't originally from my timeline, and his strange accent and vocabulary tended to affirm my hunch.

He came right to the point.

"Our mutual wetch has been lubbered by the pescos."

"Huh?"

"Mudball. The seety-bees got her."

"Oh, right."

"I need to replace her to keep the drash flowing. You interested in beng my jerson on this strand?"

"Uh, sure, I guess. But won't the cops just come after me like they did her?"

"Nugatory. The lahjoa is in. I finally decided I'd pay what I had to. Hurts, but's that the cost of doing malinkey. You won't get any arazoak from them anymore. What do you say? Are you tangled?"

"I'll need a discount on the stuff I use personally."

"We're staunch!"

And so I started my new career as a midlevel dealer, the interface between Bonnaroo and the lesser runners such as I had been. It proved a lot less demanding and better paying than my old position. And there were other satisfactions. I got to sample all the new drugs, uncut, before anyone else. And also, I could boss around my old peers. The first time Marfeo had to make nice with me to get what he wanted, groveling with a surly obsequiousness, I experienced a wonderful sensation of revenge.

I could have continued on in this role, I supposed, until either my veins collapsed, I overdosed or there was a shakeup in the Crosstime Transit Bureau and the non-bent cops took over and staged an upright-citizen-pleasing purge of all us junkies, high and low. But alas, a different, unanticipated disaster intervened.

A year passed, during which I sampled and sold so many crosstime drugs that I began almost to lose sense of my own self and history. Mecca ten, blue mango, bugcrusher, ineffabilium, zogzug, cranioklept, sorolla seven... The faddish highs came and went, each one sending users in search of even greater, more esoteric kicks.

Currently, I was pushing a new one called ent-wife. I had tried it once myself, of course, and discovered that all it seemed to do was promote a kind of "green consciousness," so that you felt more or less like Swamp Thing, attuned to the Gaian biosphere. Not my bag, although I soon learned it appealed to many others. I think at one point I was supplying half the local chapter of Greenpeace.

But what neither I nor anyone else knew was that long-term use of ent-wife actually had the effect of rendering the user into a vegetable. Not mentally, but bodily. Blood replaced with a chlorophyll solution, flesh turning to pith. Users felt compelled to leave their dwellings and find a patch of dirt, where they settled down and literally put out roots and developed bark and foliage. If found within a short time of going green, they could be saved. But otherwise, the effects were irreversible. No jolt of narcan would bring the victim around. You might as well reconcile yourself to using your loved one to provide shade for a picnic.

Naturally, the media went wild, and before too long, my name became associated with the plague, thanks to various sub-dealers narcing me out. But there was never enough solid proof adduced that the DA could succeed in building a case against me. Maybe some of my legal unaccountability stemmed from Bonnaroo's payoffs. But despite my staying out of jail, the well-publicized associational trail linked me to a number of the victims, and my name became an object of hate and social-media banter. It really sucks, becoming a meme.

I knew I had to go to ground until all this blew over. Luckily I had stockpiled some drugs and cash. But just as I thought I had succeeded in finding a hiding place and erasing my footprints, my family stepped in.

My parents and other collateral relatives, all of them sober high-status and well-respected citizens, did not relish the name of Pinfold being connected in any manner with such a tragic and sordid scandal. (And come to think of it, those same "loved ones" had probably also intervened, like Bonnaroo, on my behalf with the authorities, without informing me.) Realizing that more such disgraceful public clusterfucks were likely to occur in my future if I persisted in my chosen career, and also realizing that I would probably defy any attempts at inducing me to surrender myself to professional rehab—at least at this juncture—they decided to stage another intervention, undeterred by the fact that all previous such exercises had proved futile. But this time, they were going to do things different. They brought in the big guns.

Myselves.

Avatars of Stafford Pinfold. Doppelgangers of yours truly. My crosstime twin brothers.

You remember me saying how rich my family was? Well, they could have sent for my cooperative carbon copies the long way, down the crosstime Silk Road, by dispatching emissaries in person. (Emissaries equipped with capacious wallets, I assume, since my other selves, if they held true to the template, would want to get paid for their time.) But that would have been too slow for my proactive parents. They wanted immediate action and results. Get that shithead scion straightened out now! So they paid to punch directly through to some high-divergency strands where they found acceptable and amenable versions of me that would agree to take part in their scheme. (And as I later learned, my folks had to reach out to strands that were twenty-kay or even further displaced from our home timeline. It appears that most of my nearest cousins had, disappointingly, all followed the same path I did.)

The first inkling I got of this campaign was when I was just anonymously settling into my new quarters, a single-room-occupancy hotel in the skid row of a city not to be named. (Skid rows in general were getting scarce, since unlimited fusion power, courtesy of the Pinfold clan, had sent the global economy into overdrive, allowing for every kind of do-gooder ameliorative social program imaginable.) I was lying down and preparing to take a hit of my new favorite drug, blammo, which caused the user to experience a wildly orgasmic condition for about three eternal hours, when a knocking sounded at the door. Before I could even tell whoever it was to go away, the door opened.

I saw myself, grinning and flourishing my room key. He said, "I told the clerk I locked myself out, and he gave me the spare. He was a little perturbed by the fact that he never saw me leave the hotel, but you have to believe your eyes."

I was momentarily croggled, just gawping, but then my temporarily undrugged mind quickly provided the most likely explanation. My duplicate's healthy tan, sedate clothing and a general sense of smug superiority provided all the clues I needed.

"My family put you up to visiting me, didn't they? You're here to 'talk some sense into me.'"

He took out a luxurious linen pocket handkerchief, unfolded it and placed it on the bed before deigning to sit down on the stained comforter atop the spavined mattress. He crossed one leg over the other, exposing elegant stockings.

"Yes, I'm here to present to you the wisdom of altering your ways. If only you'd agree wholeheartedly to give up your addictions, you could find yourself in as enviable a position as I myself occupy. Surely my simple presence is the most powerful argument."

I had been listening to this doppelganger for only about sixty seconds, and I already hated him. Hated myself.

"Part of the family business, I take it?"

"Yes, indeed. Vice-president in charge of Mars expansion."

"Big salary, beautiful wife, respect of the community?"

My double cast his eyes downward in a gesture of modesty. "All of that. And such pleasant accoutrements could be yours as well, if only—"

I didn't let him finish. I yelled, "You can take all your designer socks and Mars money and stuff them up your ass!" Before he knew what I was doing or could react, I had pinned my wimpy duplicate in a wrestling hold—his squash-racket-bolstered muscles were no match for the prowess of someone who had often had to subdue wild-eyed junkies intent on disemboweling their gracious dealer—and then I pushed the tab of blammo down his throat.

Well, I should have known that violence would not solve my problem. It never succeeds, except when it does. But unfortunately, this was not one of those situations. A few hours later, as my double lay drooling on the floor, four more of my avatars showed up. Hollywood Me, Rock Star Me, Preacher Me and Scientist Me. While one of the newcomers was ministering to visitor number one, injecting him with some kind of bring-down counter-agent, the other three lashed into me with accusations, complaints, cajoling and berating.

"Staff, how could you treat one of our own avatars so disrespectfully?"

"Don't you ever want to make something good of yourself?"

"What about contributing to the cultural heritage of the species?"

"Aren't you tired of living such a miserable, grungy, dangerous, painful lifestyle?"

"Shouldn't you be leaving these juvenile practices behind?"

"Man, you are so uncool and blozarty!"

I just closed my eyes and capped my ears with my hands. Pretty soon, the room was full of about a dozen of my goody-goody selves, all haranguing me. What this all must've been costing my folks, I couldn't imagine. Just the ability to summon and transport distant avatars at the drop of a hat was mindboggling, never mind any kind of compensations they were receiving.

Finally I couldn't take any more. Making sure I had my wallet and phone, I dashed out of the room without any of my other possessions, headed straight to the bus station and took the first bus out to a random destination.

Surprisingly, I wasn't followed, but I soon realized that there was no need, since as soon as I used either my phone or my cards, I could be traced. So I got off ahead of where my ticket said I was going, withdrew all my money as cash, bought a burner phone and then took a different bus to another set of anonymous lodgings.

But that only staved off discovery of my den for a week. The enormous detective resources of Pinfold Fusion Consortium eventually resulted in them tracking me down.

Into my flop came my parents. But they weren't my mom and dad from this continuum; they were doppelgangers of my parents. And they looked like they had been through hell and back. I knew my original folks hadn't weathered whatever these guys had gone through.

"Son," my alternate mother implored, "just look at us. Our sorry state is all your fault! We're from a timeline where you became a byword for infamy. Do you know how many people have died? All thanks to your drug dealing! A thousand times worse than the ent-wife mess. And how we suffered for your sins! Won't you spare your own parents this fate?"

My alternate father put his manly arm around his wife's shoulders. "There, there, dear. Don't let yourself get worked up. I'm sure that this Stafford will benefit from the tragedy of our own son's behavior. He'll listen to reason and his sense of filial duty will prevail."

They were an affecting and pitiable sight, but I hardened myself. It wasn't me who had fucked them up so bad. Well, at least in some existential sense it wasn't, although it also was. But I resented my own folks for really playing dirty, by dragging in these pathetic losers.

"Whatever trip you two are on, I wish you'd share it. You are so far from reality, you must be halfway to Alpha Centauri."

My mom began to weep and wail, and dad cursed me out. They finally left, but only to be replaced by another pinch-hitting pair, employing a different tack. I ignored their arguments and logic and tirades, as well as those of the next five or six sets of doppelganger progenitors. The multiverse was really chapping my ass! Finally, after they had grown hoarse and tired and defeated, they all gave up and left me to stew in my own juices. Fine by me. That was all I had ever asked of anyone.

I was just trying to motivate myself to go on the lam again, to avoid more such encounters, when the door started to swing slowly open and I braced myself for more interference with my chosen lifestyle. But this time when the intruder appeared on the threshold, I was truly taken aback, experiencing a visceral punch to the gut.

The new interventionist was Gramma Atchison.

Abigail Atchison, my mom's mother, had been fifty years old when I was born. She had dropped out of school as a teenager, for reasons of poverty, then raised my mom while squeaking by as a single mother. Then my mom had the miraculous fate-changing luck to marry into the Pinfold tribe. Gramma's life immediately turned around. All her worries and physical insecurities immediately vanished. But so did the necessity of any hard work, the practices she was accustomed to and which gave her life meaning. She foundered for a while and got morally lost, maybe even developing a drinking habit, from the whispers I heard. Then I was born, and she had something—someone—to devote all her energies to. Sober and sensible and redeemed, she took over the raising of infant and toddler and child me, which was perfectly acceptable to my folks.

I didn't mind, either. In fact, I loved Gramma Atchison more than anyone. My childhood had been an idyll of love and joy and fun and exploration and freedom and learning. I had been prepped for a great life as a wise adult.

And then Gramma died in a car crash. I was sixteen, three years before I turned to dope. Maybe the sports injury excuse had been just the trigger for unleashing a deeper, buried sorrow that needed the drugs as compensation or solace. Whatever.

And now here Gramma was. Amazingly, she looked hardly any older than the sixty-six years she had accumulated when she died, although nearly well over a decade had passed in our native timeline. They must have found this Gramma in a continuum that was chronologically retarded from ours. I knew she had been cynically selected especially for her familiar looks, but I still couldn't help the fact that her face struck me like a hammerblow.

"Stuffie, my baby."

Gramma often called me "Stuffie."

"Stuffie, how it pains Gramma's heart to see you like this. The stories your parents have told me! Won't you think about changing your ways? For old Atchie's sake?"

I often called her "Atchie."

But this wasn't my Gramma! My Gramma had died and deserted me. She got creamed by a drunk driver blowing through a stop light. (I never did learn to drive. Wonder why…)

I hardened my heart and turned my face to the wall. "Forget it, lady! You ran out on me and those days are gone. It's just me alone against the world now."

Gramma allowed herself to weep quietly a little. Then she got a tissue out of her capacious nana purse, wiped her eyes, blew her nose, then left without another word.

I had expected more wrangling, the hard sell. But I remembered that Atchie had never believed in such coercion, and so her actions were totally consistent with her character, even across several timelines.

However, the next Gramma Atchie to show up was rather different.

This grandmother wore an eye patch, smoked a cigar, had biceps like a stevedore's and wore literal combat boots.

"Up on your feet, you ungrateful twerp! Do you think we ever could have beaten back the invaders from Frolix-8 if we had all been as spineless as you? You're a disgrace to the name and reputation of General Stafford Pinfold, savior of the Jovian Battalion! You make me wanna puke!"

I skittered off the bed and into a corner of the room. "Hey now, wait just a minute! I don't know where you're coming from, but we don't have any space monsters here. Maybe I would've been different if we had, just like your Stafford was. But I'm just what my world made me."

Gramma regarded me with a steely eye, then spat in my direction. "Aw, what's the use? You can't make a tiger out of a mouse!" She stormed out as if in a cloud of gunsmoke.

No sooner had she left than cyborg Gramma arrived. You really don't know creepy until you've seen the beloved face of your maternal grandmother affixed to a combination of tank chassis and sexbot. When this Gramma spoke, she sounded just like Siri—if Siri had gargled with razor blades and barbed wire.

"Grandchild Unit! We can relieve you of all your weaknesses. Just consent to a small suite of neurosomatic modifications. Abandon the ills of the flesh!"

I shrieked like a little girl who had a dead rat dropped down her shirt. I made a superhuman leap I never imagined I could perform, right over the Gramma-borg, and was out the door.

But unlike with my doppelgangers or with my many parental visitors, the Grammas elected to pursue me. Original Gramma returned from her temporary failure, then Soldier Gramma and Cyborg Gramma; they all were hot on my heels as I raced through the grungy skid-row streets, much to the stunned amazement of all the pedestrians and drivers and shopkeepers.

"Stafford! Come back! We love you and want to help you!"

My breath pounded, hard and labored. The voices behind me grew in volume and I dared to look backwards for a moment.

There were now dozens of Gramma Atchisons chasing me! Scores in fact! More popping up every moment, until it seemed like hundreds had ported in from across the multiverse.

Stumbling, aching, sniveling, half-blinded by fear, I turned down an alley to escape them all.

Dead end with tall brick facades on three sides.

I collapsed against a rusty dumpster, amidst a pile of rotting, stinking organic debris that had spilled out in transit. My mind was disintegrating at this confrontation with my childhood bastion of safety and affection transmogrified into a hundred horrible aggressive incarnations, all clamoring for my moral and bodily reformation. I closed my eyes and waited for their vengeance.

When nothing happened for about three minutes, I opened my eyes a slit.

The Grammas filled the alley in massed ranks, extending back to the street and beyond. The frontline presented a bizarre and motley array of the woman I had childishly loved in a dozen different guises. Then the Grammas parted to let one special Gramma through.

It was Shoggoth Gramma. A giant semi-transparent gelatinous green mass that slurped as it moved, with the face of Abigail Atchison duplicated a hundred times, floating all around inside the protoplasmic bulk.

The Gramma from ten million divergences away.

When Shoggoth Gramma spoke, powdered mortar sifted out of the enclosing brick walls.

"No more half-measures! I will fix the boy!"

Before I could move or protest, I was engulfed, along with the whole dumpster, by the blob-like Gramma.

Strange matter filled my nostrils and mouth, and I couldn't breathe, so I did the only sensible thing: I passed out.

I was five years old again, sitting in Gramma's lap, and she was reading me a wonderful story that went on and on endlessly. Her familiar kind voice recounted infinite wonders and miracles, adventures and exploits, all limning my bright future. I wanted it never to end.

When I came to myself again, I lay in a familiar room. Beautiful sunlight poured through the curtain-framed windows. This had been my own bedroom during summers when I returned from college to my parents' mansion in Woodside, California, a whole continent away from that gruesome alley where I had been emblobbed. I was dressed in clean pajamas, swathed in clean sheets and feeling healthier and saner than I had felt in many a year. I was curious and perplexed, but not angry or resentful. The good feelings felt weird.

I got cautiously out of bed and went downstairs to the dining room, where I found my parents—my real, original parents—having breakfast.

"Have a seat, Staff," my dad said jovially.

"It's good to have you back, son," said my mom.

No mention was made of my intervention ordeal. We started talking about inconsequential stuff. I learned more about my various cousins' recent marriages than even the paparazzi would have wanted to know. And before I quite realized it, I was agreeing to accompany my dad into the office, "just to lend your perspective on a few things."

It was only after a year of my new stable, happy and prosperous life had gone by that I realized I was in no danger of backsliding into my old ways. The impulse to do dope had been erased. Those druggy years seemed like a dream. Not a nightmare, precisely, but a dream of some other me. I guess I had had a multiversal experience without ever leaving my native continuum.

I never saw any of my alternate Grammas again, and the family never spoke of my intervention. But once in a while I did experience a vivid flashback to that moment in the alley, surrounded by hundreds of grandmothers and being engulfed by one special avatar.

And in those moments, a small portion of my left forearm would turn a translucent green, and the face of Abigail Atchison would swim up out of my interior and wink at me both affectionately and with a certain stern remonstrative look.

# DAYS OF MAGIC, NIGHTS OF WAR

## CLIVE BARKER

I dreamed I spoke in another's language,
I dreamed I lived in another's skin,
I dreamed I was my own beloved,
I dreamed I was a tiger's kin.

I dreamed that Eden lived inside me,
And when I breathed a garden came,
I dreamed I knew all of Creation,
I dreamed I knew the Creator's name.

I dreamed – and this dream was the finest –
That all I dreamed was real and true,
And we would live in joy forever,
You in me, and me in you.

# ALTERNATE
# HISTORIES

"It is impossible that ours is the only world; there must
be world after world unseen by us, in some region or
dimension that we simply do not perceive. Even though
I can't prove that, even though it isn't logical—I believe it."

**Philip K. Dick,** *The Man in the High Castle*

# A BRIEF HISTORY OF THE TRANS-PACIFIC TUNNEL

## KEN LIU

**At the** noodle shop, I wave the other waitress away, waiting for the American woman: skin pale and freckled as the moon; swelling breasts that fill the bodice of her dress; long chestnut curls spilling past her shoulders, held back with a flowery bandanna. Her eyes, green like fresh tea leaves, radiate a bold and fearless smile that is rarely seen among Asians. And I like the wrinkles around them, fitting for a woman in her thirties.

"*Hai.*" She finally stops at my table, her lips pursed impatiently. "*Hoka no okyakusan ga imasu yo. Nani wo chuumon shimasu ka?*" Her Japanese is quite good, the pronunciation maybe even better than mine—though she is not using the honorific. It is still rare to see Americans here in the Japanese half of Midpoint City, but things are changing now, in the thirty-sixth year of the Shōwa Era (she, being an American, would think of it as 1961).

"A large bowl of tonkotsu ramen," I say, mostly in English. Then I realize how loud and rude I sound. Old Diggers like me always forget that not everyone is practically deaf. "Please," I add, a whisper.

Her eyes widen as she finally recognizes me. I've cut my hair and put on a clean shirt, and that's not how I looked the past few times

I've come here. I haven't paid much attention to my appearance in a decade. There hasn't been any need to. Almost all my time is spent alone and at home. But the sight of her has quickened my pulse in a way I haven't felt in years, and I wanted to make an effort.

"Always the same thing," she says, and smiles.

I like hearing her English. It sounds more like her natural voice, not so high-pitched.

"You don't really like the noodles," she says, when she brings me my ramen. It isn't a question.

I laugh, but I don't deny it. The ramen in this place is terrible. If the owner were any good he wouldn't have left Japan to set up shop here at Midpoint City, where the tourists stopping for a break on their way through the Trans-Pacific Tunnel don't know any better. But I keep on coming, just to see her.

"You are not Japanese."

"No," I say. "I'm Formosan. Please call me Charlie." Back when I coordinated work with the American crew during the construction of Midpoint City, they called me Charlie because they couldn't pronounce my Hokkien name correctly. And I liked the way it sounded, so I kept using it.

"Okay, Charlie. I'm Betty." She turns to leave.

"Wait," I say. I do not know from where I get this sudden burst of courage. It is the boldest thing I've done in a long time. "Can I see you when you are free?"

She considers this, biting her lip. "Come back in two hours."

• • •

From *The Novice Traveler's Guide to the Trans-Pacific Tunnel*, published by the TPT Transit Authority, 1963:

*Welcome, traveler! This year marks the twenty-fifth anniversary of the completion of the Trans-Pacific Tunnel. We are excited to see that this is your first time through the Tunnel. The Trans-Pacific Tunnel follows a Great Circle path just below the seafloor to connect Asia to North America, with three surface terminus stations in Shanghai, Tokyo, and Seattle. The Tunnel takes the shortest path between the cities, arcing north to follow the Pacific Rim mountain ranges. Although this course increased the construction cost of the Tunnel due to the need for earthquake-proofing, it also allows the Tunnel to tap into geothermal vents and hot spots along the way, which generate the electrical power needed for the Tunnel and its support infrastructure, such as the air-compression stations, oxygen generators, and sub-seafloor maintenance posts.*

The Tunnel is in principle a larger—gigantic—version of the pneumatic tubes or capsule lines familiar to all of us for delivering interoffice mail in modern buildings. Two parallel concrete-enclosed steel transportation tubes, one each for westbound and eastbound traffic, 60 feet in diameter, are installed in the Tunnel. The transportation tubes are divided into numerous shorter self-sealing sections, each with multiple air-compression stations. The cylindrical capsules, containing passengers and goods, are propelled through the tubes by a partial vacuum pulling in front and by compressed air pushing from behind. The capsules ride on a monorail for reduced friction. The current maximum speed is about 120 miles per hour, and a trip from Shanghai to Seattle takes a little more than two full days. Plans are under way to eventually increase maximum speed to 200 miles per hour.

The Tunnel's combination of capacity, speed, and safety makes it superior to zeppelins, aeroplanes, and surface shipping for almost all trans-Pacific transportation needs. It is immune to storms, icebergs, and typhoons, and very cheap to operate, as it is powered by the boundless heat of the Earth itself. Today, it is the chief means by which passengers and manufactured goods flow between Asia and America. More than 30 per cent of global container shipping each year goes through the Tunnel.

We hope you enjoy your travel along the Trans-Pacific Tunnel, and wish you a safe journey to your final destination.

• • •

I was born in the second year of the Taishō Era (1913), in a small village in Shinchiku Prefecture, in Formosa. My family were simple peasants who never participated in any of the uprisings against Japan. The way my father saw it, whether the Manchus on the mainland or the Japanese were in charge didn't much matter, since they all left us alone except when it came time for taxes. The lot of the Hoklo peasant was to toil and suffer in silence.

Politics were for those who had too much to eat. Besides, I always liked the Japanese workers from the lumber company, who would hand me candy during their lunch break. The Japanese colonist families we saw were polite, well-dressed, and very lettered. My father once said, "If I got to choose, in my next life I'd come back as a Japanese."

During my boyhood, a new prime minister in Japan announced a change in policy: natives in the colonies should be turned into good subjects of the Emperor. The Japanese governor-general set up village schools that everyone had to attend. The more clever boys could even expect to attend high schools formerly reserved for the Japanese and then go on to study in Japan, where they would have bright futures.

I was not a good student, however, and never learned Japanese very well. I was content to know how to read a few characters and go back to the fields, the same as my father and his father before him.

All this changed in the year I turned seventeen (the fifth year of the Shōwa Era, or 1930), when a Japanese man in a Western suit came to our village, promising riches for the families of young men who knew how to work hard and didn't complain.

• • •

We stroll through Friendship Square, the heart of Midpoint City. A few pedestrians, both American and Japanese, stare and whisper as they see us walking together. But Betty does not care, and her carelessness is infectious.

Here, kilometers under the Pacific Ocean and the seafloor, it's late afternoon by the City's clock, and the arc lamps around us are turned up as bright as can be.

"I always feel like I'm at a night baseball game when I go through here," Betty says. "When my husband was alive, we went to many baseball games together as a family."

I nod. Betty usually keeps her reminiscences of her husband light. She mentioned once that he was a lawyer, and he had left their home in California to work in South Africa, where he died because some people didn't like who he was defending. "They called him a race traitor," she said. I didn't press for details.

Now that her children are old enough to be on their own, she's traveling the world for enlightenment and wisdom. Her capsule train to Japan had stopped at Midpoint Station for a standard one-hour break for passengers to get off and take some pictures, but she had wandered too far into the City and missed the train. She took it as a sign and stayed in the City, waiting to see what lessons the world had to teach her.

Only an American could lead such a life. Among Americans, there are many free spirits like hers.

We've been seeing each other for four weeks, usually on Betty's days off. We take walks around Midpoint City, and we talk. I prefer that we converse in English, mostly because I do not have to think much about how formal and polite to be.

As we pass by the bronze plaque in the middle of the square, I point out to her my Japanese-style name on the plaque: Takumi Hayashi. The Japanese teacher in my village school had helped me pick the first name, and I had liked the characters: "open up, sea." The choice turned out to be prescient.

She is impressed. "That must have been something. You should tell me more about what it was like to work on the Tunnel."

There are not many of us old Diggers left now. The years of hard labor spent breathing hot and humid dust that stung our lungs had done invisible damage to our insides and joints. At forty-eight, I've said goodbye to all my friends as they succumbed to illnesses. I am the last keeper of what we had done together.

When we finally blasted through the thin rock wall dividing our side from the American side and completed the Tunnel in the thirteenth year of the Shōwa Era (1938), I had the honor of being one of the shift supervisors invited to attend the ceremony. I explain to Betty that the blast-through spot is in the main tunnel due north of where we are standing, just beyond Midpoint Station.

We arrive at my apartment building, on the edge of the section of the city where most Formosans live. I invite her to come up. She accepts.

My apartment is a single room eight mats in size, but there is a window. Back when I bought it, it was considered a very luxurious place for Midpoint City, where space was and is at a premium. I mortgaged most of my pension on it, since I had no desire ever to move. Most men made do with coffinlike one-mat rooms. But to her American eyes, it probably seems very cramped and shabby. Americans like things to be open and big.

I make her tea. It is very relaxing to talk to her. She does not care that I am not Japanese, and assumes nothing about me. She takes out a joint, as is the custom for Americans, and we share it.

Outside the window, the arc lights have been dimmed. It's evening in Midpoint City. Betty does not get up and say that she has to leave. We stop talking. The air feels tense, but in a good way, expectant. I reach out for her hand, and she lets me. The touch is electric.

• • •

From *Splendid America*, AP ed., 1995:

*In 1929, the fledging and weak Republic of China, in order to focus on the domestic Communist rebellion, appeased Japan by signing the Sino-Japanese Mutual Cooperation Treaty. The treaty formally ceded all Chinese territories in Manchuria to Japan, which averted the prospect of all-out war between China and Japan and halted Soviet ambitions in Manchuria. This was the capstone on Japan's thirty-five-year drive for imperial expansion. Now, with Formosa, Korea, and Manchuria incorporated into the Empire and a collaborationist China within its orbit, Japan had access to vast reserves of natural resources, cheap labor, and a potential market of hundreds of millions for its manufactured goods.*

*Internationally, Japan announced that it would continue its rise as a Great Power henceforth by peaceful means. Western powers, however, led by Britain and the United States, were suspicious. They were especially alarmed by Japan's colonial ideology of a "Greater East Asia Co-Prosperity Sphere," which seemed to be a Japanese version of the Monroe Doctrine and suggested a desire to drive European and American influence from Asia.*

*Before the Western powers could decide on a plan to contain and encircle Japan's "Peaceful Ascent," however, the Great Depression struck. The brilliant Emperor Hirohito seized the opportunity and suggested to President Herbert Hoover his vision of the Trans-Pacific Tunnel as the solution to the worldwide economic crisis.*

• • •

The work was hard and dangerous. Every day men were injured and sometimes killed. It was also very hot. In the finished sections, they installed machines to cool the air. But in the most forward parts of the Tunnel, where the actual digging happened, we were exposed to the heat of the Earth, and we worked in nothing but our undershorts, sweating nonstop. The work crews were segregated by race—there were Koreans, Formosans, Okinawans, Filipinos, Chinese (separated again by topolect)—but after a while we all looked the same, covered in sweat and dust and mud, only little white circles of skin showing around our eyes.

It didn't take me long to get used to living underground, to the constant noise of dynamite, hydraulic drills, the bellows cycling cooling air, and to the flickering faint yellow light of arc lamps. Even when you were sleeping, the next shift was already at it. Everyone grew hard of hearing after a while, and we stopped talking to each other. There was nothing to say, anyway; just more digging.

But the pay was good, and I saved up and sent money home. However, visiting home was out of the question. By the time I started, the head of the tunnel was already halfway between Shanghai and Tokyo. They charged you a month's wages to ride the steam train carrying the excavated waste back to Shanghai and up to the surface. I couldn't afford such luxuries. As we made progress, the trip back only grew longer and more expensive.

It was best not to think too much about what we were doing, about the miles of water over our heads, and the fact that we were digging a tunnel through the Earth's crust to get to America. Some men did go crazy under those conditions and had to be restrained before they could hurt themselves or others.

• • •

From *A Brief History of the Trans-Pacific Tunnel*,
published by the TPT Transit Authority, 1960:

*Osachi Hamaguchi, prime minister of Japan during the Great Depression, claimed that Emperor Hirohito was inspired by the American effort to build the Panama Canal to conceive of the Trans-Pacific Tunnel. "America has knit together two oceans," the Emperor supposedly said. "Now let us chain together two continents." President Hoover, trained as an engineer, enthusiastically promoted and backed the project as an antidote to the global economic contraction.*

*The Tunnel is, without a doubt, the greatest engineering project ever conceived by Man. Its sheer scale makes the Great Pyramids and the Great Wall of China seem like mere toys, and many critics at the time described it as hubristic lunacy, a modern Tower of Babel. Although tubes and pressurized air have been used for passing around documents and small parcels since Victorian times, before the Tunnel, pneumatic tube transport of heavy goods and passengers had only been tried on a few intracity-subway demonstration programs. The extraordinary engineering demands of the Tunnel thus drove many technological advances, often beyond the core technologies involved, such as fast-tunneling directed explosives. As one illustration, thousands of young women with abacuses and notepads were employed as computers for engineering calculations at the start of the project, but by the end of the project electronic computers had taken their place.*

*In all, construction of the 5,880-mile tunnel took ten years between 1929 and 1938. Some seven million men worked on it, with Japan and the United States providing the bulk of the workers. At its height, one in ten working men in the United States was employed in building the Tunnel. More than thirteen billion cubic yards of material were excavated, almost fifty times the amount removed during the construction of the Panama Canal, and the fill was used to extend the shorelines of China, the Japanese home islands, and Puget Sound.*

• • •

Afterward we lie still on the futon, our limbs entwined. In the darkness I can hear her heart beating, and the smell of sex and our sweat, unfamiliar in this apartment, is comforting.

She tells me about her son, who is still going to school in America. She says that he is traveling with his friends in the southern states of America, riding the buses together.

"Some of the friends are Negroes," she says.

I know some Negroes. They have their own section in the American half of the City, where they mostly keep to themselves. Some Japanese families hire the women to cook Western meals.

"I hope he's having a good time," I say.

My reaction surprises Betty. She turns to stare at me and then laughs. "I forget that you cannot understand what this is about."

She sits up in bed. "In America, the Negroes and whites are separated: where they live, where they work, where they go to school."

I nod. That sounds familiar. Here in the Japanese half of the City, the races also keep to themselves. There are superior and inferior races. For example, there are many restaurants and clubs reserved only for the Japanese.

"The law says that whites and Negroes can ride the bus together, but the secret of America is that law is not followed by large swaths of the country. My son and his friends want to change that. They ride the buses together to make a statement, to make people pay attention to the secret. They ride in places where people do not want to see Negroes sitting in seats that belong only to whites. Things can become violent and dangerous when people get angry and form a mob."

This seems very foolish: to make statements that no one wants to hear, to speak when it is better to be quiet. What difference will a few boys riding a bus make?

"I don't know if it's going to make any difference, change anyone's mind. But it doesn't matter. It's good enough for me that he is speaking, that he is not silent. He's making the secret a little bit harder to keep, and that counts for something." Her voice is full of pride, and she is beautiful when she is proud.

I consider Betty's words. It is the obsession of Americans to speak, to express opinions on things that they are ignorant about. They believe in drawing attention to things that other people may prefer to keep quiet, to ignore and forget.

But I can't dismiss the image Betty has put into my head: a boy stands in darkness and silence. He speaks; his words float up like a bubble. It explodes, and the world is a little brighter, and a little less stiflingly silent.

I have read in the papers that back in Japan, they are debating about granting Formosans and Manchurians seats in the Imperial Diet. Britain is still fighting the native guerrillas in Africa and India but may be forced soon to grant the colonies independence. The world is indeed changing.

• • •

"What's wrong?" Betty asks. She wipes the sweat from my forehead. She shifts to give me more of the flow from the air conditioner. I shiver. Outside, the great arc lights are still off, not yet dawn. "Another bad dream?"

We've been spending many of our nights together since that first time. Betty has upset my routine, but I don't mind at all. That was the routine of a man with one foot in the grave. Betty has made me feel alive after so many years under the ocean, alone in darkness and silence.

But being with Betty has also unblocked something within me, and memories are tumbling out.

• • •

If you really couldn't stand it, they provided comfort women from Korea for the men. But you had to pay a day's wages.

I tried it only once. We were both so dirty, and the girl stayed still like a dead fish. I never used the comfort women again.

A friend told me that some of the girls were not there willingly but had been sold to the Imperial Army, and maybe the one I had was like that. I didn't really feel sorry for her. I was too tired.

• • •

From *The Ignoramus's Guide to American History*, 1995:

*So just when everyone was losing jobs and lining up for soup and bread, Japan came along and said, "Hey America, let's build this big-ass tunnel and spend a whole lot of money and hire lots of workers and get the economy going again. Whaddya say?" And the idea basically worked, so everyone was like: "Dōmo arigatō, Japan!"*

*Now, when you come up with a good idea like that, you get some chips you can cash in. So that's what Japan did the next year, in 1930. At the London Naval Conference, where the Big Bullies—oops, I meant "Great Powers"— figured out how many battleships and aircraft carriers each country got to build, Japan demanded to be allowed to build the same number of ships as the United States and Britain. And the US and Britain said "fine".*[1]

*This concession to Japan turned out to be a big deal. Remember Hamaguchi, the Japanese prime minister, and the way he kept on talking about how Japan was going to "ascend peacefully" from then on? This had really annoyed the militarists and nationalists in Japan because they thought Hamaguchi was selling out the country. But when Hamaguchi came home with such an impressive diplomatic victory, he was hailed as a hero, and people began to believe that his "Peaceful Ascent" policy was going to make*

---

1    The Washington Naval Treaty of 1922 had set the ratio of capital ships among the US, Britain, and Japan at 5:5:3. This was the ratio Japan got adjusted in 1930.

Japan strong. People thought maybe he really could get the Western powers to treat Japan as an equal without turning Japan into a giant army camp. The militarists and nationalists got less support after that.

At that fun party, the London Naval Conference, the Big Bullies also scrapped all those humiliating provisions of the Treaty of Versailles that made Germany toothless. Britain and Japan both had their own reasons for supporting this: They each thought Germany liked them better than the other and would join up as an ally if a global brawl for Asian colonies broke out one day. Everyone was wary about the Soviets, too, and wanted to set up Germany as a guard dog of sorts for the polar bear.[2]

Things to Think About in the Shower

1. Many economists describe the Tunnel as the first real Keynesian stimulus project, which shortened the Great Depression. The Tunnel's biggest fan was probably President Hoover: he won an unprecedented four terms in office because of its success.

2. We now know that the Japanese military abused the rights of many of the workers during the Tunnel's construction, but it took decades for the facts to emerge. The bibliography points to some more books on this subject.

3. The Tunnel ended up taking a lot of business away from surface shipping, and many Pacific ports went bust. The most famous example of this occurred in 1949, when Britain sold Hong Kong to Japan because it didn't think the harbor city was all that important anymore.

4. The Great War (1914–1918) turned out to be the last global 'hot war' of the twentieth century (so far). Are we turning into wimps? Who wants to start a new world war?

---

2 Allowing Germany to re-arm also let the German government heave a big sigh of relief. The harsh Treaty of Versailles, especially those articles about neutering Germany, made a lot of Germans very angry and some of them joined a group of goose-stepping thugs called the German Nationalist Socialist Party, which scared everyone, including the government. After those provisions of the treaty were scrapped, the thugs got no electoral support at the next election in 1930, and faded away. Heck, they are literally now a footnote of history, like this one.

● ● ●

After the main work on the Tunnel was completed in the thirteenth year of the Shōwa Era (1938), I returned home for the first and only time since I left eight years earlier. I bought a window seat on the westbound capsule train from Midpoint Station, coach class. The ride was smooth and comfortable, the capsule quiet save for the low voices of my fellow passengers and a faint whoosh as we were pushed along by air. Young female attendants pushed carts of drinks and food up and down the aisles.

Some clever companies had bought advertising space along the inside of the tube and painted pictures at window height. As the capsule moved along, the pictures rushing by centimeters from the windows blurred together and became animated, like a silent film. My fellow passengers and I were mesmerized by the novel effect.

The elevator ride up to the surface in Shanghai filled me with trepidation, my ears popping with the changes in pressure. And then it was time to get on a boat bound for Formosa.

I hardly recognized my home. With the money I sent, my parents had built a new house and bought more land. My family was now rich, and my village a bustling town. I found it hard to speak to my siblings and my parents. I had been away so long that I did not understand much about their lives, and I could not explain to them how I felt. I did not realize how much I had been hardened and numbed by my experience, and there were things I had seen that I could not speak of. In some sense I felt that I had become like a turtle, with a shell around me that kept me from feeling anything.

My father had written to me to come home because it was long past time for me to find a wife. Since I had worked hard, stayed healthy, and kept my mouth shut—it also helped that as a Formosan I was considered superior to the other races except the Japanese and Koreans—I had been steadily promoted to crew chief and then to shift supervisor. I had money, and if I settled in my hometown, I would provide a good home.

But I could no longer imagine a life on the surface. It had been so long since I had seen the blinding light of the sun that I felt like a newborn when out in the open. Things were so quiet. Everyone was startled when I spoke because I was used to shouting. And the sky and tall buildings made me dizzy—I was so used to being underground, under the sea, in tight, confined spaces, that I had trouble breathing if I looked up.

I expressed my desire to stay underground and work in one of the station cities strung like pearls along the Tunnel. The faces of the fathers of all the girls tightened at this thought. I didn't blame them: who would want their daughter to spend the rest of her life underground, never seeing the light of day? The fathers whispered to one another that I was deranged.

I said goodbye to my family for the last time, and I did not feel I was home until I was back at Midpoint Station, the warmth and the noise of the heart of the Earth around me, a safe shell. When I saw the soldiers on the platform at the station, I knew that the world was finally back to normal. More work still had to be done to complete the side tunnels that would be expanded into Midpoint City.

• • •

"Soldiers," Betty says, "why were there soldiers at Midpoint City?"

*I stand in darkness and silence. I cannot hear or see. Words churn in my throat, like a rising flood waiting to burst the dam. I have been holding my tongue for a long, long time.*

"They were there to keep the reporters from snooping around," I say.

I tell Betty about my secret, the secret of my nightmares, something I've never spoken of all these years.

• • •

As the economy recovered, labor costs rose. There were fewer and fewer young men desperate enough to take jobs as Diggers in the Tunnel. Progress on the American side had slowed for a few years, and Japan was not doing much better. Even China seemed to run out of poor peasants who wanted this work.

Hideki Tōjō, Army Minister, came up with a solution. The Imperial Army's pacification of the Communist rebellions supported by the Soviet Union in Manchuria and China resulted in many prisoners. They could be put to work, for free.

The prisoners were brought into the Tunnel to take the place of regular work crews. As shift supervisor, I managed them with the aid of a squad of soldiers. The prisoners were a sorry sight, chained together, naked, thin like scarecrows. They did not look like dangerous and crafty Communist bandits. I wondered sometimes how there could be so many prisoners, since the news always said that the pacification of the Communists was going well and the Communists were not much of a threat.

They usually didn't last long. When a prisoner was discovered to have expired from the work, his body was released from the shackles and a soldier would shoot it a few times. We would then report the death as the result of an escape attempt.

To hide the involvement of the slave laborers, we kept visiting reporters away from work on the main Tunnel. They were used mainly on the side excavations, for station cities or power stations, in places that were not well surveyed and more dangerous.

One time, while making a side tunnel for a power station, my crew blasted through to a pocket of undetected slush and water, and the side tunnel began to flood. We had to seal the breach quickly before the flood got into the main Tunnel. I woke up the crews of the two other shifts and sent a second chained crew into the side tunnel with sandbags to help with plugging up the break.

The corporal in charge of the squad of soldiers guarding the prisoners asked me, "What if they can't plug it?"

His meaning was obvious. We had to make sure that the water did not get into the main Tunnel, even if the repair crews we sent in failed. There was only one way to make sure, and as water was flowing back up the side tunnel, time was running out.

I directed the chained crew I'd kept behind as a reserve to begin placing dynamite around the side tunnel, behind the men we had sent in earlier. I did not much like this, but I told myself that these were hardened Communist terrorists, and they were probably sentenced to death already, anyway.

The prisoners hesitated. They understood what we were trying to do, and they did not want to do it. Some worked slowly. Others just stood.

The corporal ordered one of the prisoners shot. This motivated the remaining ones to hurry.

I set off the charges. The side tunnel collapsed, and the pile of debris and falling rocks filled most of the entrance, but there was still some space at the top. I directed the remaining prisoners to climb up and seal the opening. Even I climbed up to help them.

The sound of the explosion told the prisoners we sent in earlier what was happening. The chained men lumbered back, sloshing through the rising water and the darkness, trying to get to us. The corporal ordered the soldiers to shoot a few of the men, but the rest kept on coming, dragging the dead bodies with their chains, begging us to let them through. They climbed up the pile of debris toward us.

The man at the front of the chain was only a few meters from us, and in the remaining cone of light cast by the small opening that was left I could see his face, contorted with fright.

"Please," he said. "Please let me through. I just stole some money. I don't deserve to die." He spoke to me in Hokkien, my mother tongue. This shocked me. Was he a common criminal from back home in Formosa, and not a Chinese Communist from Manchuria?

He reached the opening and began to push away the rocks, to enlarge the opening and climb through. The corporal shouted at me to stop him. The water level was rising. Behind the man, the other chained prisoners were climbing to help him.

I lifted a heavy rock near me and smashed it down on the hands of the man grabbing onto the opening. He howled and fell back, dragging the other prisoners down with him. I heard the splash of water.

"Faster, faster!" I ordered the prisoners on our side of the collapsed tunnel. We sealed the opening, then retreated to set up more dynamite and blast down more rocks to solidify the seal.

When the work was finally done, the corporal ordered all the remaining prisoners shot, and we buried their bodies under yet more blast debris.

*There was a massive prisoner uprising. They attempted to sabotage the project, but failed and instead killed themselves.*

This was the corporal's report of the incident, and I signed my name to it as well. Everyone understood that was the way to write up such reports.

I remember the face of the man begging me to stop very well. That was the face I saw in the dream last night.

• • •

The Square is deserted right before dawn. Overhead, neon advertising signs hang from the City's ceiling, a few hundred meters up. They take the place of long-forgotten constellations and the moon.

Betty keeps an eye out for unlikely pedestrians while I swing the hammer against the chisel. Bronze is a hard material, but I have not lost the old skills I learned as a Digger. Soon the characters of my name are gone from the plaque, leaving behind a smooth rectangle.

I switch to a smaller chisel and begin to carve. The design is simple: three ovals interlinked, a chain. These are the links that bound two continents and three great cities together, and these are the shackles that bound men whose voices were forever silenced, whose names were forgotten. There is beauty and wonder here, and also horror and death.

With each strike of the hammer, I feel as though I am chipping away the shell around me, the numbness, the silence.

*Make the secret a bit harder to keep. That counts for something.*

"Hurry," Betty says.

My eyes are blurry. And suddenly the lights around the Square come on. It is morning under the Pacific Ocean.

# THIRTY-SIX ALTERNATE
# VIEWS OF MOUNT FUJI

## RUMI KANEKO
## TRANSLATED BY PRESTON GRASSMANN

**When Miko** Otomo began working for the Cultural Properties Protection Division of Tokyo, she had been surprised by the apathy and boredom of her colleagues. It was true that many of the artifact queries were either disappointing or of minor historical interest, but there were occasional moments of discovery. She would, for instance, never forget the twenty-thousand-year-old painted beads discovered in an abandoned house in Okinawa, or the ancient clay figurines known as *dogu* casually perched on the counter of an antique store in Shibuya.

Today, while her bored colleagues stared blankly at their screens, she could feel that same sense of excitement as she looked over her new claims—three prospects in one day. Among the most recent documents was a katana that its owner had said was from the Muromachi period, a piece of furniture from the Heian era, and an intriguing but doubtful claim for an undiscovered woodblock print reported to be from Hokusai himself.

She put aside the first two for later.

The third claim was addressed to her, written on a handmade parchment that was rare in the current market. Miko could tell, just by the weight and feel of the paper, that it was more akin to eighteenth-century ukiyo-e prints than anything contemporary. The return address was in Golden Gai, a scruffy neon-lit neighborhood in central Shinjuku known for its miniature standing bars and pedestrian alleys. Miko knew the area well enough to realize that the numbers on it were outdated long before it had become a haven for sightseers and heavy drinkers.

Was this an elaborate joke? If so, a lot of work had been put into it.

One thing was certain—the sender knew something about her area of expertise.

The envelope was also made from older material—tracing its firm edge with a finger, she thought of paper lanterns, shoji screens, and Edo-era umbrellas.

Returning to the letter, she studied the handwriting. It was written in an elegant semi-cursive form called gyosho, an older style that contrasted to the simple lines of modern calligraphy. There was no doubt the sender was a skilled practitioner of the art.

*Dear Dr Otomo,*

*As history tells us, the process of industrialization in Japan began during the Meiji Restoration—a pivotal point in the future of our nation. As we shrugged away the feudal warlords, we turned to the Western world, adopting a European vision of the future. Of course, there were choices that had to be made, and those choices had undoubtedly given us the benefit of rapid advancement. But what if this was an incomplete version of history, one which has always existed parallel to our current understanding? Let us for a moment imagine, as we historians often do, a Japanese society with a vision independent of our western counterparts.*

*As a historian, I'm sure you know that the Edo era, with its silk reeling and spinning, was already advancing new technologies, and that the potential for new inventions was growing in other industries as well. As an example, let us look at all the possibilities of geothermal energy, capable of fostering entirely new forms of mechanized production. Imagine whole cities lit up by the fires churning below us, by steam and heat born of the Earth—a power far more stable than solar energy or the wind.*

*I hope you will give me a chance to prove to you that such a world is not the mere fancy of an old man steeped in nostalgia, but that there is a civilization, sequestered from our current view, that is part of our history too. As noted in the attached documentation, I have in my possession several artifacts that will, with careful examination, provide the evidence of my claim.*

*Yours sincerely,*

*Katsuhiro Sawa*

• • •

Miko hadn't been to this part of Shinjuku for many years. Bright neon signs buzzed beneath the sounds of enka singers, bad karaoke, and jazz, while the smell of plum wine, sake, and whiskey permeated the dry winter air. It felt as if the pandemic had never existed here, that it belonged to an earlier age or some alternate version of the city she knew.

Before coming here, she'd done some background research on Dr Sawa. He had been a lecturer at Tokyo University for several years, but his relativistic approach to history had been too radical for the traditions of the institution. He would often quote Derrida and cite deconstructionist philosophy when talking about the past, referring to history as a fiction that was always being rewritten. His testing method was theoretical instead of fact-based, requiring his students to speculate on how single changes in the past could alter the present world or the future.

Miko covered her face with her mask and walked quickly,

turning corners until she reached the shop. It was located at the dark end of a closed-off lane, in a ramshackle building that tilted against its neighbors like an ill-fitting puzzle piece. When she arrived, there was only a faint light on the second floor. As she knocked on the door and waited, she became aware of a sudden quietness around her, like a radio tuning through static. Some time passed before she heard a faint stirring, the ponderous weight of feet on old wood. A voice that seemed as frail and cracked as the building came through the wooden slats.

"Dr Otomo?"

"Yes, that's me," she said.

The door unlocked and the old man stood at the entrance, wearing a shortened leather jacket over a gold kimono. It was covered in copper-colored designs that resembled clockwork gears and airships. She recognized the style as an Edo-period haori, a thigh-length piece tied together with two cords at the front, but the rest was clearly cosplay. He wore a watch with vacuum tubes attached to it, glowing with fluorescent orange numbers. If she'd had any doubts about the letter before, they were confirmed here. She had pinned her hopes on the mysterious presentation of the letter and its uncanny source, rather than heeding the rational explanation: that the doctor had lost touch with reality.

He smiled and bowed politely. She thought of the pseudo-Victorian cosplay of her youth, the alternate histories played out in the streets of Harajuku.

"Dr Sawa," she said. "Thank you for your letter."

"Thank you for coming," he said, sweeping his hand toward a tan-colored vintage couch that looked like a blend of Victorian and traditional Japanese craftsmanship. "Make yourself at home. I'll get you some tea."

She sat down and surveyed the room. Some of it seemed to belong to a much older era—classic furniture made of cypress, cedar, and ash, mixed in with other common woodwork designs from the seventeenth century. She also noticed small furnishings that looked authentic, like lanterns, sewing boxes, and jewelry chests made in a popular style called kusemono. But scattered throughout the room were artifacts that were clearly mock-historical. She saw aviator's goggles bearing a samurai family crest, a leather harness etched with an image of a dirigible, a cane topped with a brass falcon's head, brass rings with gears.

He returned to the room, smiling broadly as he poured tea from a gold-plated pot. She stared at the glowing numbers on his vacuum-tube watch.

"It's quite a piece, isn't it? There's a built-in accelerometer in here that lights up the display when it's turned."

"Amazing. You have quite a collection here," she said.

"It's amazing what kind of relics you can gather in a lifetime."

But then she noticed a large shelf of books nearby—a collection of Edo-era art books that she didn't recognize. As a specialist of that period, she was surprised by the unfamiliar titles.

"I've never seen those volumes. Where did you get them?" she asked.

He shrugged his shoulders. "Here and there," he said. "But these are the last of their kind."

She began to wonder if they were also part of his fake-relic collection.

"I see," she said as she continued reading the unfamiliar titles.

"But you came to see my Hokusai prints," he said, pushing a thin folder across the table in front of him. She watched him as he put on gloves and slowly opened the file. He smiled broadly as he slid the first print forward.

"'The Great Wave off Kanagawa,'" he said.

She sighed and shook her head. "I can tell you right now, that isn't real."

He lifted a gloved hand and said, "Please—give me a chance. I'm sure you can see that this isn't new."

"It looks old, but you don't expect me to believe this is from the Edo era?"

"Take a closer look," he said. He slid the image forward and took off his gloves.

She reluctantly put on the gloves and peered more closely. She was startled by its quality. She knew that its size, roughly thirty-six centimeters by twenty-six centimeters, and the material of the print was easy enough to fake. But then she looked at the faded image—most of the colors were in shades of Prussian blue and ink, made from plant-based dyes that would gradually fade when exposed to light. They were, like the wood-block prints from the eighteenth and nineteenth centuries, uniformly faded. She knew how hard that would be to fake with a wood-block print. Some parts of the image were the same as the original, with Mount Fuji in the background, framed by a claw-like crest of waves. What was different here, and all the more remarkable for mimicking the geometrical proportions of the original, was a cluster of airships dotting the distant sky. In the foreground, there should've been two *oshiokuri bune*—traditional boats filled with fishermen toiling among the waves. Instead, this image depicted a single steam-powered ship rendered in faded blue dye, so out of place in the context of Floating World art, but so authentic-looking.

"Dr Sawa, I grant you, whoever made this has forgery skills, but it can't be an original Hokusai."

"I'm quite certain that it is. And it's not the only one," he said, retrieving another print.

This one was made to resemble another image from Hokusai's "Thirty-six Views of Mount Fuji." Called 'Fine Wind, Clear Morning,' it depicted Mount Fuji at dawn. At the peak of the mountain, she could see the same stylized streaks of snow, the same wisps of trailing cloud drifting through a dark-blue sky. But at the base of the mountain, surrounded by the trees of Aokigahara, there was a bustling city. The buildings were in a similar style to Edo architecture, with its dominance of wood and verandas, but unlike many of the structures of that period, these were bereft of Western influence. They blended with the surrounding landscape, with an organic sweep that seemed as expansive as the forest it replaced. And yet these were just mundane details compared to the rest of the image. There were winged objects floating above the city, flying machines that resembled prehistoric birds. In the foreground, a colossal train waited at a station, where a crowd was waiting to board. Running up one side of the mountain, merging with the forest around it, were a series of towers that appeared to be releasing steam into the dawn sky.

"These aren't real, Dr Sawa. Did you invite me here to show me these?" she asked.

"Doctor, bear with me for a moment. What you're seeing is an artifact from a parallel world, an alternate version of our history. And it's just as real as our own past."

"I'm sorry Doctor, I know about your deconstructionist theories and your postmodern philosophy of relative history, but these are nothing more than quasi-Victorian fantasies."

He shook his head. "I'm sure you know that most of those fantasies come from a mix of nostalgia and an ethnocentric view of history. But the fact is, such visions are also an acknowledgement that our version of history is inadequate. It's the awareness of a deeper truth: that the past is filled with potential realities beyond our own."

"I'm afraid that's not enough to convince me that these are real."

Dr Sawa held up his palm and pointed at the city on the print. "Take them with you. The paper and the inks are easy enough to authenticate. It won't be long before you'll be able to appreciate the truth of what I'm saying."

"I admit these are remarkable fakes, Doctor, but that's all they can be. Why did you choose me? There are plenty of other experts in the city."

He nodded slowly and turned his attention back to the print. "You're an expert on the Edo era, with a specialization in paper and prints. I've read all of your articles and research papers on authentication—I respect your eye for detail and appreciate your passion. But like me, you've courted your own share of controversy, haven't you? As I recall, you wrote a paper about the semiotics of history and how all objects possess a residue of their context."

She was surprised he had read her academic work on semiotics—her publications were hard to find. "I appreciate the kind words, Doctor, but that was meant to be a practical application for appraising artifacts."

"So is this," he said, with a quiet certainty that she hadn't heard until now. He leaned forward and said: "Every artifact contains a world, and a reflection of the dreams in which it was conceived."

He was quoting her own text.

"I'm flattered, Dr Sawa," she said, feeling off-balance. It was true that her intuitive approach to artifacts had been criticized, but that was nothing compared to a relativistic view of history. "But I'm not sure that applies here."

"Of course it does. Look at this print again. What do you see?" He pointed to a group of thin towers painted along the base of the mountain.

"Based on what you said earlier, I would guess they're drawing geothermal energy from below, channeling it to fuel all the industries of the city."

"And these winged machines?"

"They look like ornithopters."

"Right again. And how can a city like this exist next to Mount Fuji? The volcanic—"

She pointed at a series of thinly painted cracks at the base of the mountain. "Are those meant to divert the flow?"

"Correct—they're channels. The molten rock powers turbines that can generate enough energy to power several cities. And now you see why I chose you."

He opened other Hokusai prints to show her—"A Sketch of the Mitsui Shop," "Sunset Across the Ryōgoku Bridge," "Tea House at Koishikawa," "Watermill at Onden," "Shore of Tago Bay," and "Nihonbashi Bridge"—all of them with the same kind of alternate-world imagery.

She had no doubt that Dr Sawa had convinced himself that this make-believe world was real, and that nothing she would say could change that.

"Are all of these objects from the alternate past?" she asked, pointing to the cane and the books on the shelf.

"Most of them are. This one is a new acquisition." He reached for an orb-shaped object that sat on a nearby shelf. "It's a form of himitsu-bako—a puzzle box made of brass instead of wood."

Most himitsu-bako were made of layers of overlapping wood, designed to open with a sequence of movements on its surface. This looked nothing like that, Miko thought. Although it appeared to be a solid sphere at first, she noticed hairline grooves cut through it, like the longitude lines of a globe. But as Dr Sawa began to move his fingers over the brass, the surface shifted, unfolding like a mechanical origami flower. Five tapered sections became petals and flanged outward in tiny bursts of steam. A koto sound began to play inside it.

"It's quite remarkable," she said.

"As you might know, the steam engine was developed by Thomas Newcomen in 1712. That is true in that version of Edo as well, but the imported technology was adapted in ways we haven't been able to manage here."

"Why is that, do you think?" she asked, realizing she was being drawn into his fantasy world.

"A good question. Japan never faced a financial crisis in the seventeenth century and didn't need to sell off its natural resources as we did in our world—copper, zinc, and silver exports were minimal, and we used them to build technologies that later became popular throughout the world," he said, lifting the toy in his palm as it continued playing out its tune.

"The Sony Walkman of the Edo era," she said.

"You might say that." He smiled as he placed it on the counter.

"Well," she began, trying to navigate her way through a strange maze of curiosity and doubt. "Thank you for inviting me here, Doctor. I'll take these prints, as requested, and examine them."

He handed her the file and bowed. "At your leisure," he said.

She returned the gesture. "I'll come back soon."

"I know you will," he said.

• • •

As she closed the door, she couldn't shake the feeling that something was off. She looked down the street, silent now as the signs hovered over the Golden Gai like neon ghosts. Trying to retrace her steps, she encountered narrow streets she didn't remember seeing, with signs that seemed too large and opulent for this district. But then she noticed that one of the signs was made of vacuum tubes, like Dr Sawa's watch. How had she missed that before? She huddled further into her jacket and walked quickly. Something wasn't right. She thought of her words—*Every artifact contains a world*—written at the beginning of her career. They began to take on a new meaning, as if to prove Dr Sawa's own theories of relative history. Was her own mind playing tricks on her now?

She could no longer hear the cars in the distance, the sound of singing, the voices of drinkers. She tried to retrace her steps back through the streets, but everything seemed slightly out of step from her memory. And then, in the sky between the buildings, she saw something pass in a sliver glint of light. She shook her head. *It couldn't have been,* she thought—a dirigible in the shape of a tear lingered in her mind's eye like a splinter.

When she emerged from the Golden Gai, the streets were quiet. She looked around for the subway sign, but it was gone. Instead, she saw a familiar tower, its distant peak pouring steam into a starlit sky. Below her, she heard a faint whirring sound and felt the ground tremble as something passed beneath her. She thought of pneumatic tubes, of Alfred Beach's dreams of New York in the nineteenth century.

*It won't be long before you'll be able to appreciate the truth of what I'm saying.*

With shaking hands, she opened Dr Sawa's file. There were no longer any towers or dirigibles or machinery of an alternate Japan.

Instead, they were the original woodblock prints of Hokusai.

# THE CARTOGRAPHY
# OF SUDDEN DEATH

## CHARLIE JANE ANDERS

**Ythna came** to the Beldame's household when she was barely old enough to walk. They took her from the nursery block in the middle of the night, with nothing but the simple koton robe she was wearing, and carried the tiny girl to a black shiny vehicle, a Monopod. Sitting in the back, wearing a neat gray uniform and matching black gloves and shoes, was an Officiator, who asked the young Ythna some questions. The next thing she knew, she was riding a white cage on a wire over the mountains, up to the gilded fortress where she would serve the Beldame for the rest of her days, if she was lucky.

Ythna forgot the Officiator's face, or whatever else he said to her, but she would always remember what he said as she stepped, barefoot, out of the cage as the sun rose over the golden house. He knelt before her and spoke gently: "You are but one of a thousand retainers to the Beldame. But each of you is a finger, or a toe. Your movements are her movements. Do not make her a disgrace."

Ythna lived in a tiny yellow dormitory room with nine other small children, all of them sharing white-and-red uniforms and eating from the same dispensary. Ythna learned to read and write basic Gaven texts, and worked in the cavernous kitchen and boiler room of the golden fortress, which was called Parathall. At night, the other children teased Ythna and pinched her in places where the bruises wouldn't show on her golden-brown skin, under her retainer uniform. Two girls, the pale, blonde Maryn and the olive-toned Yuli, appointed themselves the rulers of Children's Wing, and if Ythna didn't please Maryn and Yuli she found herself sealed inside a small wooden linen box, suffocating, sometimes overnight.

Every moment when people weren't looking, Ythna wept into her loose sleeve. Until one day when she brought some hot barley wine to the Beldame herself, doing the five-point turn as she'd been taught, ending up on one knee with the tray raised before the wrought iron chair.

Ythna was eight or nine years old, and she made sure not to look at the Beldame's white round face, as she knelt. But in Ythna's eagerness to avoid looking on her mistress, she found herself gazing, instead, at the papers the Beldame was studying. Ythna started reading them, until the Beldame noticed.

"You can read that?" the Beldame said.

Ythna nodded, terrified.

"And tell me, what do you think of it?" the Beldame asked.

Ythna stammered at first, but at last she shared a few thoughts about the document, which dealt with the rebellious offworld colonists, and the problems with maintaining order in the fringes of the Empire here on Earth. The Beldame asked more questions, and Ythna answered as best she could. After that, the Beldame sent her away—but then Ythna found herself chosen to bring food and drink to the Beldame often. And sometimes, the Beldame would invite her to sit for a moment at her feet, and talk to her.

Years passed. One day, word came that the Beldame was going to be elevated to the Emperor's Thousand, so she would be in the same direct relationship to the Emperor that the Beldame's thousand retainers were to her. There would be a massive ceremony at the

Tomb of the Unknown Emperor, at which the Beldame would be given a steel thimble, symbolizing the fact that she was becoming one of the Emperor's own fingers. Ythna couldn't even imagine that she could be one-thousandth of the woman who was one-thousandth of the Emperor. She watched the sunrise between the mountain peaks below the Beldame's arched picture windows and laughed at the floor brush in her hand.

"A lot is going to change for all of us," said Maryn, who had grown into a striking young woman who still bossed around the other retainers. "Strange foods, new places. All the more reason to keep our behavior perfect. The Beldame is counting on us."

Ythna said nothing. She was still smaller than Maryn, barely noticeable except for her ribbons of long black hair, down to her waist, and the way she ran through the stone passages of the fortress, her bare feet as silent as snow melting, when nobody else was around.

The day came nearer, and they all traveled for a week by steam truck and Monopod to the Tomb of the Unknown Emperor. At last, they saw it in the distance, looming over the plains: a great structure, shaped like an old letter M, with two great pillars supporting the black canopy. The Unknown Emperor had lain in state for over a hundred years there, behind a faceless statue that raised one hand to the people who'd served him without knowing his name.

They all lined up in rows, the thousand of them, at the base of the Tomb, while the Beldame climbed to the very top. Some of the retainers were playing small bells, and sweet smoke was coming up out of brass pipes all around them. The Officiators were leading Ythna and the others in ceremonial chants. Ythna could see the tiny figure of the Beldame, emerging on top of the structure, as the Emperor himself bestowed the thimble on her. A voice, one of the Chief Officiators, spoke of the hundreds of years of tradition they honored today.

Ythna thought that she could not be any more deliriously proud than she was at this moment, watching her friend and mistress elevated. Her only wish was that she could see the Beldame Thakrra up close at this moment, to behold the look on Thakrra's face.

A second later, Ythna had her desire. The Beldame lay on the ground directly in front of her, lying on her back, her small body broken by the fall from the top of the structure. Her gentle, lined face was still recognizable, inside her brocaded robe and twelve-peaked silken hat, but she had no expression at all, and blood was leaking out all over the ground, until it lapped against Ythna's bare feet. She could not help but panic that maybe her selfish wish had caused this to happen.

Next to Ythna, Maryn saw the Beldame's corpse and began wailing in a loud, theatrical fashion. The other retainers heard Maryn and followed her lead, making a sound like a family of cats. Ythna, meanwhile, could barely choke out a single tear, and it hurt like a splinter coming out.

Frantic to avoid seeing the Beldame like this, Ythna looked up—just as a strange woman stepped out of the nearest pillar in the Tomb. The woman had long curly red hair under a pillbox hat shaped like one of the lacquered discs where the Beldame had kept her spare monocles. She had a sharp nose and chin, and quick gray eyes. And she wore a long black coat, with embroidered sleeves and shoulders, and shiny brass buttons with cords looping around them. She looked like a commanding general from an old-fashioned foreign army.

The red-haired woman stepped forward, looked around, and took in the scene. Then she said a curse word in a language that Ythna had never heard, and slipped away around the side of the Tomb, before anybody else noticed her.

· · ·

Hours went by. Ythna felt as though her ribcage were as barbed and twisted as the ends of the Beldame's beloved wrought-iron chair. She knelt on the ground, in the Beldame's dried blood, weeping, though the Beldame's body was long gone. Nearby, Yuli and Maryn were making a huge show of singing the Bottomless Grief Spiral chant along with the Officiators. But Maryn kept whispering to Yuli that maybe they should make a break for it—retainers whose mistress died could not count on being given new positions elsewhere, and the alternative was Obsolescence.

"We can't escape," Yuli whispered back. "Not with everybody watching. And where would we go? There is no place to hide in the entire Empire, from sea to pole to sea."

Ythna couldn't stop wondering about the red-haired woman, who wore no uniform Ythna recognized, and who had all but spat on the ground on seeing the gathered retainers and Officiators. She finally crept over to the pillar she'd seen the woman step out of, and started feeling around for a hinge or join, some evidence of a passageway. The Tomb had many hidden ways in and out—that was how the Emperor's body had been deposited there without anyone seeing his face—but if there was a doorway here, then Ythna could not find it. She tried to shake the granite edge of the pillar with her fingertips, as if she could bring down the mighty Tomb by herself.

"What do you think you are doing?"

Ythna turned to see one of the Obfuscators watching her. Trex. He'd arrived with the others, to take charge of the scene, and keep the retainers in order. He was a tall, solidly built man with a sallow face and black hair and eyes. And he was holding a fully charged valence gun, aimed at her. She could smell the burnt-shoe odor from a few feet away, and if he fired she would be a pile of dust in seconds. He had the black chestpiece and square helmet that indicated he was one of the Emperor's personal Obfuscators, empowered to create order in just about any way he deemed necessary.

Ythna backed against the pillar, stuttering and trying to think of what to say. "There was a woman, a stranger. Not one of our party. She came out of this pillar right after the Beldame was killed." She described the woman and her clothing as best she could, and the Obfuscator Trex seemed to be listening carefully. At last, he nodded and indicated for her to rejoin the others.

"Tell nobody else what you saw," added Trex. Then he stalked away, his back and legs as stiff as one of the supply robots carrying fuel and food up the mountainside to the Golden Fortress.

The retainers all started to freeze as the sun got lower on the horizon, since they were wearing light koton ceremonial gowns designed for comfort in the noon sun. The patch of dried blood had gone crisp, but the smell of newly slaughtered cattle still hung in the air. Nobody had yet decided what to do with these surplus retainers. Yuli and Maryn still debated running away.

Someone gave the retainers hot barley wine, to warm them up, which just reminded Ythna of the Beldame Thakrra all over again, and she found herself crying harder than ever as she drank from the communal jug. Some time later, she needed to relieve herself, and couldn't bear to soil the same ground where the Beldame had bled to death. She begged an Obfuscator until he gave her permission to go around the Tomb to the front entrance, where some simple latrines had been set up. Ythna thanked him profusely.

The latrines were lined up like sentry boxes, perpendicular to the front pillar of the Tomb. Beyond them, there was the edge of a dense forest of oaks, birches, and pines, stretching all the way to the distant white mountains. A chill wind seemed to come from the woods as Ythna slipped inside one of the latrines, hiking up her shift. When she came out again, the red-haired woman was there.

The woman gestured for Ythna to be silent. "I've been observing you," she whispered, with an accent that Ythna couldn't place. "You're cleverer than the rest. And you're actually grief-stricken for the poor dead Beldame. All your friends are just pretending. I want to help you."

"You killed her," Ythna said. "You killed the Beldame. I saw you step out of the tomb right after she fell."

"No, I swear I had nothing to do with her death," the woman said sadly. "Except that it created a door for me to step through. That's how I travel. My name is Jemima Brookwater, and I'm from the future."

Ythna studied the strange red-haired woman for a moment. Her black boots were shiny but scuffed, her puffy pants had a grass stain on one knee, and her fine velvet coat had a rip in the side, which had been hastily sewn and patched. Whatever this woman was—crackwit, breakbond, or something else—she was not an assassin. But maybe Ythna should tell Trex in any case.

"It was good to meet you, Jemima," Ythna said. "I should go and rejoin the others. Be safe." She turned to go back around the tomb toward the other retainers, whom she could hear chanting the grief spiral with dry, exhausted throats.

"Let me help you," Jemima said again.

Ythna turned back. "Why would you want to help me?"

"I told you, I travel by using the openings created when someone important dies unexpectedly. And I feel bad about that. So I made a vow: every time I travel, I try to help one person, one deserving person."

"And how would you help me?" Something about this woman's way of speaking reminded Ythna of the Beldame, except that Jemima was more animated and lacked the Beldame's dignity.

"I don't know. You tell me. It's not really helping if I decide for myself what sort of help you need, is it?"

Ythna didn't say anything for a moment, so Jemima added: "Tell me. Your mistress, Thakrra, is dead. What do you want to do now?"

Nobody had ever asked Ythna what she wanted, in her entire life. But more startling than that was to hear Jemima say Thakrra was dead, by name, because it hit her all over again: the feeling of hopelessness. Like she had swallowed something enormous, that she could never digest even if she lived forever. She heard the droning chant from the plains on the other side of the tomb, and all of a sudden the voices sounded genuinely miserable instead of forced and dried out.

"There is nothing you can do for me," Ythna said, and turned to leave in the shadow of the great crisscrossing limbs of the Tomb.

The woman chased after her, speaking quickly. "That's just not true," she said. "I really don't want to tell you what you should do, but I can help with anything you choose. For example, I can get you out of here. That forest is full of landmines, but I know a secret underground passage, which archaeologists discovered hundreds of years from now. And I could forge whatever documents you might need. Your Empire outlawed proper computers. They keep obsessive records on paper, but with a few major flaws. You can be anyone."

Ythna turned back one last time, tears all over her face. "I cannot be anyone," she said. "I can only be what I am: one small piece of the Beldame. Who do you belong to? Are you completely alone? You seem like someone who just comes and goes, like a ghost. And you want me to become a ghost as well. I can't. Leave me alone."

"Listen." Jemima grabbed Ythna's arm. They were almost back within view of the massed group of retainers, Obfuscators, and Officiators. "This is not going to go well for you. I've read the history books. I know what happened to a retainer whose master or mistress died suddenly, without making arrangements first. If you're lucky, you get reeducated and sent to a new household, where you'll be the lowest status and they'll treat you like dirt. If you're unlucky…"

Ythna tried to explain, with eyes full of tears and a voice suddenly hoarse from crying and chanting, that she didn't care what happened to her. "I can't just dishonor the Beldame by running away. That would be worse than enduring any abuse. If you know so much, then you have to understand that."

At last, Jemima let go of Ythna's arm, and she turned to go back to the others before she was missed.

"At least I tried," Jemima said. "I do admire your conviction."

"There she is," a voice said from behind them. "I told you. I told you she was conspiring. All along, conspiring. And scheming." Maryn stood at the edge of the tomb, pointing at Ythna and Jemima. Beside her, Obfuscator Trex advanced, raising the brass rod of his valence gun. Maryn was a foot shorter than Trex and wore simple robes—like Ythna's—next to Trex's bulky chrome-and-leather uniform. But Maryn's excitement and triumph made her seem twice as big as the strong, fussy man.

Jemima grabbed Ythna and pushed her behind herself, so that Jemima could take the brunt of Trex's first shot and Ythna would have an extra few seconds to live.

"The penalty for conspiring to assassinate a Beldame is death," Trex said, chewing each syllable like a nugget of fat. "I am mightily empowered to carry out the sentence at once."

"I don't want any reward," Maryn said. Everybody ignored her.

"Wait," Jemima said. "You are being duped here. I know you're an intelligent man. I've read about you. Trex, right? I know all about your illustrious career. And I have a perfectly sensible explanation for everything you've witnessed." Jemima was reaching into a tiny holster hidden in the braided piping on the side of her velvet coat, reaching for an object the size of her thumb. A gun.

"Please," Ythna said to Trex. "We didn't conspire. I only just met this woman."

But Trex aimed his valence gun, sparks coming from the connecting tubes, and said, "You are both found guilty, and your sentence is—"

Ythna closed her eyes, waiting for a sizzling noise and the acrid stench of Jemima being torn molecule from molecule. Instead, she heard Maryn scream and thrash the air. When Ythna opened her eyes, Trex's headless body was falling to the ground, and Trex's head was rolling to a stop at Maryn's feet, an expression of supreme disgruntlement forever sealed on Trex's face.

A man wearing a black uniform, as simple as Trex's was ornate, was running away, sheathing a bloody sword of a curved design that Ythna had never seen before. An opaque helmet, shaped like a teardrop, obscured the man's features.

Jemima gave another one of her foreign curse-words and ran after the man. Ythna took one look at the headless Obfuscator and the wailing Maryn—whose screams were likely to bring everybody running—and followed Jemima.

The man with the sword reached the outermost pillar of the M-shaped tomb, and ran through the wall without breaking stride. One moment he was there, the next he was gone. Jemima and Ythna reached the wall a moment later, and Jemima ran straight for the spot where the man had vanished. And then she, too, was gone. Ythna's momentum carried her forward before she could even think about the insanity of what she was doing. She hit the massive-blocked granite wall at the same point as the other two, and felt a sensation like a million tiny hands tugging at her. And then her senses were stolen away, one by one. But not before she had a glimpse of a million bright threads of different colors, crisscrossing around her in the midst of infinite darkness.

• • •

Ythna foundered, unable to see, hear, or touch anything for an age, until those same tiny hands grabbed her and shoved her forward, into the light.

For a moment, Ythna was dazzled and had pins and needles in her hands and feet, then she slowly regained her sight. She was lying on the floor of a long high-vaulted chamber, open to the air on one side and closed off on the other. A giant terrace, or balcony, then. The walls to her left were incredibly ornate, with what looked like molded silver encrusted with countless priceless jewels—and yet, someone had gone to great trouble to make that opulence look as ugly as possible. The silver was smudgy gray, the rubies and diamonds were as dull as you could make them. To Ythna's left, past the railing, she could see an endless phalanx of people in retainer outfits, not all that different from what she wore every day, marching forward to the grim, repetitive droning of horns.

Next to Ythna, Jemima was on her knees, covering her face with one hand, and saying "No, no, no, no, please no," over and over again.

"What is it?" Ythna said. "What's wrong?" She put one hand on Jemima's epauletted shoulder.

"This is the worst place," Jemima said, uncovering her face and gesturing past the balcony at the thousands of people walking in neat rows. "I'm sorry. This is my fault. I shouldn't have brought you here. I wanted to help you, and I've just made everything worse."

"What place? Where are we?" Ythna was still having a hard time thinking straight after the disorientation of passing through the senseless tangle of threads.

"Roughly seventy years after your time. The Glorious Restoration. The worst period in the history of the Gaven Empire." Jemima straightened up a bit on her haunches. "An attempt to restore traditional values to an empire that had grown decadent. They've probably executed another Chief Officiator, and that's what made the door we just came out of. And those people down there? They're marching to the death camps."

"We're in the future," Ythna said, and now she was pulling her own hair to try and get her head straight.

The whole thing sounded mad. But they weren't at the Tomb of the Unknown Emperor anymore, and the more she looked at the scene outside, the more she noticed little incongruities.

Like, the retainers marching forward across the square wore simpler uniforms than she'd ever seen before, with a different insignia. The banners hanging on the outer wall of the courtyard, opposite the balcony, listed a different Imperial Era: the Great Rejoicing Era, not the Bountiful Era that Ythna was used to. So there was a different Emperor on the throne. But the banners looked old. And the Obfuscators herding these retainers across the courtyard wore helmets with weird spikes on them, and their chestpieces were a blockier design as well, aimed at protecting against a different class of weapons. Their valence guns were much smaller and could be carried with one hand, too. There were other details, but those were the ones that jumped out at Ythna.

"How did we get here?" Ythna said.

"I told you," Jemima said. "That's how I travel. But I've never killed anyone to open a portal. Trex was supposed to live another few decades, and become the Chief Obfuscator to the Emperor Maarthyon. And I'm sorry, but Beldame Thakrra always died on that day. Her death is in my history book, and I'm pretty sure it was an accident."

Jemima was searching the terrace for clues to the exact date, while trying to stay out of sight from the people below, or on the other balconies further along. "If we know what day this is, then we can know when the next significant death will be," Jemima said. "We need to get the blazes out of here."

"And any death of an important person will make a door?" Ythna said.

"It must be an unexpected death," Jemima said. "Something that creates a lot of causal torsions." Ythna must have looked confused, because she added: "A lot of adjustments. Like ripples."

"So you really are a ghost," Ythna said. "You belong to no one, you travel through death, and you come and go without being seen. I feel sorry for you."

Jemima didn't have anything to say. For the second time in half an hour, she had lost her unflappable good humor. She stared at Ythna for a moment.

Then she turned and pointed with one slender gloved finger. "Over there. He's making for that dais. We must stop him, or he'll ruin absolutely everything."

The man with the opaque tear-shaped helmet had his sword out again, with traces of Trex's blood still on it. He was running along another terrace, just around a corner of the giant building from the one where Jemima and Ythna stood. And when Ythna leaned dangerously out into the open, over the stone railing, she could see the man's destination: a dais facing the courtyard, where a bald, sweaty man sat watching the thousands of people being herded away to the slaughter. The man's robes, dais, and throne were like the walls of this chamber: ornate, but ugly and drained of color. Everything about him was designed to show off wealth, without sharing beauty.

At least twenty Obfuscators and Officiators stood between the man with the sword and the man on the throne, who had to be a Vice Emperor. They all aimed their valence guns at the assassin, who raised a long metal brace strapped to his left forearm, which he held in front of him like a shield. The valence guns made the scorching sound Ythna had heard before, but without effect. The man's forearm glowed with a blue light that spread in front of him and seemed to protect him. He reached the first of the Obfuscators, and put his sword through her stomach in an elegant motion that did not slow his run at all.

"How is he doing that?" Ythna said. "With the valence guns?"

Then she turned and realized Jemima wasn't next to her anymore. She was already at the far end of the terrace, opening a hidden door she'd found, which led to the next terrace along. Jemima was rushing toward the assassin and the Vice Emperor. Ythna did her best imitation of Jemima's strange foreign swear word—"fth'nak"—and ran after her.

In the next terrace, a group of Officiators were holding up ceremonial trowels, symbolizing the burial of the past and the building of the future, and they gasped when two strange women came running into the space, a tall redhead in a fancy coat and a small dark girl in old-fashioned retainer clothes.

"The Vice Emperor," Jemima gasped without slowing her run. "I'm the only one who can save him."

For a moment, Ythna thought the Officiators might believe Jemima and let her pass. But they fell back on an Officiator's ingrained distrust of anyone or anything that didn't instantly fit, and reached out to try and restrain both Ythna and Jemima. They were too slow—Jemima had almost reached the far wall, and Ythna was slippery as a wet goose—but they called for Obfuscators to help them. By the time Ythna reached the far wall, where Jemima was trying to open the next door, people were firing valence guns at her from the courtyard below. The balcony next to them exploded into chunks of silver and bejeweled masonry.

"Don't worry," Jemima said. "They mass-produced those guns cheaply in this era. At this range, they couldn't hit a Monopod."

She got the door to the next terrace open, and they were facing three Obfuscators aiming valence guns. At point-blank range.

"Guh," Jemima said. "Listen. That reprehensible man over there is about to assassinate your Vice Emperor." By now they were close enough to have an excellent view, as the last few of the Vice Emperor's Obfuscators fought hand-to-hand against the sword-wielding assassin, surrounded by the fresh corpses of their brethren. "I can stop him. I swear to you I can."

These Obfuscators hesitated—long enough for Jemima to pull out the thumb-sized gun hidden in her coat's braid and shoot them all with it. There was a bright pink flash in front of each of them, just before they all fell face down on the ground.

"Stunned," she said. "They'll be fine."

Then she lifted one arm, so that a bit of lace cuff flopped out of her velvet sleeve, and aimed at the top of the ceremonial gate between the courtyard and the Vice Emperor's dais. A tiny hook shot out of her lace cuff, with a steel cord attached to it, and it latched on to the apex of the gate's arch, right on top of the symbol for Dja-Thun—or the unbroken chain of thousands from Emperor to gutterslave. "Hang on tight," Jemima said, right before she grabbed Ythna's waist and pressed a button, sending them sailing through the smoky bright air over the men shooting valence guns at them. The sun lit up Ythna's face in mid swing, the same way it once had from the Beldame's window.

By the time they reached the dais, dismounting with only a slight stumble, the assassin had killed the last Obfuscator, and was advancing on the Vice Emperor, who cowered on his massive gray-gold throne.

"Listen to me," Jemima shouted at the man. "You don't want to do this. You really, really do not. Time-travel via murder is a dead end. Literally. You'll tear the map apart, and none of the major deaths of history will happen on schedule. You'll be every bit as lost as I will."

The man turned to salute Jemima. "Professor Brookwater," he said in a low voice, only slightly muffled by his milky helmet. "You are one of my all-time heroes. But you don't know the full potential of what you discovered. I sincerely hope you do get home someday."

Jemima shot at him and missed. He spun, low to the ground, and then pivoted and took the Vice Emperor's head clean off. Almost at once, Ythna could see an indistinct doorway appear on the elaborately carved side of the gray dais: like a pinwheel with too many spokes to count, opening outwards and showing a secret pathway through death and time. Somehow, Ythna couldn't see these doors, until she had already passed through one.

The assassin ran into the pinwheel and vanished. The remaining Obfuscators and retainers were crying out from the courtyard below, and a hundred valence guns went off all at once. The dais was collapsing into rubble. Ythna was paralyzed for a moment, until Jemima grabbed her and threw her into the doorway the assassin had created.

• • •

The next thing Ythna knew, she landed facedown on a hard cement surface, outdoors, under a nearly cloudless sky. In front of her was a big chain-link fence, with men in unfamiliar uniforms walking past it, holding big bulky metal guns. She heard a voice saying indistinct words over a loudspeaker. She turned and saw a row of giant rocket ships looming in the distance, with a flaming circle painted on each gunmetal shell and a mesh of bright scaffolding clinging to their sides.

She couldn't see the assassin with the sword, but Jemima was crouched next to her, looking pissed off and maybe a little weepy.

"It just gets better and better," Jemima said. "This is—"

"I know where we are, this time," Ythna said. "The Beldame showed me pictures. This was the last great assault on the Martian

Colony. The Emperor Dickon's great and glorious campaign to bring the principle of Dja-Thun to the unruly people on Mars. This happened decades before I was born."

"It's happening right now," Jemima said, looking in all directions for the man they'd been chasing. "I wonder who just died here."

"What did you mean, about the map?" Ythna said. "You said he was tearing the map apart."

"I've got a history book," Jemima said without pausing her search. "I know the major deaths, down to the exact place and time. Every time I travel, I chart where each death leads. I'm deciphering the map slowly, but this cad will render that impossible. I've done twenty-eight trips so far, including today."

"How many people have you helped?" Ythna said. "Twenty-seven?"

"Twenty-five," Jemima said.

"And how did that turn out for them?"

"No idea. People like you don't get mentioned in the history books, even if I found an updated version. No offense. But if I ever get home, I can try to look up some detailed records, and try to find out what happened to all of you."

Jemima cursed again in her own language: "Fth'nak." An old-fashioned wheeled vehicle was rolling toward them, with figures in bulky black armor, holding big oily guns. The jeep rumbled, a cloud of dust in its wake, as it grew bigger until it was right in front of them. On the side of the jeep was the round, fiery insignia of the Age of Advancement, the Emperor Dickon's era. The men in the front of the truck wore the same image on their helmets.

Jemima started to try and explain their presence to these men, but they cut her off.

"Desertion is a capital crime, as you are no doubt aware," the man in the truck's passenger seat said. "But you're lucky. The *Dauntless* is short-crewed and ammunition is precious. So I'm going to pretend you didn't just try to run away. That's a one-time offer, good only if you come with me right now. Your new home lifts off tomorrow morning at oh-five-hundred hours."

And that's how Jemima and Ythna found themselves in a bare gray cage with a tiny window that gave them a partial view of the nearest rocket, a snub-nosed, squat monstrosity with nine thrusters arrayed like petals. Ythna rubbed the bruises she'd gotten from the guards' rifle butts and rough hands.

"At least they don't think we're spies," said Ythna. "Or they'd have just executed us."

"They assume that nobody could ever get this far inside their security perimeter undetected," said Jemima. "So they reached for the next logical explanation: we must be members of the galley crew, who tried to make a break for it. Instead of executing us, they'll just send us up in one of those ships, probably in irons in case we actually are saboteurs."

"The Beldame told me that this campaign was a terrible waste. The whole assault force died without ever reaching Mars, because the colonists had superior weapons. They used technology that the Empire had rejected as impure," said Ythna. "It was one of the Beldame's lessons that she liked to tell: A just cause becomes unjust when it costs too much human life."

"The Beldame sounds like she was a wise woman," said Jemima.

Ythna was sure she was going to look up and see a sarcastic leer on Jemima's sharp face, but there was none. Instead, Jemima just nodded, then walked to the window and studied the rocket they were soon going to be chained up in the belly of.

"I don't want to die in a pointless war that was lost before I was born," Ythna said.

"Really? I thought you didn't want anything, one way or the other," Jemima said, still facing the window. "Isn't that what you said? And how is this different from what would have happened to you if we had never met? You would have been sent to work for some new master, who might have worked you to death in a year or two. Or you could have been marked for Obsolescence, and died sooner. This is the same."

"It's not the same at all," Ythna said. Just when she had thought Jemima was starting to treat her like an adult.

"Isn't it?"

Ythna changed the subject. "So if everybody on board the rocket ship dies, can we use that to escape?"

"No," said Jemima. "Their deaths won't be significant. Or terribly unexpected. I can only use a single sudden death that changes lots of other people's fates."

"That's a stupid rule."

Jemima shrugged. "It's a science that won't exist for hundreds of years. Like I said: causal torsions. Think of causality as a weave that holds all of us fast, and occasionally gaps appear that you can slip through."

"So how are we going to escape before they put us on that rocket?"

"First things first." Jemima came and stood in front of Ythna, so she was silhouetted by the setting sun through the small window, and put her right hand out, palm up and at an angle. "I really do want to help. So far, all I've done is make things worse for you. If you'll let me, I'll do whatever I can. You're a smart person and you care about other people. You deserve better. And the Gaven Empire could use a million more like you."

"How does the Empire end?" Ythna said.

"It dies," Jemima said. "Everything dies eventually. You were born in the Golden Century, which was a relatively stable era. After that, there was a twenty-year fall into decadence and social decay, followed by the Glorious Restoration, which you saw. That lasted about fifty-seven years, and was followed by the Perfect Culmination, the most exact implementation of the ideal of Dja-Thun on Earth. Which lasted about as long as you'd expect. After that, there were about 150 years of slow decline, until the whole thing fell apart and your people begged the off-world colonists to come and save them. That's the executive summary, anyway."

"Okay," Ythna said, taking Jemima's hand in both of hers. "I want to make a difference. Give me a new identity, and put me where I can make a difference."

"Very well," Jemima said. "Done."

Jemima searched through what seemed to be a million hidden pockets sewn into the lining of her giant coat until she found a device, perhaps twice the size of your fingernail. With this gadget, she opened the lock on their cage, and then she used her tiny stun gun on the two guards in the hallway outside, who were already half asleep in any case.

"Now what?" Ythna said. "Do we wait for that man in the helmet to arrive and murder someone else?"

"He's long gone, whoever he was," Jemima said. "But we don't need him to kill anybody. The *Dauntless* is launching tomorrow, which means I know what day this is. And someone very famous is going to die, all on his own, in the next couple days. Come on." She unlocked the front door of the holding facility with her lockpick. "We've got a lot of distance to cover. And first, we have to break out of a maximum-security launch site."

• • •

Beldame Thakrra's grave wasn't nearly as fancy as the Tomb of the Unknown Emperor. They had built her a big stone sphere with a metal spike sticking through it, befitting the rank she'd attained in the moment just before she died. And there was a bust in front, with a close enough likeness of her face, except that she looked placid and sleepy, instead of keen and on the verge of asking another question. The sphere was a little taller than Ythna, and the spike soared over her head. The tomb was surrounded by other, grander memorials, as far as Ythna could see.

The sphere and the bust of Thakrra were both covered with a thick layer of grime. Nobody had visited the Beldame's tomb for decades. Maybe never. Ythna pulled a cloth out of her new, sharp-creased black uniform trousers and started to wipe the tomb so it looked fresh and clean, the way the Beldame had always kept her house. "It's good to see you again," she whispered.

Jemima came up behind Ythna while she was still wiping. "Here." She handed Ythna a stack of official-looking cards. "It's all correct. You're a Vice Officiator named Dhar. That's your name from now on. You were part of a secret mission for the Vice Emperor Htap, and everybody else who knew about that mission is dead now. Such things were common in the final days of the Perfect Culmination, sad to say. In any case, you can present these anywhere and if they need a new Vice Officiator, they'll take you on."

"Thank you," Ythna said. "But I can't go anywhere until I finish the ritual of mourning for the Beldame. I've waited much too long as it is."

"There's no rush whatsoever," Jemima said. "In fact, if I were you, I would lay low for a few more weeks before trying to travel. Oh, and if anybody asks you about the past hundred years of history, just pretend you have a head injury from that secret mission."

"What about you?" Ythna said. "Are you going to risk traveling right now?"

"Can't hang about," Jemima said. "This is the furthest forward in time I've reached in forever. And there's a death next week that I'm hopeful will send me even further ahead." She looked out at the rows of ziggurats, spheres, and statues, stretching out past the misty horizon. "I've jumped through time twenty-nine times. Twenty-nine times, and each time I find myself stuck in the Gaven Empire. There's something I'm doing wrong, and I can't figure out what it is."

"Maybe if you find that man with the helmet," Ythna said, "you can ask him."

"If I find that man again," Jemima said, "I shall have to kill him. Goodbye, Ythna. Have a great life. For me."

They embraced. Ythna watched Jemima walk away across the rows of memorials and reliquaries, the rulers and saints of the Empire resting in glory. Jemima's long black coat swished as she strode, jauntily, like someone who knew just what she was about. One arm swung back and forth, as if she had an invisible cane swatting aside the ghosts of this place. Ythna stared until all she could see was Jemima's red curls and black hat amidst the big gray shapes. Then she turned back toward the Beldame, whose stone face still looked much too complacent. Ythna wiped the bust down one more time, then sank to her knees and began the slow, mournful chant of indelible grief.

# THE RAINMAKER

## LAVIE TIDHAR

**Near Inhambane** in Mozambique there is a cliff overlooking a low sand beach which floods during high tide. Into the cliff, the Portuguese colonial authorities in times past had dug a shaft through the rock. It was down that hole that various unwanted prisoners were lowered, bound hand and foot, during low tide. The prisoners would be left on the tiny beach to await their death, and it was into that hole, one sunny day in mid-November, that they had lowered the Rainmaker.

• • •

This was long before we found out the truth, you understand. The story's all there, in the classified files. How Fogg, in love, covered up for the Vomacht girl. How he conspired with Oblivion, who loved him with an unrequited love. The Vomacht girl had disappeared after the Second World War, and it took the Old Man nearly a century to catch her. Now the Old Man was dead, and Fogg and the girl were gone into that place where it all Changed, and they had vanished – or so we believed – forever. It was a violent century, but then, aren't they all?

Only Oblivion remained, the new head of the Bureau.

This is the Bureau for Superannuated Affairs, you understand, the one deep under Whitehall, with the plant that never dies standing in the dusty hallway. But you know all this, about the Change, and quantum mutations, and the Übermenschen. Vomacht created them, in that farmhouse, in 1926, and changed them – changed us all. There is a place where it is always summer... but you know all this, and if you don't, it doesn't matter anyway. It never did.

• • •

"You have to understand, this was, what, the mid 80s?" Spit says. "It was the height of the civil war, and that in turn was just a proxy of the Cold War. The Soviets funded FRELIMO, so we funded RENAMO through the South Africans and the Rhodesians. The whole place descended into chaos and over one million people died. It's not a war anyone really thinks about. It was just one of those things that happen, in Africa."

"You were no longer with the Bureau at that time?"

"No, that's right. I went freelance. But I suppose you never really leave the Bureau, do you. The Old Man got in touch through our man in Nairobi. What was his name."

"Jeffries? I met him in Bangkok, in the 60s," Oblivion says.

"He looked like a cadaver," Spit says. "Yellow skin taut over a skeleton. I met him in downtown Nairobi, in one of the hotels. The smoke of his cigarette never waned. In a way, it reminded me of Fogg."

A look of momentary pain suffuses Oblivion's face and then is gone, and Spit thinks maybe she'd imagined it. They're sitting in the Bureau's debriefing room, deep under Pall Mall.

"Jeffries died not that long after," Oblivion says. "I think he had cancer."

Spit shrugs. She doesn't understand why they have to do this. Old cases, obsolete histories. Names and faces ground into dust.

She feels *old*. The Übermenschen never age, outwardly, but she still feels the weight of years, the overcrowding of memories. She wants to be back with Whirlwind, back on the farm in Kenya, with nothing but the never-ending skies overhead, like a clean slate.

"Jeffries. He was Foreign Office, wasn't he?" she says, reluctantly.

"Maybe. But he was the Old Man's creature all the same."

Spit tries to remember. The opulent hotel, all dark wood and plush chairs, a full afternoon tea service on the table. Deferential servers who were probably all informants for the Kenyan DSI. White men in suits, smoking, reading out-of-date copies of the *Guardian* and the *Daily Mail*. Jeffries, like an animated corpse, looking at her balefully across the table.

"It's about the Rainmaker, you see." Almost apologetically. "We hear he's… active, again. The Old Man just wants you to keep an eye on him. Find out what he's up to. That sort of thing." Fingers like claws around his cigarette. "I'm told you have a history together."

"I wouldn't go that far," Spit told him.

"But you knew him?" Oblivion says.

"I ran into him." Her distaste is evident in her voice. "Macau in '64, I think. I'm sure it's all in your files."

Oblivion frowns, turns a page. This is how the Bureau does things, has always done them, Spit thinks, with a bitterness that only grew throughout the long years. Files and paperwork, case histories. The Bureau are incessant watchers, *voyeurs* of historical events. Spit just wishes she could forget all of it, moments in which all the actors are gone, whose only remaining witness is herself. She thinks of that poem Larkin wrote, about the Übermenschen. "We weren't meant to lie so long…" she says.

"Excuse me?"

"Nothing, Oblivion."

"Tell me about Macau."

Spit shrugs. "What's to tell?"

She thinks of Macau, then. The humidity and the warm sea, and how the firecrackers echoed through the streets and reminded her of distant gunshots, other wars. She'd met him at the floating casino.

• • •

His real name was Enrique Hernando and he was one of only three Portuguese Übermenschen the Bureau had records of. He grew up in Beja, fought across the border in the Spanish Civil War, though no one was sure, later, on which side. He wasn't really on anyone's radar, much. One of those profiles in Lieber's *Le Dictionnaire Biographique des Surhommes* with a question mark next to their name, like that Bogdan, the entertainer. No one was sure what he did during World War Two.

Then, after the war, the rumours. That he was seen in Moscow; that he'd met with Beria himself. Deep-cover agents found drowned in freak rainstorms. Bad weather seemed to follow wherever he went. He was never much more of a legend. In the mid 50s the Bureau got the chance to debrief a Soviet defector, codenamed Trilby. The man claimed Hernando had been captured and tortured by French Allied forces during the war, and that, always a Communist sympathiser, by the time he'd reached Moscow and Beria's hands he had developed an intense hatred of the West.

Trilby, however, was suspicious as a source. Later rumours had the Rainmaker working for Salazar's secret police, a sort of trouble-shooter for the Portuguese colonies. The truth, as always, was probably something in between. Spit met him at the Macau Palace.

"You the English girl?"

He was a short, skinny guy. He wore a pornstar moustache at the time, though he later shaved it off. His cheeks were hollow, with a few days' growth of bristles. Outside, it was raining. It was monsoon season. His eyes were feverish bright.

"You're him? The Rainmaker?"

"I don't make the rain," he said. "I just tend to be around when it happens." He smiled as he said it, but the smile never reached his eyes. They ordered drinks.

• • •

"What were you drinking?" Oblivion says.

Spit shrugs. "Scotch, I think."

Oblivion makes a note.

"Is it somehow important?"

"No, no," he says. "Just a detail."

"Whatever."

• • •

"I've just got back in from Peking," the Rainmaker said. "Did you know the Chinese have more Übermenschen than any other country? They have great plans, great plans."

"Only because they have the largest population," Spit said, not particularly impressed. "Do you have anything I could actually *use*?"

"That depends."

"Depends on what?"

There was something about him that really got under your skin. He smelled of wet leaves and dog fur. He never blinked and, whenever you looked into his eyes, all you saw was the reflection of rain clouds. Around them in the casino, wealthy ex-pats and rich Chinese played baccarat and dai-siu.

"I hate them," the Rainmaker said. "All of them."

She didn't ask who.

At the end of the evening, he passed her an envelope. She

passed him one back, full of cash. It was that kind of arrangement. They parted ways and that was the last she saw of him, at least for a couple of decades.

• • •

"Do you know what was in the envelope?"

"I never even looked."

"Really."

"I didn't care, Oblivion. I figured it was some photos, something compromising we could use to put the pressure on someone high up in the Central Committee. I went out that night, found someone, got drunk, got laid."

"Yes," he says. "Yes, you're quite right, Spit."

"What *is* this about?"

"Let's get back to Mozambique, then," Oblivion says, ignoring her.

"It wasn't Mozambique, not at first," she says, correcting him. "After meeting Jeffries, I did keep my eyes open. Whirlwind and I had just got together then. We went freelance, mostly. She got gigs from the Agency, I moonlighted for MI6, though you know how cheap those bastards are."

"And the rest of it?"

"You know all this."

"You ran guns."

"Yes."

She thinks about that time. Africa, during the Cold War. All that money, all those arms flooding in. The Israelis were selling Uzis and the Russians were offloading Kalashnikovs by the boatload. The Americans shipped in land mines and even the North Koreans got involved, providing training and provisions. Everyone had a slice of the pie. Meanwhile Ian Smith was fighting a war in Rhodesia, Samora Machel was fighting in Mozambique, the South Africans were fucking up anyone who had the wrong skin colour, and Idi Amin, well . . . he was just being Idi Amin.

"See, it wasn't a *cold* war, not there," she says. "It was a playground, Russia and America both playing chess using Africa as a board. There was so much *money*, Oblivion!"

"And you didn't take sides."

"Fuck, no."

"You were essentially mercenaries?"

"Fuck you," Spit says. "Is it any better to always just take orders? At least we got to choose what jobs we wanted to do."

"We tried to do good," he says. They look at each other, until Spit shakes her head.

"You were always a strange sort of idealist, Oblivion," she says. "What was it? For queen and country?"

"For king and country, in the old days," he says.

"You *saw* what they did to Turing!"

"That was... Times were different, then."

"You *saw*."

He turns a page. "The Rainmaker," he says.

Spit sits back, sighs. "We got word he was down in Zaire. The Americans were funding that psycho, Mobutu, and he meanwhile was robbing the country blind. Whirlwind had good contacts with the Company there... Anyway, next thing we know, there's a freak flood and a whole platoon of Katanganese rebels ends up floating belly-up in the middle of a forest. I mean, can you imagine that? By the time we got down there, he was long gone. Next we heard about him, he's in Banda's Malawi, and a boat full of vacationing Soviet mercenaries ends up capsized in the middle of the lake, with no survivors. I mean, I was beginning to *like* this guy, Oblivion. He just took whatever job there was, and he was neat about it."

"*Neat?*"

"He did clean jobs. You know that's not exactly *my* style."

"What happened then?"

"We tracked him down to Rhodesia. He was holed up in Bulawayo, lying low. Word was he had a big gig coming up in Mozambique. Then, I get a summons from Jeffries again…"

• • •

She did look in the envelope, that time in Macau. Of course she did.

It showed a girl in a light dress stepping out of a doorway into a busy street. The street was somewhere in northern China, and the people walking around looked cold and downbeat in their blue workers' uniforms. The door itself was not connected to anything. It was just a door. Through it, if one magnified the photo sufficiently, one could see the Alps, far in the distance, and the sun, shining down on an old white farmhouse, and a hovering butterfly. Green grass and yellow sun and blue skies and white clouds – a perfect summer's day.

And the girl was *smiling*.

"We've been after that bitch for years," Spit says. "The Vomacht girl. Sommertag."

"Her name was Klara. Is Klara."

"The Vomacht girl," Spit says. "Stepping out from her little fucking quantum hiding place into the middle of a street in China, without a fucking care in the world."

Oblivion looks pained. "You knew?"

"Of course I fucking knew. What did you *do*, Oblivion? Did you destroy the photo? You knew the Old Man wanted her, and you knew if he got her, she'd have given up Fogg."

"His only crime was to love her," Oblivion says. "Well, that and high treason. We never *asked* to be heroes. It wasn't—"

"Fair? *Please*. Life isn't *fair*, Oblivion. Doesn't matter *what* you are. So you, what, you did a little bit of treason of your own? Destroyed the photo?"

"We're not *perfect*, Spit! Fogg wasn't... I'm not... Even you—"

"No," she says, with unexpected bitterness. "No, Oblivion. I was just your *tool*."

• • •

"We want you to run him to ground," Jeffries said, and coughed. Little globules of blood mottled his shaking hand.

"Why? Is it still about the p—"

"Find him and kill him. You can do that, can't you, Spit? You're good at that sort of thing."

"Listen, you weasel-faced..." She calmed herself down. "Listen, Jeffries. I don't work for you anymore. Any of you. I don't take *orders*."

He tried to smile, but it wasn't pretty and she wished he hadn't. "It's very much a request. A *favour*."

"Why?"

"I don't know. To be honest with you, I don't really care."

She looked at him. Really looked at him. What did she really know about Jeffries? He'd been around a long time but he wasn't one of *them*; he was just... just a person. He lived, he aged and he was going to, very soon, die.

"Is this... Is this from the Old Man?" she said.

"What do you think?"

"I think you're full of shit."

He laughed. She couldn't read his face and she hated him a little for it.

"Just do it," he said. "What do you care? To you we're all..." He waved his hand, like pushing away smoke.

"But he's not one of you. The Rainmaker."

"What do you care?"

"I probably don't," Spit said. She got up to leave. "I'll be seeing you, Jeffries."

"No," he said. "No, I doubt that you will."

• • •

By the time they got to Bulawayo, they just missed him. They followed flash floods and freak rains, circling via Apartheid South Africa to Swaziland to Mozambique, the Rainmaker always one step ahead, always leaving the drowned in his wake. A banker in Johannesburg, face down in the tub as rain flooded his home. A party of four in Ezulwini, a head-on collision in a sudden shower of rain that made the road deadly. A Moroccan arms dealer in Maputo. Spit and Whirlwind followed the shore along the Indian Ocean, heading north. They finally caught up with him just outside Inhambane.

• • •

Spit wishes she could say there had been some grand gesture, some triumph of good over evil, but the whole thing felt grubby and sordid when it happened. They'd cornered the Rainmaker by the ocean. Whirlwind attacked from the sea, and for a moment Spit, hidden in the hill above, could only admire her partner's graceful, inhuman form, the violence of wind as it attacked air and water particles, tearing across the ocean towards the land, and the small figure of the Portuguese.

It began to rain, then, the sky clouding over in a grey sheet. The sky rumbled, and lightning began to flash down, hitting sea and earth with a sort of beautiful, illuminating violence. Spit hawked phlegm, willed herself a weapon. When she spat, the material underwent a metamorphosis, glycoproteins and water hardening into something hard and strong like a bullet. She missed the Rainmaker by an inch and he turned and saw her. She could read nothing in his face. Lightning flashed nearby, too close, the electric discharge making her short hair stand on end. Then Whirlwind had come ashore and the force of her wind tore the Rainmaker from his place and tossed him in the air, like a ragdoll. The rain lashed violently down, and all about them people must have stared, nearby, at this freak spot of weather in the middle of a calm and sunny day. Then Spit spat again, and the shot caught the Rainmaker in the calf and he cried out in agony and fell from on high as Whirlwind released him. The two of them converged on the fallen figure, staring down at him, Spit and Whirlwind, Whirlwind and Spit.

• • •

"But it was never the Old Man, was it?" Spit says, "These were never his orders. He had nothing to do with it."

Oblivion frowns. Turns the page. Says nothing.

"He didn't know about the Rainmaker. And why did the Rainmaker have to die, anyway? What business was he of ours? Unless there *was* a reason. Unless the Rainmaker made contact again, like he did all those years before, in Macau. What did he have to sell, Oblivion? What did he have to sell the Bureau that you were so desperate to cover up?"

"You're making a lot of suppositions, Spit," he says, mildly.

"You brought it up. I was happy to leave it all in the past, where it belongs."

"If you had… suspicions," he says, turning his eyes on her with an intensity she has always found disconcerting, now and then, "why didn't you say something?"

Spit shrugs. What could she tell him? She should have done.

Gone to the Old Man. Confronted Oblivion. Something. But the truth was that she hadn't. She...

"It was just a job," she says.

He nods. "And did he speak to you? At the time?"

"Do you mean, do I *know*?"

"I suppose."

Spit rubs her eyes. She hates the cold, has not missed England. She wants to be back in Kenya, on the farm, with Whirlwind...

"I suppose," she says, a little sadly.

●  ●  ●

Near Inhambane in Mozambique, there is a cliff overlooking a low sand beach which floods during high tide. Into the cliff, the Portuguese colonial authorities in times past had dug a shaft through the rock. It was down that hole that various unwanted prisoners were lowered, bound hand and foot, during low tide. The prisoners would be left on the tiny beach to await their death, and it was into that hole, one sunny day in mid-November, that Whirlwind and Spit lowered the Rainmaker.

He didn't bother struggling. He was only semi-conscious for most of the time, unable to control the rains, if he ever did. He mumbled something, though. He didn't ask why – why they were doing it, why to him. In the world of the Übermenschen, innocence has long stopped being an operable word. What he said was, "Did you ever think about what it means?"

"What?" Spit said, distracted. Whirlwind stood on the edge of the hole, looking down onto the small sand beach. They were waiting for the tides.

"What we are. What we represent."

"Who gives a shit?" Whirlwind said. Spit loved her accent, that American twang. Americans never much bothered about what things *meant*; they only cared about what things *were*, and usually how you could get something useful out of them. They looked to the future while the British looked to the past. She had no idea what the Portuguese looked for. It'd never even crossed her mind to wonder.

"You… should," the Rainmaker said, and he tried to laugh, but it didn't quite come out. "We're different. Changed."

"No shit."

"I was hoping to find out… what it all meant. Why us. If there was a… purpose." He looked almost sad, lying there. "I guess I… won't, now. Tell Oblivion I… I made a mistake."

That attempt at a laugh again.

"Tell him there's a… a place. A place where… it is always summer. The door: look for the door. She's—"

"Oh shut up," Whirlwind said, and kicked him, savagely, in the ribs. Spit winced. They picked up the Rainmaker and dragged him to the hole. They looked at each other, then just got on with it. They lowered him down and watched him as he lay, helpless, on the tiny beach. Already the tide was coming in, wavelets nibbling at the debris line, and soon it would fill up and take the Rainmaker away. Spit thought it was no more than he deserved, considering. It occurred to her it could have been her in his place, but she put the thought away for another time.

They watched him go. They watched him for a long time.

● ● ●

"A door," she says. "I think he was hoping for some sort of impossible escape, but it was just a fantasy. We watched him drown and the corpse go out to sea. Then we got the hell out of there, Oblivion, and I put the whole thing out of my mind. Until now. Why did you have to bring it up?"

"Oh," he says. "No reason." He makes a vague gesture. "Old paperwork. You know how it is. You can't find anything in this place."

"She's gone, Oblivion. Fogg's gone. It's over. I know you loved him. I know you covered up for him. But there's no need now, not anymore, is there?"

"No," he says. "No, I suppose not."

"Is that it?" Spit says. "Only I have a plane to catch and—"

"No, no," he says. "You've been very helpful. Thank you for coming in, and—"

"Yeah," Spit says. "I'll see you, all right? Send my regards to James."

"Charles," he says, distractedly. And: "We're separated."

"Oh. I'm sorry."

"It happens."

"I'll see you." She gives him a quick peck on the cheek. "I'll show myself out."

When she's gone, Oblivion just sits there, for a long moment, staring at the file. A piece of paper stuck between the others seems to catch his attention. Almost reluctantly, his long, slim fingers reach for it. Almost unwillingly, or anyway without, it seems, his direct control, he slides it out from the file.

The photo was taken with one of those new digital cameras, ultra-high definition, as though it's more real than what it portrays. He stares at it. Taps his fingers on the tabletop. The date in the bottom-left corner's one week ago.

The photo shows a rainy street scene, somewhere near Waterloo. A double-decker bus is parked by the kerb, and a couple of drivers huddle against the railway arches, smoking cigarettes. A train passes overhead, frozen in transit. An old pub sign is partially visible right-of-frame, spelling out *–n The Wall*.

Set into the same brick brown wall, to right of frame, a door seems to have materialised. It is partially open, and if you peer through the doorway you can just make out a clear blue sky, a yellow sun, green grass, a white farmhouse. Smoke rises out of the farmhouse chimney. A butterfly hovers over the grass. You can almost smell it, the sweet, perfumed air of a perfect summer's day. Stepping out of the door, arms outstretched, is a young girl in a light summer dress, and she is smiling.

Oblivion tap-tap-taps on the tabletop distractedly. He stares at the empty chair which Spit vacated. In his eyes there is a lost, uneasy look.

Then he scribbles a final note on the page, and closes the file.

# THE IMMINENT WORLD

## D.R.G. SUGAWARA

The fires of war
Fade into such small embers
Like fallen petals

Drifting in the ruins
Of some other history
An alternate now

How did we arrive
In this version of the world
Unreal to us all

Are we like blossoms
Scattered by the whims of time
Forever adrift

Or the tree itself
Tangled branches dividing
Reaching for the sky

Knotted roots beneath
Searching for the sustenance
So often denied

Perhaps we are all
A part but never apart
Blossom, branch, and root as one

And this moment holds
Another version of now
Waiting to be born

# FRACTURED REALITIES

"There are no rules of architecture for
a castle in the clouds."

G.K. Chesterton

# #SELFCARE

## ANNALEE NEWITZ

**Wildfire season** turned sunset a rotten orange that seeped in through the shop windows and spread across the floor in lurid streaks. Edwina leaned on the poured-concrete counter, watching women walk past outside, pushing strollers whose fabric gently strobed with the names of their nannyshare agencies. Usually they veered off to buy groceries at Whole Foods, currently bathed in a hellish glow. But sometimes they peered inside, looking beyond her to stare at rows of glass bottles full of creams and aromatherapies and anti-aging remedies. A small, tasteful sign in the window guardedly alluded to the services they offered at Skin Seraph:

Feel younger with a moisture peel
Indulge in a revitalizing mask
Try cool sculpting for clean lines
Even out your natural color with melanin toners
#skinseraph #selfcare #youdeserveit

Customers trickled in all day. Women asked for less hair and men asked for more. White people wanted to be tan, and brown people wanted to be paler. Older people wanted tight, matte skin and younger people wanted plump, dewy cheeks like on K-beauty Instagram. Edwina's job wasn't to help them. She was a "customer care associate," which mostly meant she babysat the system that texted appointment reminders. Occasionally she took calls from harried assistants trying to rebook their bosses. Her physical presence wasn't necessary, but her boss Isobel wanted Skin Seraph to feel elite and expensive. That's why she'd hired an actual human to stand here on the premises instead of outsourcing to Task Rabbits like Edwina's cousins in the Philippines.

Sometimes customers would ask if she used any of the products. Edwina had tried most of the Skin Seraph-branded masks, so she could say honestly that she did. She liked the company's signature citrus-and-cinnamon scent. But she'd never had a chemical peel or Botox or laser color correction. Most customers were looking for something way out of Edwina's price range. She tried to be nice to everyone, because this was a decent on-site job with health insurance and a 401K plan. There were limits, though. She wasn't going to do free brand repping like Daisy, the staff clinician. Daisy's self-care videos blew up pretty regularly, and they were full of artfully deployed Skin Seraph products. That's why Daisy got bonuses while Edwina never would.

Isobel ran fifteen Skin Seraph stores in three countries, but she still found time to micromanage their bonus system. All the employees had to install this humiliating productivity app called MakeMeProud that tracked how many people they'd converted into loyal customers and pushed leaderboard updates to them every hour. Daisy always won because she had incredible numbers from her socials. The app could see who clicked "buy" after watching the clinician apply toning snails to her face on Instagram. But since Edwina worked at the front desk, it was hard to prove she'd triggered a sale. The one time she used the app to log a $500 purchase of foot cream, Isobel rejected it because "merely operating the cash register is not the same thing as brand conversion." Edwina had given up at that point. Her salary wasn't great, but it was good enough. At least Isobel didn't leave screamy voicemails for her like she did for the high-performing clinicians.

Edwina sighed, rested both elbows on the counter, and let her shoulders rise up until it felt like they were touching her ears. A cute person with a dog stood outside talking to someone remote. Maybe they were arranging a dinner date. Or having a conference with fifty people in Shenzhen. Idly, Edwina wondered what time it was in Shenzhen. Was it morning there? She blinked up an interface in her contacts and searched for the answer.

Outside, the sunset was browning into twilight, and the cute person wandered away. Edwina would be closing soon, leaving a few dim lights strategically trained on their most expensive products, which had been decanted into crystal polygons that shot rainbows onto the white display shelves. As she wiped Instagram out of the air, she noticed a woman staring into the window directly at her. Something was wrong with her skin, which maybe made sense because she was staring into a skin care boutique. Edwina squinted into the smoky shadows, blinking all the feeds out of her contacts. Was that a sunburn or some kind of scarring? The woman placed her hands on the glass, leaning in so close that her breath made a frosty, opaque circle. Now Edwina was sure the darkness was messing with her vision, because it really looked as if tiny cracks were growing outward from the woman's fingers.

No. It was actually happening.

She heard the unmistakable cry of glass fracturing, and the threadlike fissures spread faster, forming a snarled pattern like a medieval street map full of twisted roads. The woman continued to gaze at Edwina, hands and breath at the center of this bizarre form of vandalism. Edwina jumped out of her chair, flicking the emergency call screen into her left eye. But something kept her from pinching the button.

Hesitantly, she approached the woman. Her skin—it wasn't skin at all. There was no skin. The woman's muscles moved wetly, beaded with clusters of yellow collagen, veins and arteries a throbbing lace across her cheeks and neck. Her lidless blue eyes were set into sockets the color of rubies. Her lips slithered with fat.

The jagged cracks had wound their way to the edges of the window frame.

"Get the fuck away from here!" Edwina screamed without thinking. "I'm calling the police right now!"

The woman smiled, squeezing the tissues of her face into a new configuration of oil and blood. All around her, the glass whined and sagged, on the verge of collapsing into a million shards.

"Go away! Leave right now!" Edwina realized distantly that her voice was rising to a higher and higher pitch.

She reached up to pinch the button that would call Skin Seraph's private security service. Before her fingers could rub together, the woman disappeared. It was as abrupt as a bad special effect: she was there, and then she was gone. Shaking, Edwina reached out to touch the glass where the woman's hands had been. The windows were perfectly smooth.

Daisy came racing out of the back, where she'd been assisting with the day's last chemical peel. Perfect pink ringlets bobbed around her pink face. "Are you okay, Edwina?"

"There was—there was a person messing with the windows."

Daisy made a big show of opening the door and looking up and down the street, now glowing with LEDs from the Whole Foods parking lot. "Was it that homeless lady again?" she asked. "The one with the cute cat?"

With no other way to explain what she'd seen, Edwina nodded. "I think maybe it was her, yeah."

"She used to stay down in the Mission at the BART station, but now she climbs the hill to Noe Valley because people in this neighborhood have more money." Daisy sighed. "I have to admit it's relatable."

Edwina kept staring at the place where the woman had been, and Daisy finally went back to her chemical peel, still talking about homeless people. Except that woman hadn't been carrying a cat. She might not even have been real. Edwina sat back down behind the desk and put her head in her hands, wondering if she'd finally gone crazy.

Half an hour until closing. There were no more tasks in her queue, and the last client of the day was with Daisy. She had no reason to be here other than to lock up. Pulling up a chat window, Edwina texted her best friend Alyx. They ran social for a few Memegen brands, and were always online.

> Edwinner: I think this job is starting to drive me insane.
> Alyx777: Too many face transplants? That shit is grisly.
> Edwinner: I seriously thought I saw a woman breaking our windows. I actually screamed or something? Daisy came running in, and now I feel like an idiot. I guess I'm hallucinating now.
> Alyx777: Dang! You got Daisy to notice something other than her follow count?
> Edwinner: Haha yes! But now I feel really weird. Do you want to hang out in a couple of hours and watch the new episode of Fae Killers?
> Alyx777: YASSSSSS luv u!

Talking to Alyx always made Edwina feel better. Maybe her job arranging appointments to revamp people's faces was bizarre, but it was practically mundane compared to Alyx making tax payment apps into loveable personalities on WimWam. Edwina sent some music to her earbuds and swiped more coin into her streaming account so they could watch Fae Killers uninterrupted.

• • •

By the time she returned to work after the long Memorial Day weekend, Edwina had chalked up the window incident to exhaustion and put it out of her mind. The wildfire smoke had cleared briefly, and Jupiter rose like the business end of a bright laser pointer in the sky over Whole Foods.

She blinked up two windows. In one, she stacked the week's appointments, and in the other she chatted with Alyx. They were excited about a new marketing campaign where the nannyshare app Babyfren came out as a Fae Killers superfan. In Babyfren persona, Alyx posted a video about how all infants secretly want Fae Killers' naughty shape-shifter Puck to be their daddy. It instantly sucked up a thousand new Babyfren subscribers in San Francisco alone. Edwina had to admit the video was pretty hilarious, especially when the infant drew a big circle around Puck's "tight fae butt." Idly, Edwina wondered if Babyfren got a kickback from Fae Killers, or if maybe Memegen represented Fae Killers too. She was about to ask Alyx when a dark silhouette blocked Jupiter's light.

It was the skinless woman again, raw face like a popped blister around her pus-slicked smile. "Hello," she mouthed silently to Edwina, pressing her hand to the windowpane farthest from the front desk. She spread her fingers wide, trailing them behind her along the glass as she walked. Nothing cracked in her wake. The apparition paused in front of Edwina and rubbed both palms over the window as if washing it, but she left swirls of thick mud behind instead of soap. This time, Edwina didn't pull up the alarm, and she didn't scream. The woman swayed, almost dancing as she drew great arcs of wet brown curds over a display of snail masks. Just as the stuff blocked Edwina's view of the Whole Foods parking lot, a smell hit her.

Anyone who rode the BART train in San Francisco knew it. People dug communal cesspits in the tunnels. Apparently using them was better than getting chipped and monitored at the city's homeless facilities. And now the whole waiting room, with its clean white walls and spotless bottles of cream, was permeated by the unmistakable, heavy reek of day-old human shit.

Edwina's eyes started to water. Only the most intense odors from the street could overpower the atomizer that perpetually emitted Skin Seraph's aromatherapy mist. This had to be real. Should she call somebody? The woman grinned at her again, distorting the arrangement of blood vessels in her neck, and completed her work with a flourish of excrement in the shape of a blooming flower. And then, just like last time, she winked out.

"What… the… fuck?" It was Daisy's voice behind her.

Edwina jumped. "What? What is it?"

Daisy had dyed one ringlet sparkly gold and wore two jeweled nourishment patches under each eye. "Is that… shit smeared all over the windows?"

Two women in spa robes and revitalization socks padded into the front room behind Daisy. "Oh my god!" one of them cried, putting a hand to her mouth and dislodging the depilation caterpillar on her upper lip. The other woman's face was still wrapped tightly in quick-heal bandages and she couldn't say anything. Instead, her eyes widened and she made a mewing noise in her throat. Then the bandages over her mouth went puffy and gray as ribbons of vomit slid down her neck. She ripped the bandages off, revealing a sticky red chin and an even more disgusting smell as she dripped onto the floor.

"Mrs Landsdale!" Daisy screamed. "You can't take those off!" She raced to help her client, grabbing a handful of soothing wipes from the counter and pulling the still-gagging woman into the back. "Ms Desai, why don't you lie down again in the garden suite while my colleague cleans up?" She shot a meaningful look at Edwina over her shoulder.

"It's that hobo who begs in front of Whole Foods, isn't it?" Ms Desai asked conversationally as Daisy and Mrs Landsdale disappeared into a treatment room. "I don't know why they let her sit there. It's private property."

Edwina had finally processed what was happening. The woman was real. The shit was real. A woman had just vomited on the floor. And now she was going to have to be nice to a client while she cleaned everything up.

"I don't know who it was. She didn't look homeless." The words felt algorithmically generated by her mouth as she looked for cleaning supplies under the front desk.

Ms Desai leaned on the counter, readjusting the caterpillar over her upper lip. "You should report her to the police. You guys have a security camera out there, right? Just take a screenshot from it and make a report. That's what my neighbor did when people kept stealing her Amazon packages, and they caught the guys. If the police have a face, they can find people anywhere."

Edwina hefted the motorized window washer in one hand, its plastic tank sloshing with Clorox-spiked fluid, and looped the hose over her shoulder. She could plug it in outside. "Well, I have to do some cleaning, Ms Desai. If you go back to the garden suite, I'm sure Daisy will be right with you."

She didn't bother to wish Ms Desai a nice evening.

Soapy water cascaded over the glass, and Edwina used the hose to chase wafers of caked excrement into the gutter. As she followed the edges of the shit flower with needles of spray, Edwina realized that Ms Desai had a point. She could review security footage and figure out what she'd actually seen. At least, once she was done here. Edwina sighed and wished Skin Seraph's protective gloves didn't cost twenty dollars each. It would come out of her paycheck.

• • •

The windows still looked spotty when Mrs Landsdale walked through the lobby with Ms Desai. Both were dressed in those yoga pants that transformed from opaque fabric into mesh netting when exposed to perspiration. Mrs Landsdale's bandages were newly applied. Daisy had given both women free youth-restoration elixir gift packages, gently strobing with luminescent jellyfish protein in their frosted bottles.

"My skin may never recover from that," Mrs Landsdale said in a voice that was meant to be overheard. "I could have been seriously injured."

Ms Desai shot Edwina a sympathetic look. "I hope you catch her. It's horrifying what those people think they can do."

They drifted outside, discussing whether to hire a rideshare or walk up the hill to their neighborhood.

As they passed out of earshot, Edwina caught Mrs Landsdale's parting salvo. "Did that girl just sit there while a hobo destroyed her shop?" she asked with exaggerated incomprehension. "Why didn't she do anything? Is she profoundly basic? I'm never going to that place again."

"Same," said Ms Desai. "We can always go to Nature's Blessing in the Marina."

Edwina made sure she'd sprayed every fleck of ordure off the windows before returning inside to start the shutdown routine. Daisy was still banging around in back, so she walked to the garden suite to check on her. Daisy was kneeling next to the orchid display, carefully emptying several tiny trash containers into a scented plastic bag. She looked sweaty and her ringlets had wilted.

"Hey, I'm going to start closing up. Are you almost done?"

Daisy looked up, and Edwina braced herself for rage. Instead, her colleague's face was streaked with tears. "I'm done." Her voice was hoarse.

"Are you okay?"

Daisy shook what remained of her curls. "Of course I'm not okay. Mrs Landsdale is one of my best clients. I've gotten a ton of referrals from her."

Edwina flashed on the conversation she'd just overheard between Mrs Landsdale and Ms Desai, and felt an unfamiliar flare of sympathy for Daisy. Clinicians worked for those bonuses, and Skin Seraph wasn't a just day job for Daisy. It was her career.

"I bet she'll forget about it tomorrow when she tries that elixir," Edwina said with forced cheerfulness.

Daisy shook her head. "I hope so. That wasn't some free sample. I gave her the good shit."

"I dunno. I think I'm the true judge of good shit now." Edwina cracked a grin and Daisy let out a laugh-sob noise that turned into a genuine laugh. It was the first time Edwina had ever seen her without absolutely perfect makeup and structured hair.

Daisy slung the bag of trash over her shoulder and cocked her head at Edwina. "Do you want to drink some of those CBD coolers that Isobel and Brad left in the fridge?" she asked. "I really need to relax." Isobel and her boyfriend Brad, whom she'd hired as some kind of nebulous marketing manager, always kept drinks on hand for pop-up influencer parties.

Edwina blinked up her chat with Alyx, which had mostly degenerated into poop emoji. "Can I invite my friend Alyx? I told them to meet me after work."

"The more the merrier."

• • •

The three of them sat on massage chairs in the restoration room, drinking and watching Fae Killer memes on YouTube. That's when Edwina remembered the security camera footage. She had two witnesses now, and wanted to see what they thought.

She and Daisy swiped through Skin Seraph's dashboard lazily, digging into several maintenance menus before they found the security cam file. It was set to delete anything older than a week, so her first encounter with the woman was gone. But this afternoon's encounter was there. They watched the scene unfold with mouths open. The webcam was positioned over the door, which meant most of the action at the windows happened at the edge of the video. Still, they could zoom in to see a person touching the windows, face averted, her movements a jerky blur.

"Is this in fast motion or something?" Alyx asked. "It looks weird."

Daisy fiddled with the controls and brought up the timestamp. "Nope," she said. "She's just moving really fast."

And then they came to the part where the woman winked out. It happened on film just the way it had in real life: she was there and then not there. Except now it was easier to blame on bad video than it had been when the actual scene was streaming into her eyes.

"There must be something wrong with the webcam," Daisy said uncertainly.

"Yeah it's glitchy," Alyx agreed. They chugged more CBD cooler, and looked over at Edwina. "Right? It's glitchy."

Edwina debated whether to agree with them or come out and say it. She took another swig of CBD, looked at Alyx's lean face with their jet-black eyes, and Daisy's pale, de-sparkled cheeks. "That's actually what I saw too. She moved really fast and then she disappeared. Daisy, remember how last week I said I thought I saw a woman breaking the window? It's the same one. She disappeared then too."

Daisy set her bottle down carefully. "So, what is this? Some kind of... fae?"

None of them laughed.

Alyx pulled their mobile out of a back pocket and unfolded it on the table between them. "So obviously fae aren't real," they said. "But it could be somebody in a costume fucking around with the camera, right? Let's see if there are other reports like this on Nextdoor. People freaking love to report vandalism there. There's also a feed from San Francisco city government where people submit cleanup requests." Alyx already had six feeds going on the mobile.

"You don't think fae are real?" Daisy asked, using the very serious voice she usually reserved for talking to customers about gold flake masks.

Edwina and Alyx glanced at each other and then at Daisy. "I mean, I love Fae Killers, but that's not real life," Edwina said.

"Well, no, that's not real life," Daisy agreed. "But there are definitely fae here in San Francisco."

Edwina's heart sank. She was just starting to like Daisy, and now she felt herself withdrawing. It wasn't as if she was some kind of douchey skeptic who hated all people with New Age beliefs, but it was going to be hard to solve this mystery if Daisy blamed it on ancient aliens.

Alyx broke through Edwina's disappointment spiral. "What do you mean when you say there are fae here in the city?" they asked.

Daisy shrugged. "Don't you run socials for brands? You must have seen Fae Twitter. A lot of companies hire fae consultants now to help them with outreach because dreamwalking is a great way to raise brand awareness."

"I've heard of that, but I thought it was like hiring astrologers or something." Alyx looked nonplussed.

Something about Edwina's expression and Alyx's tone had gotten through to Daisy. She dropped her eyes and picked at one of her nails. "I guess it's like that. Some people believe fae are real, though." Daisy laughed nervously. "It's probably like those magicians in Vegas who turn people into giant pigs, but then it turns out to be a hologram, right?"

"Wait, did that happen? A magician turned somebody into a holographic pig?" Edwina was eager to change the subject. "I'm looking that up on YouTube right now."

After she found it, they spent another hour clicking on even more bizarre magician videos. Then it was time to head home. Daisy hopped in a rideshare while Alyx and Edwina walked down the hill to catch BART.

At the West Oakland stop, Alyx hugged Edwina goodnight, but kept a warm hand on her arm as they separated. "I'll use some of the algorithms we have at work to look for reports on that shit-smearing lady, okay? I bet somebody has reported her, and then at least you'll know more."

Edwina nodded. "Thanks. I'm still stuck in this weird energy from what Daisy said about the fae."

"Social media people have a zillion superstitions," Alyx laughed. "Gotta pray to the mushroom people if you wanna go viral, man."

"I guess so." Edwina managed a smile, but she couldn't stop thinking about the skinless woman who had shattered and unshattered a window. Like she was casting a spell. Edwina glanced up at Jupiter, still burning brightly overhead, and remembered how the collagen had glistened in the woman's cheeks as she said hello. Maybe it wasn't a spell. Maybe it was a curse.

• • •

The next day at work was a lot more fun than usual because Edwina finally had an office friend. Now she and Daisy could roll their eyes at each other when there was a particularly rude client, and she had somebody to grab a turmeric latte with at Martha & Brothers up the street. Daisy snuck a look at her socials as they waited in the coffee queue behind three women with four Babyfren carriages between them.

"Oh shit, Edwina," she said with a quaver. "Ohhhhh shit." Her eyes had that foggy look of somebody accessing a lot of feeds on their contacts.

A chill crept up Edwina's arms. "What is it?"

"Mrs Landsdale posted a seriously psycho review of Skin Seraph on Mommyland and it's blowing up everywhere."

"Omigod let me see."

Daisy flicked the link to Edwina's contacts. It was posted in the San Francisco shopping forum, and already had thousands of upvotes after only an hour.

### Disgusting experience at Skin Seraph—DO NOT GO THERE

I have been going to Skin Seraph in Noe Valley for more than a year, and have always had a pleasant enough experience but NEVER AGAIN. Last night a hobo attacked the windows and smeared them with excrement, and the management did NOTHING. The entire place smelled terrible, and made me extremely ill. My skin peel was ruined and my doctor says I may have scarring. THIS IS UNACCEPTABLE AND DANGEROUS. This is a medical establishment and the management has NO SECURITY. The girls who work at the store did nothing to stop it, and then they rinsed the windows with nothing more than a little tap water. Can you believe it? That window is probably coated in all kinds of disgusting microbes now, and who knows how much has been tracked inside to infect everyone who goes there. I'm warning you, as a concerned mother, to avoid this

place. It's another case of a local store becoming a chain
and the service suffering as a result. I'm also contacting the
city to recommend an inspection IMMEDIATELY.

The comment section was filled with outrage and
recommendations for other local skin spas. When she got tired of
blinking through them, Edwina looked up to see that Daisy had
the same expression she'd worn last night when she was cleaning
up in back. Her eyes were going red.

"At least she didn't name me," Daisy said shakily. "There's that.
She didn't link to me or say I had personally done anything wrong."

Edwina touched Daisy's shoulder. "Nobody will be able to
track this back to you. Skin Seraph might be canceled for a few
days, but you're not."

Daisy looked vague again, and then refocused her eyes on
Edwina. "Good. I gained a bunch of followers for this video I posted
yesterday. So far, I'm fine."

Then they both checked Skin Seraph's socials, and it was
a bloodbath. Followers had plummeted, and people were
screaming at them about how they were unsanitary and
disgusting and doomed. There was some conspiracy group that
was fixated on the term *seraph* as a sign of Satanism, and now
the store was on their radar too. Skin Seraph's timeline was
full of reminders that "the Beast can't hide" and vague threats
to Isobel and Brad. Somebody had even dug up Isobel's mobile
number and was urging people to text her about the dangers of
consorting with devils.

"These guys don't even understand that seraphs are angels,"
Edwina grumbled. She got a half-hearted laugh out of Daisy.

"They are idiots, but Mrs Landsdale is a huge influencer on
Mommyland. She could actually kill the brand."

"I wonder what Isobel and Brad are going to do? Do you think they know about this?"

Daisy looked at her like she was basic. "Edwina. Of course they know. I'm sure they're having a very bad meeting with their marketing people right now."

Most of the afternoon appointments were canceled, so Edwina and Daisy did a deep clean on the garden suite and unpacked a new display of frog milk bottles. They got a memo from Isobel around three p.m.

**To: All Staff**
**From: Isobel Chang**
**Subject: Exciting changes!**
We are pleased to announce that Margot Redberry is taking over as Skin Seraph's new marketing manager. Brad will be stepping down to focus on special projects, working closely with our partners in the Philippines to develop new markets. Please take a moment to congratulate Margot. We're so excited to have her in this big new role!

"Wow—she fired her own boyfriend!" Edwina exclaimed. "This must be really bad."

"Uh, yeah. Did you see the story in *Teen Vogue*? Basically it's quoting Mrs Landsdale's post and then linking to a bunch of other people talking about how the Skin Seraph stores have all become super unsanitary. Also they're saying the frog milk line is made with endangered tree frogs or something?" Daisy looked dubious. "I'm pretty sure that's not true. All this stuff is biomimetic. It imitates animal proteins, but it's made in labs."

Edwina stared out the front window. There was one smeary spot left in the corner, where the skinless woman had pressed her fingers last night. Were they going to lose their jobs? She still needed a hefty amount to build a solid nest egg for graduate school, and she didn't want to go back to gigging for a dollar a minute.

As if she'd read Edwina's mind, Daisy pulled out her mobile and spread it open to a page full of task offers in San Francisco. But then she wiped those away and opened up her Twitch dashboard. "Want to see something totally secret?"

"Sure!"

Daisy poked at an unpublished video called "Sweety Quest." It was a teaser for a new streaming romance series, starring Daisy, the hapless heroine looking for snuggles in the big city. Sponsored by Sugardew, the new Korean-style face-care brand. "They hired me to do a show about their new line of nightlife skin products— like all the stuff you need for going out and recovering afterwards. Isn't it dope? I'm a real influencer now!" Daisy made a face. "I mean, I know that sounds awful but I'm really excited. I get to write and direct all the episodes, and they said I can do queer content and have lots of stories about women of color."

Maybe Daisy believed in fae, Edwina thought, but she was also a genuinely nice person. It was hard not to like somebody who was promising to make romances that pandered charmingly to your exact demographic. She smiled. "Wow, congrats! Are you allowed to rep other brands while you're here, though?"

Daisy looked around, as if Isobel might jump out of that memo and scream at them. "I was worried about that, but I think now… well, now might be a good time to think about finding other brands to rep? You know what I mean?"

Edwina hung her head. "Yeah. I know. I have no idea what I'll do if this job goes away."

Impulsively, Daisy hugged her. "Maybe it will be fine here. But if not, I know you'll find something."

• • •

That night, Daisy came along with Edwina and Alyx to an old bar in the Mission where the drinks were strong and grizzled millennials sat around debating politics with their thick phones propped on the tables next to their face masks. The wildfire smoke was back again.

"I love this place," Edwina said. "It's been around for forty years—like since the early 2000s. It's the real San Francisco." She finished her scotch in two gulps and ordered another one.

Alyx sipped slowly on a rum and coke. "So I found out something pretty interesting about Skin Seraph today while everybody was losing their shit about… the shit." They raised an eyebrow.

Edwina sighed. "I don't know if I can take more Satanist conspiracy stuff."

"Did you know that Isobel hired a fae-owned firm to promote Skin Seraph last year when she took the chain national?" Alyx asked. They flipped open their mobile on the bar so the two women could look over their shoulder at what was onscreen. It was a tweet from a brand consultancy called Witchy Wonders, announcing that they'd just signed a contract with Skin Seraph to "sprinkle a little fairy dust on their already excellent brand." Alyx thumbed to the next screen. It was a PDF of the actual contract. "Obviously you never saw this," they said. "But Memegen has access to a lot of private corporate information. It looks like Isobel has been hemorrhaging money, missing bill payments. And she stopped paying this Witchy Wonder contract too."

Daisy sucked in her breath. "Oh no. She didn't pay her brand consultant?"

Edwina was starting to feel drunk, but it wasn't from the scotch. It was this conversation. "Okay, so you're saying that fae are real, and they are brand consultants in San Francisco." Her voice came out a lot more evenly than she expected it would.

"I mean, yeah?" Daisy arched a perfectly gilded eyebrow. "I told you last night."

"Like actual fae, with actual magic powers? Not cosplayers or pagans?"

"I don't know about powers, but they are contractors," Alyx said. "And I can definitely understand being pissed when you don't get paid. Contractors are always the first to get screwed."

"Tell me about it," Daisy groaned.

Edwina thought about the three years she'd worked as a Task Rabbit after college, and how grateful she'd been to get hired as a staffer at Skin Seraph. "I mean, I get why this Witchy Wonders person is angry, but she's going to ruin a lot of people's lives. It's not just Isobel. There are hundreds of Skin Seraph employees all over the world."

"I'm going DM them," Alyx said, fingers twitching midair.

"What? No!" Daisy yelped.

But Edwina was curious. "Do it!" she said. "See if you can find out how bad the contract violation is."

Alyx started giggling, eyes foggy with data. "The person running their socials remembers you, Edwina. She says she's really sorry because she liked how sparky you are." Alyx kept typing. "Okay, yeah. Yeah. This is bad. There's nothing you can do. Isobel really screwed Witchy Wonders over, like for tons of money, and Skin Seraph is going down hard. It's going to get a lot worse." Alyx's eyes cleared. "She says you should look for another job now. She's willing to give you a few days before she pulls the trigger on the next curse."

Edwina sank down on the bar stool, feeling simultaneously freaked out and vindicated. There was no way she was going to find another job with decent benefits in a few days. But it was oddly affirming to know that there was a scary magical woman roaming the city who thought she was sparky. Suddenly, she had an idea.

"Alyx, ask if she'd be willing to meet with me and Daisy to work something out. Maybe we can salvage this."

A smirk spread over Alyx's face as they typed. "She's open to talking. She says she'll meet you at Skin Seraph tomorrow when you close." They folded up the mobile and tucked it into a front pocket. "Her name is Agony, by the way."

Recalling the fae's last couple of visits to Skin Seraph, Edwina was willing to admit that Agony had earned her hyperbolic name.

"What are you thinking?" Daisy asked, picking at a piece of glitter caught in the sleeve of her sweater. "I told you I'm probably not staying at Skin Seraph. Plus, are you really going to try to bargain with a fae? That shit is dangerous."

"Listen." Edwina expertly flicked the glitter off Daisy's sleeve. "She likes me, right? I just want to see if we can get her to slow down. I need this job if I'm going to save enough to go to grad school next year. Plus, I actually like working at Skin Seraph—it's chill, and we have good benefits."

"Yeah, I get that." Daisy shot Edwina a look of sympathy.

Alyx poked Daisy's shoulder. "Don't you want to meet somebody who is a literal shit disturber? She sounds cool."

Daisy laughed. "I guess so. But I'm out if things start to get weird. And I'm not going to make any deals or bargains with her."

"Thank you!" Edwina hugged Daisy and Alyx at the same time, almost unseating herself in the process. She had no idea what she was going to say to Agony, but somehow it felt like she was making the right choice.

• • •

The next evening, Daisy kept finding excuses to sit at the front desk with Edwina, watching the sidewalk outside warily. Nearly every appointment had been canceled, so it wasn't like she had anything to do in the treatment rooms.

As daylight drained from the picture windows, a flock of green parrots crowded into the tree outside, chittering and eating the tiny red berries that grew between its spoon-shaped leaves. More kept arriving. Within minutes, it was hard to tell parrot from tree.

"That's kind of weird," Daisy said, pointing at the growing flock.

As if in answer, the door shushed open and three parrots flew inside to land next to the bottles of frog milk. Their feathered heads were as red as the berries they'd been eating. One of them immediately squirted a shit onto the pristine glass shelf.

Following the parrots inside was a woman with magenta hair in a fitted green jumpsuit embroidered with tropical flowers. She was muscular and tall, her bulky silhouette filling the doorway. She curled her hand into a gun shape, index finger pointed at the camera over the front desk, and an alert flickered in Edwina's contacts: Skin Seraph Security Feed Temporarily Offline.

"Well, that wasn't creepy at all," Daisy whispered.

"You must be Agony," Edwina said loudly. "I'm Edwina, and this is Daisy."

The fae smiled and pretended to blow smoke from the loaded barrel of her finger gun. Now that she was wearing her skin, Edwina could see that she was probably in her late twenties, with a pale brown complexion. She might be Latinx, or possibly southeast Asian. Did fae have human racial identities? Probably best not to assume.

Agony walked slowly around the store, picking up a revitalizing cream packaged in a squishy plastic bulb, peering at its warning label, then setting it back down. One of the parrots landed on her shoulder.

"I—I like your jumpsuit, Agony," Daisy said.

At last the fae looked directly at them. "Isn't it the best? I got it on sale at Wildfang." Agony finished her circuit of the room and leaned on the counter across from them. "I love your self-care videos, by the way. I've been following you for ages."

"Oh thanks!" Daisy had the desperately upbeat tone she used when Isobel visited the store and yelled at the clinicians who weren't on the MakeMeProud leaderboard.

Edwina was glad the small talk was handled. "So, Agony, I wanted to talk to you about this thing you're doing to Skin Seraph," she said.

The fae turned her gaze on Edwina, and she felt a pleasurable tingle of… something. Was that magic, or was Agony just super hot? "I told your friend Alyx that I'd give you a few days before I burn this brand down." Agony looked down and the tingle receded. "And for the record, I do feel bad about it. My boss at Witchy Wonders has this scorched-earth approach that feels very 2020. You know? She's from that extremist generation."

"Yeah," Edwina sighed. "Our boss is awful too. Obviously."

"That's why I'm going to work for myself," Daisy said. "I just got another sponsorship."

Agony shrugged. "You'll still be a contractor. That means you can get screwed by ten people instead of one. Trust me. I spend half my days chasing down payments for the company. And when they don't pay, well… I have to deal with that too."

"Why do you work there, then?" Edwina was genuinely curious.

"I love doing socials and events. I figure I'll work at Witchy for a couple more years, build up my portfolio, and then get a staff job at a marketing or design firm. I need some health insurance and stability."

Daisy was losing her anxiety frown. "I hear that. I'm going to miss the health insurance here."

Cocking her head, Agony blinked up something on her contacts. "Your numbers are amazing, Daisy. You should come to this healer pop-up I'm organizing. We need somebody to talk about nourishing beauty products."

Edwina watched the two women talking shop and wished they could be friends. Agony might be a fae with supernatural powers—or a really good cosplayer with a camera-killing device hidden up her sleeve—but her job situation sounded a lot like theirs. There had to be some way to get her on their side. Suddenly she had an idea. "Remember how Wooden Board Café had that whole scandal where the dude who owned it was forcing everyone to do creepy stuff like compete for overtime bonuses and clean the bathroom when he was in the stall taking a dump?"

"Ugh!"

"Yes!"

She had their full attention. "Well, Wooden Board is still open now, right? That's because the workers all joined a class-action suit, and the dude decided to settle by quitting and giving them the business. So they became a worker-owned cooperative. Everybody has a share in the shop. It worked out great and they started selling those really amazing cheese tarts." Edwina paused. "We could do that."

Daisy was dubious. "But Skin Seraph is an international chain. We can't turn it all into a co-op."

"No, you mean with the Skin Seraph workers at this one shop, right?" Agony continued to blink up feeds as she thought it over. "It might even work, because your boss could get rid of the shop that got her in trouble in the first place. She could do a total rebrand."

"Okay, sure. But what would we do with a shop?" Daisy asked.

Edwina's heart began to pound, and she realized with surprise this mattered a lot to her. "We all need jobs. Daisy, you want to be a self-care influencer, and this shop is the perfect place to build your brand and make video. Agony, you want to do events? We've got amazing spaces here for retreats, classes, and pop-ups. Listen. How often do you have the chance to grab prime retail real estate that has suddenly become garbage? Isobel has a dozen other outlets—

she doesn't need the hassle of dealing with all the fallout from Agony's curse. We'd be doing her a favor. And we—we could make a really great store. We don't have to do it forever. But wouldn't it be nice to build a business where all the workers would be owners, so we could give ourselves good health benefits and vacation time and stuff?"

Daisy looked thoughtful. "We could get rid of Isobel's shitty bonus system, too."

Agony waved her hand to dismiss whatever she was accessing online. Nobody said anything for a minute while two parrots fluttered down to the counter. The third, still on Agony's shoulder, spoke first. "These humans have good hearts," the bird said. "You can trust them."

Another bird cackled. "Or you could swindle them! They're credulous!"

Agony rolled her eyes. "We've talked about this, Loudface. That's an inside-your-head thought."

Edwina glanced at Daisy, worried the talking animals might be triggering her anti-fae feelings. But she was toying with one of the free sample packets they kept behind the counter, seemingly oblivious to the possibly-magic, possibly-trained-parrot scenario.

And then Daisy said the last thing Edwina expected. "You know what? Fuck it. I'm in. Let's do this. Let's make a store."

"YESSSS!" Edwina did an awkward wiggly dance. "We can do this! What do you say, Agony?"

The fae looked at Loudface, then behind her through the windows, seeming to measure the armies of pedestrians swarming Whole Foods across the street. When she turned back around, she was smiling. "We're going to need a lawyer. And a business manager."

It was weird how you could want something badly, and not realize exactly what it was until you found yourself in a completely anomalous situation. Edwina drummed her fists on the counter in triumph. "I have a couple friends who might be able to help. They just got their MBAs and have done some start-up stuff."

"My mom is a labor lawyer," Daisy said haltingly. "This might be the only time she will ever understand my job."

Agony's smile turned hard. "And I can make your boss very... receptive to our offer."

"We'll need to ask the other workers if they want to join us, too," Edwina said.

"After my next curse, though? Because we don't want to tip our hand."

"Yeah, that makes sense."

"Hey, do you want me to do it right now? It's going to be super gross and scary."

Edwina looked at Daisy. "Do you want to? I want to."

Daisy shrugged and then grinned a little. "No more poop, though, okay?"

Agony crooked her finger and they followed her outside onto the sidewalk, facing the illuminated interior of a business they were about to claim as their own. The fae raised her arms, fingers spread wide, and Venus became visible in the evening sky.

That's when the fat, warm drops of blood began to fall.

# A WITCH'S GUIDE TO ESCAPE: A PRACTICAL COMPENDIUM OF PORTAL FANTASIES

## ALIX E. HARROW

GEORGE, JC—THE RUNAWAY PRINCE—J FIC GEO 1994

**You'd think** it would make us happy when a kid checks out the same book a zillion times in a row, but actually it just keeps us up at night.

*The Runaway Prince* is one of those low-budget young adult fantasies from the mid-nineties, before J.K. Rowling arrived to tell everyone that magic was cool, printed on brittle yellow paper. It's about a lonely boy who runs away and discovers a Magical Portal into another world where he has Medieval Adventures, but honestly there are so many typos most people give up before he even finds the portal.

Not this kid, though. He pulled it off the shelf and sat cross-legged in the juvenile fiction section with his grimy red backpack clutched to his chest. He didn't move for hours. Other patrons were forced to double back in the aisle, shooting suspicious you-don't-belong-here looks behind them as if wondering what a skinny black teenager was *really* up to while pretending to read a fantasy book. He ignored them.

The books above him rustled and quivered; that kind of attention flatters them.

He took *The Runaway Prince* home and renewed it twice online, at which point a gray pop-up box that looks like an emissary from 1995 tells you, "The renewal limit for this item has been reached." You can almost feel the disapproving eyes of a librarian glaring at you through the screen.

(There have only ever been two kinds of librarians in the history of the world: the prudish, bitter ones with lipstick running into the cracks around their lips who believe the books are their personal property and patrons are dangerous delinquents come to steal them, and witches.)

Our late fee is twenty-five cents per day or a can of non-perishable food during the summer food drive. By the time the boy finally slid *The Runaway Prince* into the return slot, he owed $4.75. I didn't have to swipe his card to know; any good librarian (of the second kind) ought to be able to tell you the exact dollar amount of a patron's bill just by the angle of their shoulders.

"What'd you think?" I used my this-is-a-secret-between-us-pals voice, which works on teenagers about sixteen per cent of the time.

He shrugged. It has a lower success rate with black teenagers, because this is the rural South and they aren't stupid enough to trust thirty-something white ladies no matter how many tattoos we have.

"Didn't finish it, huh?" I knew he'd finished it at least four times by the warm, well-oiled feel of the pages.

"Yeah, I did." His eyes flicked up. They were smoke-colored and long-lashed, with an achy, faraway expression, as if he knew there was something gleaming and forbidden just beneath the dull surfaces of things that he could never quite touch. They were the kinds of eyes that had belonged to sorcerers or soothsayers, in different times. "The ending sucked."

In the end, the Runaway Prince leaves Medieval Adventureland

and closes the portal behind him before returning home to his family. It was supposed to be a happy ending.

Which kind of tells you all you need to know about this kid's life, doesn't it?

He left without checking anything else out.

• • •

GARRISON, ALLEN B—

THE TAVALARRIAN CHRONICLES—v. I-XVI—F GAR 1976

LE GUIN, URSULA K—

A WIZARD OF EARTHSEA—J FIC LEG 1968

He returned four days later, sloping past a bright blue display titled THIS SUMMER, DIVE INTO READING! (who knows where they were supposed to swim; Ulysses County's lone public pool had been filled with cement in the '60s rather than desegregate).

Because I am a librarian of the second sort, I almost always know what kind of book a person wants. It's like a very particular smell rising off them which is instantly recognizable as *Murder mystery* or *Political biography* or *Something kind of trashy but ultimately life-affirming, preferably with lesbians.*

I do my best to give people the books they need most. In grad school, they called it "ensuring readers have access to texts/materials that are engaging and emotionally rewarding," and in my other kind of schooling, they called it "divining the unfilled spaces in their souls and filling them with stories and starshine," but it comes to the same thing.

I don't bother with the people who have call numbers scribbled on their palms and titles rattling around in their skulls like bingo cards. They don't need me. And you really can't do anything for the people who only read Award-Winning Literature, who wear elbow patches and equate the popularity of *Twilight* with the death of the American intellect; their hearts are too closed up for the new or secret or undiscovered.

So, it's only a certain kind of patron I pay attention to. The kind that let their eyes feather across the titles like trailing fingertips, heads cocked, with book-hunger rising off them like heatwaves from a July pavement. The books bask in it, of course, even the really hopeless cases that haven't been checked out since 1958 (there aren't many of these; me and Agnes take turns carting home outdated astronomy textbooks that still think Pluto is a planet and cookbooks that call for lard, just to keep their spirits up). I choose one or two books and let their spines gleam and glimmer in the twilit stacks. People reach towards them without quite knowing why.

The boy with the red backpack wasn't an experienced aisle-wanderer. He prowled, moving too quickly to read the titles, hands hanging empty and uncertain at his sides. The sewing and pattern books (646.2) noted that his jeans were unlaundered and too small, and the neck of his T-shirt was stained grayish-yellow. The cookbooks (641.5) diagnosed a diet of frozen waffles and gas-station pizza. They *tssk*ed to themselves.

I sat at the circulation desk, running returns beneath the blinky red scanner light, and breathed him in. I was expecting something like *Generic Arthurian retelling* or maybe *Teen romance with sword-fighting*, but instead I found a howling, clamoring mess of need.

He smelled of a thousand secret worlds, of rabbit-holes and hidden doorways and platforms nine-and-three-quarters, of Wonderland and Oz and Narnia, of anyplace-but-here. He smelled of *yearning*.

God save me from the yearners. The insatiable, the inconsolable, the ones who chafe and claw against the edges of the world. No book can save them.

(That's a lie. There are Books potent enough to save any mortal soul: books of witchery, augury, alchemy; books with wand-wood in their spines and moon-dust on their pages; books older than stones and wily as dragons. We give people the books they need most, except when we don't.)

I sent him a '70s sword-and-sorcery series because it was total junk food and he needed fattening up, and because I hoped sixteen volumes might act as a sort of ballast and keep his keening soul from rising away into the ether. I let Le Guin shimmer at him, too, because he reminded me a bit of Ged (feral; full of longing).

I ignored *The Lion, the Witch, and the Wardrobe*, jostling importantly on its shelf; this was a kid who wanted to go through the wardrobe and never, ever come back.

• • •

GRAYSON, DR BERNARD—WHEN NOTHING MATTERS ANYMORE: A SURVIVAL GUIDE FOR DEPRESSED TEENS— 616.84 GRA 2002

Once you make it past book four of the *Tavalarrian Chronicles*, you're committed at least through book fourteen when the true Sword of Tavalar is revealed and the young farm-boy ascends to his rightful throne. The boy with the red backpack showed up every week or so all summer for the next installment.

I snuck in a few others (all pretty old, all pretty white; our branch director is one of those pinch-lipped Baptists who thinks fantasy books teach kids about Devil worship, so roughly ninety per cent of my collection requests are mysteriously denied): *A Wrinkle in Time* came back with the furtive, jammed-in-a-backpack scent that meant he liked it but thought it was too young for him; *Watership Down* was offended because he never got past the first ten pages, but I guess footnotes about rabbit-math aren't for everyone; and *The Golden Compass* had the flashlight-smell of 3:00 a.m. on its final chapter and was unbearably smug about it. I'd just gotten an inter-library-loaned copy of *Akata Witch*—when he stopped coming.

Our display (GET READ-Y FOR SCHOOL!) was filled with SAT prep kits and over-sized yellow *For Dummies* books. Agnes had cut out blobby construction-paper leaves and taped them to the front doors. Lots of kids stop hanging around the library when school starts up, with all its clubs and teams.

I worried anyway. I could feel the Book I hadn't given him like a wrong note or a missing tooth, a magnetic absence. Just when I was seriously considering calling Ulysses County High School with a made-up story about an un-returned CD, he came back.

For the first time, there was someone else with him: A squat white woman with a plastic nametag and the kind of squarish perm you can only get in Southern beauty salons with faded glamor-shots in the windows. The boy trailed behind her looking thin and pressed, like a flower crushed between dictionary pages. I wondered how badly you had to fuck up to get assigned a school counselor after hours, until I read her nametag: Department of Community-Based Services, Division of Protection and Permanency, Child Caseworker (II).

Oh. A foster kid.

The woman marched him through the nonfiction stacks (the travel guides sighed as she passed, muttering about overwork and recommending vacations to sunny, faraway beaches) and stopped in the 616s. "Here, why don't we have a look at these?"

Predictable, sullen silence from the boy.

A person who works with foster kids sixty hours a week is unfazed by sullenness. She slid titles off the shelf and stacked them in the boy's arms. "We talked about this, remember? We decided you might like to read something practical, something helpful?"

*Dealing with Depression* (616.81 WHI 1998). *Beating the Blues: Five Steps to Feeling Normal Again!* (616.822 TRE 2011). *Chicken Soup for the Depressed Soul* (616.9 CAN). The books greeted him in soothing, syrupy voices.

The boy stayed silent. "Look. I know you'd rather read about dragons and, uh, elves," oh, Tolkien, you have so much to account for, "but sometimes we've got to face our problems head-on, rather than running away from them."

What *bullshit*. I was in the back room running scratched DVDs through the disc repair machine, so the only person to hear me swear was Agnes. She gave me her patented over-the-glasses *shame on you* look which, when properly deployed, can reduce noisy patrons to piles of ash or pillars of salt (Agnes is a librarian of the second kind, too).

But seriously. Anyone could see that kid needed to run and keep running until he shed his own skin, until he clawed out of the choking darkness and unfurled his wings, precious and prisming in the light of some other world.

His caseworker was one of those people who say the word "escapism" as if it's a moral failing, a regrettable hobby, a mental-health diagnosis. As if escape is not, in itself, one of the highest orders of magics they'll ever see in their miserable mortal lives, right up there with true love and prophetic dreams and fireflies blinking in synchrony on a June evening.

The boy and his keeper were winding back through the aisles toward the front desk. The boy's shoulders were curled inward, as if he chafed against invisible walls on either side.

As he passed the juvenile fiction section, a cheap paperback flung itself off the return cart and thudded into his kneecap. He picked it up and rubbed his thumb softly over the title. *The Runaway Prince* purred at him.

He smiled. I thanked the library cart, silently.

There was a long, familiar sigh behind me. I turned to see Agnes watching me from the circulation desk, aquamarine nails tapping the cover of a Grisham novel, eyes crimped with pity. *Oh honey, not another one,* they said.

I turned back to my stack of DVDs, unsmiling, thinking things like *what do you know about it* and *this one is different* and *oh shit.*

• • •

### DUMAS, ALEXANDRE—THE COUNT OF MONTE CRISTO— F DUM 1974

The boy returned at 10:30 on a Tuesday morning. It's official library policy to report truants to the high school, because the school board felt we were becoming "a haven for unsupervised and illicit teenage activity." I happen to think that's exactly what libraries should aspire to be, and suggested we get it engraved on a plaque for the front door, but then I was asked to be serious or leave the proceedings, and anyway we're supposed to report kids who skip school to play *League of Legends* on our computers or skulk in the graphic novel section.

I watched the boy prowling the shelves—muscles strung wire-tight over his bones, soul writhing and clawing like a caged creature—and did not reach for the phone. Agnes, still wearing her *oh honey* expression, declined to reprimand me.

I sent him home with *The Count of Monte Cristo,* partly because it requires your full attention and a flow chart to keep track of the plot and the kid needed distracting, but mostly because of what Edmond says on the second-to-last page: "… all human wisdom is summed up in these two words—'Wait and hope.'"

But people can't keep waiting and hoping forever.

They fracture, they unravel, they crack open; they do something desperate and stupid and then you see their high-school senior photo printed in the *Ulysses Gazette*, grainy and oversized, and you spend the next five years thinking: *If only I'd given her the right book.*

• • •

ROWLING, JK—HARRY POTTER
AND THE SORCERER'S STONE—J FIC ROW 1998
ROWLING, JK—HARRY POTTER
AND THE CHAMBER OF SECRETS—J FIC ROW 1999
ROWLING, JK—HARRY POTTER
AND THE PRISONER OF AZKABAN—J FIC ROW 1999

Every librarian has Books she never lends to anyone.

I'm not talking about first editions of *Alice in Wonderland* or Dutch translations of *Winnie-the-Pooh*; I'm talking about Books so powerful and potent, so full of susurrating seduction, that only librarians of the second sort even know they exist.

Each of us has her own system for keeping them hidden. The most venerable libraries (the ones with oak paneling and vaulted ceilings and *Beauty and the Beast*-style ladders) have secret rooms behind fireplaces or bookcases, which you can only enter by tugging on a certain title on the shelf. Sainte-Geneviève in Paris is supposed to have vast catacombs beneath it guarded by librarians so ancient and desiccated they've become human-shaped books, paper-skinned and ink-blooded. In Timbuktu, I heard they hired wizard-smiths to make great wrought-iron gates that only permit passage to the pure of heart.

In the Maysville branch of the Ulysses County Library system, we have a locked roll-top desk in the Special Collections room with a sign on it that says, "This is an Antique! Please Ask for Assistance."

We only have a dozen or so Books, anyhow, and god knows where they came from or how they ended up here. *A Witch's Guide to Seeking Righteous Vengeance*, with its slender steel pages and arsenic ink. *A Witch's Guide to Falling in Love for the First Time, for Readers at Every Stage of Life!*, which smells like starlight and the summer you were seventeen. *A Witch's Guide to Uncanny Baking* contains over thirty full-color photographs to ensorcell your friends and afflict your adversaries. *A Witch's Guide to Escape: A Practical Compendium of Portal Fantasies* has no words in it at all, but only pages and pages of maps: hand-drawn Middle-earth knock-offs with unpronounceable names; medieval tapestry-maps showing tiny ships sailing off the edge of the world; topographical maps of Machu Picchu; 1970s Rand McNally street maps of Istanbul.

It's my job to keep Books like this out of the hands of desperate high-school kids with red backpacks. Our schoolmistresses called it "preserving the hallowed and hidden arts of our foremothers from mundane eyes." Our professors called it "conserving rare/historic texts."

Both of them mean the same thing: We give people the books they need, except when we don't. Except when they need them most.

He racked up $1.50 on *The Count of Monte Cristo* and returned it with saltwater splotches on the final pages. They weren't my-favorite-character-died tears or the-book-is-over tears. They were bitter, acidic, anise-scented: tears of jealousy. He was jealous that the Count and Haydée sailed away from their world and out into the blue unknown. That they escaped.

I panicked and weighed him down with the first three Harry Potters, because they don't really get good until Sirius and Lupin show up, and because they're about a neglected, lonely kid who gets a letter from another world and disappears.

...

GEORGE, JC—
THE RUNAWAY PRINCE—J FIC GEO 1994

Agnes always does the "we will be closing in ten minutes" announcement because something in her voice implies that anybody still in the library in nine minutes and fifty seconds will be harvested for organ donations, and even the most stationary patrons amble towards the exit.

The kid with the red backpack was hovering in the oversize print section (gossipy, aging books, bored since the advent of e-readers with changeable font sizes) when Agnes's voice came through the speakers. He went very still, teetering the way a person does when they're about to do something really dumb, then dove beneath a reading desk and pulled his dark hoodie over his head. The oversize books gave scintillated squeals.

It was my turn to close, so Agnes left right at nine. By 9:15 I was standing at the door with my NPR tote on my shoulder and my keys in my hand. Hesitating.

It is very, extremely, absolutely against the rules to lock up for the night with a patron still inside, especially when that patron is a minor of questionable emotional health. It's big trouble both in the conventional sense (phone calls from panicked guardians, police searches, charges of criminal neglect) and in the other sense (libraries at night are noisier places than they are during the daylight hours).

I'm not a natural rule-follower. I roll through stop signs, I swear in public, I lie on online personality tests so I get the answers I want (Hermione, Arya Stark, Jo March). But I'm a very good librarian of either kind, and good librarians follow the rules. Even when they don't want to.

That's what Agnes told me five years ago, when I first started at Maysville.

This girl had started showing up on Sunday afternoons: ponytailed, cute, but wearing one of those knee-length denim skirts that scream "mandatory virginity pledge." I'd been feeding her a steady diet of subversion (Orwell, Bradbury, Butler), and was about to hit her with *A Handmaid's Tale* when she suddenly lost interest in fiction. She drifted through the stacks, face gone white and empty as a blank page, navy skirt swishing against her knees.

It wasn't until she reached the 618s that I understood. The maternity and childbirth section trilled saccharine congratulations. She touched one finger to the spine of *What to Expect When You're Expecting* (618.2 EIS) with an expression of dawning, swallowing horror, and left without checking anything out.

For the next nine weeks, I sent her stories of bravery and boldness, defying-your-parents stories and empowered-women-resisting-authority stories. I abandoned subtlety entirely and slid Planned Parenthood pamphlets into her book bag, even though the nearest clinic is six hours away and only open twice a week, but found them jammed frantically in the bathroom trash.

But I never gave her what she really needed: *A Witch's Guide to Undoing What Has Been Done: A Guilt-Free Approach to Life's Inevitable Accidents*. A leather-bound tome filled with delicate mechanical drawings of clocks, which smelled of regret and yesterday mornings. I'd left it locked in the roll-top desk, whispering and tick-tocking to itself.

Look, there are good reasons we don't lend out Books like that. Our mistresses used to scare us with stories of mortals run amok: people who used Books to steal or kill or break hearts; who performed miracles and founded religions; who hated us, afterward, and spent a tiresome few centuries burning us at stakes.

If I were caught handing out Books, I'd be renounced, reviled, stripped of my title. They'd burn my library card in the eternal mauve flames of our sisterhood and write my crimes in ash and blood in *The Book of Perfidy*. They'd ban me from every library for eternity, and what's a librarian without her books? What would I be, cut off from the orderly world of words and their readers, from the peaceful Ouroboran cycle of story-telling and story-eating? There were rumors of rogue librarians—madwomen who chose to live outside the library system in the howling chaos of unwritten words and untold stories—but none of us envied them.

The last time I'd seen the ponytailed girl her denim skirt was fastened with a rubber band looped through the buttonhole. She'd smelled of desperation, like someone whose wait-and-hoping had run dry.

Four days later, her picture was in the paper and the article was blurring and un-blurring in my vision (*accidental poisoning, viewing from 2:00-3:30 at Zimmerman & Holmes, direct your donations to Maysville Baptist Ministries*). Agnes had patted my hand and said, "I know, honey, I know. Sometimes there's nothing you can do." It was a kind lie.

I still have the newspaper clipping in my desk drawer, as a memorial or reminder or warning.

The boy with the red backpack was sweating beneath the reading desk. He smelled of desperation, just like she had.

Should I call the Child Protective Services hotline? Make awkward small talk until his crummy caseworker collected him? *Hey, kid, I was once a lonely teenager in a backwater shithole, too!* Or should I let him run away, even if running away was only hiding in the library overnight?

I teetered, the way you do when you're about to do something really dumb.

The lock thunked into place. I walked across the parking lot breathing the caramel-and-frost smell of October, hoping—almost praying, if witches were into that—that it would be enough.

• • •

I opened half an hour early, angling to beat Agnes to the phone and delete the "Have you seen this unaccompanied minor?" voicemails before she could hear them. There was an automated message from somebody trying to sell us a security system, three calls from community members asking when we open because apparently it's physically impossible to google it, and a volunteer calling in sick.

There were no messages about the boy. Fucking Ulysses County foster system.

He emerged at 9:45, when he could blend in with the growing numbers of other patrons. He looked rumpled and ill-fitting, like a visitor from another planet who hadn't quite figured out human body language. Or like a kid who's spent a night in the stacks, listening to furtive missives from a thousand different worlds and wishing he could disappear into any one of them.

I was so busy trying not to cry and ignoring the Book now calling to the boy from the roll-top desk that I scanned his card and handed him back his book without realizing what it was: *The Runaway Prince*.

• • •

MAYSVILLE PUBLIC LIBRARY NOTICE:
YOU HAVE (1) OVERDUE ITEMS. PLEASE RETURN YOUR ITEM(S)
AS SOON AS POSSIBLE.

Shit.

The overdue notices go out on the fifteenth day an item has been checked out. On the sixteenth day, I pulled up the boy's account and glared at the terse red font (OVERDUE ITEM: J FIC GEO 1994) until the screen began to crackle and smoke faintly and Agnes gave me a *hold it together, woman* look.

He hadn't even bothered to renew it.

My sense of *The Runaway Prince* had grown faint and blurred with distance, as if I were looking at it through an unfocused telescope, but it was still a book from my library and thus still in my domain. (All you people who never returned books to their high school libraries, or who bought stolen books off Amazon with call numbers taped to their spines? We see you.) It reported only the faintest second-hand scent of the boy: futility, resignation, and a tarry, oozing smell like yearning that had died and begun to fossilize.

He was alive, but probably not for much longer. I don't just mean physical suicide; those of us who can see soulstuff know there are lots of ways to die without anybody noticing. Have you ever seen those stupid TV specials where they rescue animals from some third-rate horror show of a circus in Las Vegas, and when they finally open the cages the lions just sit there, dead-eyed, because they've forgotten what it is to want anything? To desire, to yearn, to be filled with the terrible, golden hunger of being alive?

But there was nothing I could do. Except wait and hope.

Our volunteers were doing the weekly movie showing in Media Room #2, so I was stuck re-shelving. It wasn't until I was actually in the F DAC-FEN aisle, holding our dog-eared copy of *The Count of Monte Cristo* in my hand, that I realized Edmond Dantès was absolutely, one hundred per cent full of shit.

If Edmond had taken his own advice, he would've sat in his jail cell waiting and hoping for forty years while the Count de Morcerf and Villefort and the rest of them stayed rich and happy. The real moral of *The Count of Monte Cristo* was surely something more like: If you screw someone over, be prepared for a vengeful mastermind to fuck up your life twenty years later. Or maybe it was: If you want justice and goodness to prevail in this world, you have to fight for it tooth and nail. And it will be hard, and costly, and probably illegal. You will have to break the rules.

I pressed my head to the cold metal of the shelf and closed my eyes. *If that boy ever comes back into my library, I swear to Clio and Calliope I will do my most holy duty.*

*I will give him the book he needs most.*

• • •

ARADIA, MORGAN—A WITCH'S GUIDE TO ESCAPE:
A PRACTICAL COMPENDIUM OF PORTAL FANTASIES—
WRITTEN IN THE YEAR OF OUR SISTERHOOD TWO THOUSAND
AND TWO AND SUBMITTED TO THE CARE OF THE ULYSSES
COUNTY PUBLIC LIBRARY SYSTEM.

He came back to say goodbye, I think. He slid *The Runaway Prince* into the return slot then drifted through the aisles with his red backpack hanging off one shoulder, fingertips not quite brushing the shelves, eyes on the floor. They hardly seemed sorcerous at all, now; merely sad and old and smoke-colored.

He was passing through the travel and tourism section when he saw it: A heavy, clothbound book jammed right between *The Practical Nomad* (910.4 HAS) and *By Plane, Train, or Foot: A Guide for the Aspiring Globe-Trotter* (910.51). It had no call number, but the title was stamped in swirly gold lettering on the spine: *A Witch's Guide to Escape.*

I felt the hollow thud-thudding of his heart, the pain of resurrected hope. He reached towards the book and the book reached back towards him, because books need to be read quite as much as we need to read them, and it had been a very long time since this particular book had been out of the roll-top desk in the Special Collections room.

Dark fingers touched green-dyed cloth, and it was like two sundered halves of some broken thing finally reuniting, like a lost key finally turning in its lock. Every book in the library rustled in unison, sighing at the sacred wholeness of reader and book.

Agnes was in the rows of computers, explaining our thirty-minute policy to a new patron. She broke off mid-sentence and looked up towards the 900s, nostrils flared. Then, with an expression halfway between accusation and disbelief, she turned to look at me.

I met her eyes—and it isn't easy to meet Agnes's eyes when she's angry, believe me—and smiled.

When they drag me before the mistresses and burn my card and demand to know, in tones of mournful recrimination, how I could have abandoned the vows of our order, I'll say: *Hey, you abandoned them first, ladies. Somewhere along the line, you forgot our first and purest purpose: to give patrons the books they need most. And oh, how they need. How they will always need.*

I wondered, with a kind of detached trepidation, how rogue librarians spent their time, and whether they had clubs or societies, and what it was like to encounter feral stories untamed by narrative and unbound by books. And then I wondered where our Books came from in the first place, and who wrote them.

● ● ●

There was a sudden, imperceptible rushing, as if a wild wind had whipped through the stacks without disturbing a single page. Several people looked up uneasily from their screens.

*A Witch's Guide to Escape* lay abandoned on the carpet, open to a map of some foreign fey country drawn in sepia ink. A red backpack sat beside it.

# AMBER TOO RED, LIKE EMBER

## YUKIMI OGAWA

**Grandma broke.** Kind of.

It happened, unfortunately, while we were still deep in the wormhole. One moment ago the stars were rolling—or our house was spinning—and then everything suddenly just… stopped. The gravity wasn't working quite right; the house and the garden were a self-sufficient spacecraft that looked like a snow globe containing a one-story house and its neat garden as a whole, and the soil beneath us was supposed to be always "down," but right now… the whole globe was frozen at an odd angle.

"Grandma?" I called out from my room, having a bit of a trouble with the door. "Grandma?"

There was no answer.

The kitchen was empty. I went to the front door. When I shoved it open, I had only a moment to take in the mess—the water pot, shovels, and spare planters, all crammed around the steps to the door because of the wrong gravity—because I gasped and was then scrambling up to the skewed rose arch, at whose foot Grandma lay. A vine, full of weirdly long, sharp thorns, held her disconnected head up high in the air like a trophy.

"Grandma!"

I cut the vine with a shovel, making the head fall to the ground with a thud. I dragged her body and head into the house. I went back to the weird vine, retraced it and found its root, then killed it with a bigger, rusted shovel, and sprinkled some salt around the root for good measure. Grandma would have to take care of this properly later, she's the real gardener and I am just an assistant; for the moment the most important thing was to keep the damage minimal.

"Grandma!" I stumbled back into the house, calling her. "Are you okay?"

Not even a groan for an answer. I checked the head—it was covered with very bad scratches and a few long, nasty thorns. I set it aside and looked into her chest through the opening of her neck—the main clockwork was still working, but very, very slowly.

Nausea hit me hard. Her whole mechanism was a mystery to me. To fix her properly, I'd have to exit the wormhole and go see some kind of specialist. But only Grandma, with her song and her ticking, could carry us through a wormhole, or out of it.

I searched around the house; she was a machine, after all, and machines had instruction manuals. But no—all her books were about gardening, tea-blending or cooking; there was nothing that said something like IN CASE OF EMERGENCY. I couldn't find her other heads that she'd usually replace at her whim, either.

I opened the cabinet. There was enough food for me alone to stay alive for some time, but not forever. We weren't exactly hiding from the world, but we weren't seeking unwanted attention, either, and we'd chosen this wormhole just because it didn't usually have much traffic. I had no idea when possible help might pass by—if any.

I sat down on the floor beside Grandma's body. I thought I'd been helping her a lot here, in this globe of her cozy little house and her garden full of roses and herbs. Only now did I realize—I knew nothing about her. Nothing at all.

• • •

Over the next few days, I did manage to find what might be clues. Or not. A piece of smooth amber, with a tiny bug trapped at the bottom corner, in the jar full of dried beans; a tiny cluster of crystal behind her pet succulent; a large lump of boulder opal afloat in the rice container; and more of the like. I collected them and put them all together in a bowl to see if anything came up. I'd seen her using minerals as the vital part in her clockwork-like mechanism.

I picked up the amber I found first. It was almost as large as my eye, nugget-shaped and the surface very smoothly polished. A bit redder than amber I'd seen in books. A star-shaped shimmer at the edge made me imagine the bug fluttering its wings for a split second. I blinked and closed my hand around it—I didn't know why I did that; perhaps I just liked its feel in my hand.

Right then, there was a moment of impact beneath us, and our globe gave a sudden lurch. What now?

I crawled into Grandma's study—the impact had made our angle even steeper—and cautiously peered out the window; I said we weren't exactly on the run, yes, but we were *kind of* on the run, and I really hoped Grandma's least favorite person in the universe wasn't lurking out there.

It was another house, like ours. Another small-scale spacecraft. There was a part that was a bit… blurry? Opaque? Somewhere between our house and the other. Was that where the two globes had collided?

I turned the dial hidden beneath the windowsill and enlarged the visual. The opaque part seemed to be at the very edge of the globe. Our side of the globe looked intact, though; it must have been the other bubble, wrinkled and fogging the view there.

The house in the other globe was much smaller than ours. Probably a one-room structure, with only one occupant. The enlarging function of the window was up to full, so I put Grandma's binoculars to my eyes. The small house's window was not clear glass like ours but the color of thin honey, with strange cracks here and there. I'd have thought the house was abandoned if, right then, I hadn't seen a flicker behind the colored window.

Someone was alive.

Would they hear me if I shouted? Probably not—I needed Grandma ticking to interact with anything outside the globe, even if the thing on the outside was physically close enough. It was just the way things worked; this was an interstellar, inter-dimensional vehicle, and two meters away was just the same as two hundred light years away. Only Grandma's ticking mechanism could project the surface of the planet onto her garden, and only when that was happening could I touch the things on the said planet.

Now, the small globe was literally in contact with ours, but there was no way I could talk to the person there.

I set the window back to default and went back to the kitchen.

I lifted Grandma's head out of the box and stared at it. I'd thoroughly picked out all the thorns and immersed it in rosemary-scented oil for a day before boiling it in salt water. Then I'd put it in the box painted with the blackest black in the whole universe. Any kind of poison or bug could have infected it, and Grandma would have made me do this if she could speak. Now the head was still a bit swollen with excess water, and the stitches I'd made over the worst scars were beginning to open again.

I really needed Grandma. To fix Grandma.

I shook my head and peered into her eyes. They were glassy, the black color of the space around us. Then I placed her head back in the box and went to look down into her torso. There—her clock was still slowly moving, and at the center of it all, right beside her heart, was a glistening piece of obsidian, moving in a slightly different rhythm than the heart, as if its purpose was something other than keeping the clockwork going.

Hm. If her eyes, in her head, were connected with the same mineral in her body…

I dug into my pocket and found the piece of the amber I'd forgotten to put back in its original location. This was scary, I had to admit, but if I did nothing now, Grandma might never come back and then I'd die here. I held the amber firmly with three fingers, reached down into Grandma's torso and pushed the obsidian with it.

A tiny chip broke off the obsidian—my heart almost stopped— and that chip struck something somewhere in the pit of Grandma's body, after a second. That sent out a faint but carrying note, which reminded me of Grandma's song. Being that little bit of mass less, the obsidian moved more easily in its socket. I wiggled it out and tried to replace it with the amber, but the amber was too large for the hollow the obsidian had left. The amber unfurled there and split into two, dividing at that trapped insect. One half flew away, or down, farther into Grandma.

*No!*

I frantically reached out, leaned in too far. My fingers did touch that second half of the amber, but they didn't manage to close around it, and I fell through Grandma's body with it.

• • •

It could have been three seconds, or three thousand years, and then I wasn't falling anymore. I opened my eyes; the amber was floating there right in front of my face, and I grabbed at it.

I was afloat, too.

Everything around me was the color of thin honey. I held the amber in front of my eye, and realized I could see my surroundings only through that half of the fossil. I was in a strange room—a bedroom but also a study, and a workshop, so much furniture packed in. But cozy in its own way, in a way I liked. It was also better decorated than our place, though the decorative details were subtle, such as the carvings at the very edges of the shelves and doors, or the simple yet extensive embroidery on the quilt. I was so intent on taking in those details, and also quite near-sighted with my small lens of amber, that it took me a long moment to notice a girl looking up at me, gaping.

"Oh!" I almost dropped the amber, caught it just in time. "I'm sorry, am I intruding? Of course I'm intruding. Well, I wondered, is your globe okay?"

"W-what?" she slowly said. I was so glad she could speak.

"Something is wrong with your globe material, right? Isn't that why your house is stuck to the side of ours? Do you want us to help you fix it?"

The girl blinked, frowned, cocked her head, and then stared at me for a while. Then she said, "Well, yes, please."

I nodded at her. "Good. Because to do that, first, you need to help me fix Grandma."

• • •

She called herself Amber/Ember, because she could no longer remember which represented her true self. As I'd suspected, she did have clockwork installed in her chest, but had only one head, unlike Grandma.

"She probably was poisoned, your grandma," A/E said. "That weird vine you speak of made a mistake detaching her head, though, and the poison didn't get too far."

"Yes, but the edges of her neck, where it was severed, the flesh there might still be infected. I couldn't process her body like I did her head. And I can't find her other heads."

"How many does she have?"

"More than I can count."

"Wow." A/E stood out of her chair, excited. She looked short, though I couldn't compare her height with my own to know for sure. "I want to meet her. Look, I can take over her mechanism for a time and check exactly what is wrong with her."

"That would be great," I said. I'd realized that I was now an image reflected on the air of the small house; I'd always used the projected image that Grandma processed to touch things outside our globe, but now I myself was that processed image, so that probably meant part of Grandma was still working all right, except for something critical. "But how can you take over her?"

Amber/Ember almost plunged into her cabinet and started vigorously throwing the contents out onto the floor behind her. After a moment she came back out with a small pot, beaming. "Here they are!"

"Grandma would go crazy if she saw the mess you make," I said, grinning. "What are they?"

A/E held the pot up so that I could have a better look. It was full of some kind of mushrooms with red dews popping out of their caps. "We can use these to trick the clock hands: place these at intervals, both in your grandma's clockwork and mine, and when our hands pass over them the dews burst, slowing down our clocks to the same speed. After some time the juice will turn to spores and drift away, so until then is how long we have for borrowing her body."

"And how long, exactly, is that?"

A/E seemed to consider this. "Twelve hours, at most. If I persist longer than that…"

"What happens?"

Amber/Ember shrugged. "I haven't done this. I don't know."

Hm. "Well, we'll all die if we don't at least try."

"Right. Now you go back to your house, so that I can claim her."

I panicked for a moment, not knowing how to get back. But then I realized that that obsidian chip was spinning near my ear, so I flicked it upward, towards Grandma's neck. It flew up until it hit something in her mechanism and gave out a note again.

There was a second of sucking sensation, and the next moment I was lying on the floor, my legs on Grandma's lap. I stared at her like that, at where her head should be; something there was changing, like a heat haze was being generated.

A bubble slightly tinged with orange formed there on Grandma's neck, a bit larger than Grandma's head. There were pieces of grass blades and seeds, and chips of stones swirling inside the bubble, colliding with each other, with the bubble material, emitting many kinds of sounds inside. It took me some time to realize the sounds were forming words.

"Nice house," A/E was saying. "Not fancy, but well equipped and efficient."

I scrambled up onto my knees. "Thanks. I'll tell her that when she can hear me again. Do you think you can figure out what's wrong?"

"On-board diagnostics processing." The whole head-bubble blinked in red and orange. "Gosh, her body is so ancient. But still working perfectly. This is wondrous."

I kind of wished I could understand the inside of Grandma like that, too. Or not. I probably didn't. "So she isn't exactly broken?"

"One moment…" Amber/Ember's bubble seemed to rotate there on Grandma's neck. "Huh. This doesn't look very good."

"How 'not good'?"

"Those vines that severed your Grandma's neck, they left thorns of microscopic size behind, many, many of them, and they're burrowing deeper down her neck as we speak, slowly but steadily."

My own heart seemed to skip a beat. "Oh no. Is it hurting Grandma?"

"I'm not sure about that."

"Okay. So how can we get rid of them? We should get rid of them, right?"

The surface of the orange bubble trembled. "Yes. But I'm not sure if we can pluck hundreds of them in time…"

"Oh." I swallowed with an effort. Hundreds of thorns to take care of? That was impossible—at least for me. My life was at stake here, too, yes, but imagining these thorns, most likely poisonous thorns, cutting her into tatters…

"I have a pet," A/E declared.

My tears retracted for a moment. "Huh?"

"It's a worm. Polyesterworm. PETworm. I didn't intend the pun."

I stared at her.

A sharp chip of stone bounced off the top of her head-bubble, almost penetrating the orange layer. "All right. I did intend that pun. I smuggled one of them from the moon of the manufacturing station in the sash-like galaxy right outside the three-twenty-fifth portal of—"

"A/E, sorry, I'm no good with maps; that's for Grandma."

"Oh. Anyway, I put it in a cage that prevents it from growing, so it would keep my company for a long time. I thought it was a good idea at the time—worms don't bark so they're easier to smuggle, and PETworms are engineered worms and they eat just about anything."

I nodded slowly, not quite certain if I was following.

"I love it immensely. But the more I love it, the more worried I am, that I'm stealing its time by stopping its growth."

"Oh."

"So I'm going to set it free. And ask it to help us."

Following A/E's instructions I went out to the back garden, where it was cooler and damper than the front. I cut a patch of moss off the ground and placed it on a saucer. A/E detached a portion of her head-bubble and made it land on the soft surface of the moss.

She then deflated her main head-bubble, and once again I went into A/E's house via Grandma's unconscious projection. When I got to her place, A/E was cradling a sphere woven with dry vine, which looked like a tight rattan ball. Inside it was a little white worm, apparently asleep. It looked like a whiter, harder version of a silkworm. I wished I could have touched it.

She shook a branch of dried flower my way. "This is its favorite flower. You boil the water and let it cool, and then immerse the petals for a minute in that water. And place those watery petals along the edge of your grandma's severed neck."

"And what's that for?"

"For PET to start eating the flesh there. It wouldn't know the meat there is for it to eat if we simply placed it on her neck. It will start eating the petals first and then go on to eat the infected flesh, along with the tiny thorns."

"You are going to feed it with Grandma!?"

"Easy—just a little bit! And we'll return that flesh right back to her soon."

"W-what do you mean?"

"We will use the threads out of PET's cocoon and make a little neckpiece for her. That way the thorns can no longer harm your grandma's body. But we'll need to make the neckpiece really nice and pretty—like a very exquisite collet for a precious stone. She's been away from her body for too long and the shape of her neck will also have been altered slightly, so she'll need a very good reason to come back to it."

I scratched my chin, rotating there slowly. "I don't think she's the type to care about decorations. Not like you."

A/E rolled her eyes. "Are you nuts? Her garden is so meticulously planned, she'll be real mad if we try to make her wear something crude. Can you make lace?"

"Yeah, I'll manage." Grandma had taught me how. "Hey, but… that will end up with a dead moth, right? Silkworms die after turning into moths—they cannot eat or fly."

A/E made a face. "You really don't pay attention, do you? You think the manufacturer station folks would engineer such a feeble, inconvenient thing? Of course PET will live after making a polyester cocoon, and it can fly to mate many times later. Folks even use the PET poop as fuel." Then she sobered. "Hey—can you take PETmoth with you, when we've solved our problems? Take it to a planet where it can mate?"

I blinked; that sounded sweet, and sad, at the same time. "But why don't you do that yourself? It's your pet."

She shook her head behind my amber lens. "You have a better garden. I cannot keep PET here once it starts flying."

"I see." I *could* see—there was no real garden in her globe, no bushes to hide in, no branches to rest upon. "Okay. I promise to find the best world for it," I said, but realized my mistake even before A/E made a face. I tried again: "I promise I'll do my very best to take it to the best world I can manage to find for it." Our travels were weird and there was no guarantee for anything even if we had the exact coordinates—there was too much room for error. You do not make promises when you know the odds aren't exactly in your favor.

A/E nodded. "Thanks. And this will be good for my problem, too. Would you give me some of your grandma's dried herbs, please? I'll make some incense cones using them, together with the bay tree bark that I have in stock, and PET's last poop before cocoon. PET's poop will make a very good kindling, and here I need a very fast, sudden burst of heat. After the prototype incense is confirmed to work, I'd like to consult with your grandma about more optimal portions of the herbs."

"And what do the herbs do here?"

"Are you crazy? I'm burning bug poop inside a closed environment!"

My turn to make a face. "Okay, okay. And the resulting incense will help you how?"

"The heat will make the globe material soft, and the outgas will inflate that degraded part. That will work at least for the time I need to find a place to get proper repair work."

"All right, then. Let's get to work," I said.

A/E sent the sling with the flower and the sphere cage up to our house—they were small enough to physically pass through Grandma. When I poked my finger into the cage, I found that PETworm wasn't exactly hard, but felt somewhat drier to the touch than a normal silkworm. I set the sphere cage with PET still inside on the edge of Grandma's neck—it took me a while to balance it there, but once I'd got it settled, more or less, PET started nibbling on the flower petals that I'd placed, as A/E had told me it would, through a gap in the cage. When the petal beneath one gap was consumed, PET moved on to do the same with the next, moving along Grandma's severed neck that way, like some kind of small circus attraction. It was cute to watch, and I could understand A/E's fondness for it, perhaps.

When it had eaten all the petals like that, it went on to actually nibble at Grandma's flesh. After going over the flesh two rounds, PET stopped eating and just lay there, as if it knew there was no more for it to eat. I lifted the cage, and as soon as I cut it open with Grandma's scissors, the time that A/E had been holding back for the worm started overflowing, and I was barely prepared when it spit out its last poop as a worm, just before producing its cocoon material in a frenzied burst. I panicked for a moment, but then managed to place PET in a small wooden box which had once housed Grandma's collection of shell buttons, where it started wrapping itself happily. Using A/E's sling I sent the mini-ramekin holding PETpoop down to her house, along with Grandma's dried herbs. The ramekin was Grandma's favorite. I decided to tell her that I broke it and got rid of it while she was unconscious.

In no time at all PET was wrapped neatly in a slightly gray lump of threads. I took the cocoon into my hand, and for a moment, it felt so wrong to wake it up so soon. But PETmoth started wriggling inside as if wanting out. I found a place where I could start unraveling it, and pulled gently.

Its thread could be used without spinning, so I got to work right away with tatting. The more thread I used, the thinner the cocoon became, and I could soon see the moth well enough—now its wings looked actually hard, just like the material of a plastic bottle. PETmoth didn't even have to wait for its wings to dry. It flapped them once, twice, and then took off.

Then I wrapped my lace around Grandma's neck and cradled her swollen head in my arms. "Will this work?" I asked the orange bubble on the moss on the saucer when I had placed Grandma's head on the decorated neck.

"It should, though it might take time for her to kick in," said A/E, through the bubble, who had been quiet with her own craft of incense making. "Meanwhile, I might experiment with a tiny portion of my prototype incense. Shout if you need me."

"Okay. Good luck."

I sat down beside the immobilized Grandma, with A/E's small bubble between us. Grandma's hair was still a bit damp, and she didn't even blink. First thing when she woke up, I'd tell her how kind A/E had been, how helpful. They might get along with each other. Then, maybe we—

But at that moment, there was a strange lurch to the whole house, and it was A/E who shouted, not me: "Hey! I have a problem!"

"What? A/E, what's wrong?"

"The incense worked, and the globe material looks good as new—"

"Then what *is* the problem?"

The bubble on the moss shook so badly that I was afraid it might break any moment. "The force from the inflation," said A/E, breathless. "It was much stronger than I expected, and it pushed your globe away from mine! Now we're going farther and farther away from each other!"

I crawled to a window and looked out, and saw A/E outside her small house, near the part where the globe material had been degraded and welded to ours. She was right—our distance was widening at a surprising speed. How could mere incense do this? We should have consulted Grandma before the experiment.

Too late for should-haves—there was no way of stopping our globe. Grandma was still dormant, and I was helpless, hopeless, a speck of nothing in the vast expanse of nothingness.

"A/E!" I shouted, at the top of my lungs, so that my voice would reach the small bubble in the other room, even as I watched her go. "A/E," I said again, and the words after that—I hesitated, because of course, *of course* we don't make promises we cannot keep.

But A/E broke the rule herself, without hesitation. "I'll find you!" she said, her voice a shriek but strangely firm. "I'll find you, and we'll meet—"

And then, the orange bubble popped in the next room. There was only silence, for a long time.

I realized tears were streaking down my face. They were choking me and I had to gasp in fits, so it took me a long time to realize there was another gasping in the house. A few moments later the other gasps turned into a succession of sneezes.

I snapped out of my misery. "Grandma?"

"What are these spores doing in my house?" She sneezed some more. "Hold on. I'll adjust the gravity first."

Sure enough, the house slowly tilted back to its upright position. I wiped my tears on my shirt, stood up, and trotted to the other room. She was there—cocking her head this way and that, as if her neck was stiff.

"Grandma!" I almost flung myself at her, stopping myself at the last minute. "Grandma!!"

She laughed her booming laugh. "Easy! Oh well, this head is a complete mess, isn't it?" She lifted her head and placed it on the table, and walked blindly to the sink. And out of the space under it, she produced another head and put it on her neck.

"But Grandma, I'm sure I looked there. I looked everywhere for your other heads."

With her hipster-glasses head, she grinned at me. "Don't you dare assume you have access to all of my pockets." Then she touched her neck and went to look in the mirror. "Hm. I like this neckpiece. Your make?"

"Yes, Grandma." I felt a lump in my throat, and my eyes stung. "A friend helped. She's gone."

Grandma raised her brow.

I wiped my eyes with a sleeve. "Anyway. What happened? Was that vine sent by our pursuers?"

"Our pursuers?" Her eyes clicked. "Oh, no, no. It was just some failsafe function of the universe."

"Huh?"

She adjusted her avant-garde eyewear with the tinted lenses. "This is a wormhole that connects to many crazy places, yes? Worlds and dimensions, and even futures and pasts. Accidents always happen. Only one version of one entity should be in one place at a time; otherwise they'd topple the balance of the universe. So the universe just deactivates one of those versions of the same entity if they accidentally emerge in the same space."

I tried to place her words carefully in my head—but none of them made sense. I stared blankly at her.

Grandma rolled her eyes. "Anyway. Let's tidy up first. We have a lot of it to do."

"Now?" I protested, irritated and happy at the same time. "Can't we take a little break? Just a little? I badly need proper tea."

"No. We need to take inventory of the damage first. When it is done, I'll make you a very, very nice cup of tea, served with *biscuits*. I promise."

"Promise?" I asked.

"Yes. And I have never made a promise that I couldn't keep."

And then… she cocked her head in a strange way, as if savoring the feel of her new neckpiece. Her eyes glinted behind the honey-colored glasses—amber too red, like ember. At the corner of each lens, a bug that was reflected there flapped its wings. She raised a brow. "You have company."

I looked back over my shoulder. A moth with plastic wings came gliding in the air, slowly, and perched on my head, its fluffy polyester belly a soothing touch there.

I swallowed, my eyes stinging. "Grandma. Meet our new crew member, PETmoth."

# THE SET

## EUGEN BACON

**Jabari wished** his life was more interesting. He wished he could have an adventure just once, but no. He worked in radio, and you know what people said about radio people. The voice of an archangel, the face even a mother cannot love. Voice of an archangel was for him a stretch. And he definitely wore a face a mother struggled with.

He thought of his chin – no – that was his nose. He tried a smile in the mirror of his mind's eye, and all he saw was a snarl, empty eyes. Didn't his mother put him in a basket, place it on a doorstep for the Brothers of St Vincent to find? Same brothers who tried to rub onto him vocation, thinking that a motherless child was destined to heal others with the fingers of a god? Not with that smile, no. Salvation came in the choir. Jabari didn't question much, and when someone put him in the choir, he stayed in it. To his astonishment, he found that he could sing like a Tickell's blue flycatcher (without its colourful personality), and that is what earned him the brothers' fresh butter, lemons and honey to encourage a radio voice.

Now grown, Jabari saw his life in monochrome along the borders of a photograph. And it was digital – easily blurred, brushed, filtered, soft-edged or made transparent on a resizable canvas that could rotate or flip in pixel. If his life were a film, his footage would be a deleted scene in a documentary, never certainty or a prayer – where was hope? He was unimportant, a moment cluttered on a high shelf no one would notice. He was a line, gobbled thin and bounded by gaps in a fissure between now and then. He was a memory, shuffled and mismatched.

In this monochrome, a low-flying gull *kraa*-ed an unfamiliar ballad and dropped a piece of cellophane on Jabari's face. That was *all* the lens would remember: a seagull regurgitating cellulose that was permeable to air and water. The photo would never remember him, Jabari; what he was on the inside, or how he felt all the time – as if there was a taxi outside that had been waiting, clocking up stories all his life from the day he passed through a birth canal.

This is what Jabari was thinking at 5.43 a.m. precisely, lying inside a blanket on his bed – despite the alarm's wail at 5 a.m. sharp, which was an anomaly. He always set it for 6.30 a.m. He swung a leg and hit his toe against a wall. It appeared that overnight his house had turned. He smiled wryly. Was his self so bad, even the house turned away from it? Because that was the only way he could explain the difference.

*Who was he?* Jabari asked himself today, as he did other days. *Why was he?*

He hugged his knee, caressed the throbbing big toe, and glared at the damn wall. If someone snatched his personal space and put it on daytime TV, it would only exist as a scrolling ticker low on a screen in font so tiny you squinted to see it. Or as unnoticeable remnants of a soap opera played backwards with silent ads and bloopers: *Cut! Roll back!*

If he became a fly between now and everything else, would anyone notice?

Today, the shower was not right either. Jabari squealed when a squirt of scald came out where normally it spewed tepid. And the fridge! It wouldn't budge until he opened it from the right – which was pretty startling in itself.

Despite these mishaps, he was ready for his radio show. He'd already emailed the song sequence to Lamb, the sound guy at the studio:

1. "My Country" by Jamilla

2. "You Have the Roar" by Wolfbane

3. "Kwacha Kwacha" by Ingoma, his favourite by far: sweet chimes of the kora, the accompaniment of the mbira, a thumb piano, and the *tapee-tadoo-dah* of the djembe – tuned skin and rope – ushering gods with a drumbeat…

He'd also recorded his interviews with the show's special guests:

1. Shallow Feels – Jabari had tried to ask the muso hard questions about his anti-vaxxer stance. He (Jabari, not Feels) came out a bit inept. But it was a slot filler.

2. Ingoma – talking about her inspiration behind "Kwacha Kwacha", and she was ace because a) she just was b) he liked her nose ring and shaven head and c) he was impressed by the "wise" about social justice, female empowerment – the girl from the village shaking the universe kind of thing – that came out of her mouth.

He had the show order all good in his head, and in the radio planner he'd saved into the programmer. The show would start with "My Country", then a news-in-brief segment, already summarised on cue cards. He'd then play "You Have the Roar", followed by the Shallow Feels interview. Then "Kwacha Kwacha" and, finally, the Ingoma interview and a closing news summary.

Before going to the studio, he did his normal walk in the botanical gardens. He was startled that, today, there was nothing normal about the garden. First, gates that were meant to be spear-headed wrought-iron in black were now a towering platinum monolith with auto-sensors that let him through. Second, all walking paths were in sharp angles, not their normal sweep of arcs and curves. Third, the lawns were too manicured: he could have sworn they were artificial. His mental count of anomalies went on. He met no people walking toddlers or dogs. The signpost to the Visitor Centre pointed backwards. Instead of the herb garden, there was a fern gully trail. And where a visitors' café once stood was a shallow lake. He didn't mind that the café was gone – it promised a platinum experience, but the coffee there was borderline shit. You took one sip of it and spat because it tasted like something straight off a wombat's butt. Yeah, he wouldn't miss the café, but still!

And those weren't the only anomalies he saw. There were no bins – no yellows for recycled. He neared the spot where the bins once stood, squealed and fell back as a maw opened from the ground and nearly took him. Rattled, he looked around at a treeless garden shorn of acacias, banksias and eucalypti. There were no everyday sounds of honeyeaters, magpies, cockatoos or galahs, but near a brand-new water fountain he'd never seen before stood a goggle-eyed tramp bird that studied him. It was a bulbous-headed parrot-cum-pig with a puffed-out breast and spindly legs. Its pink tongue dangled out of the side of its closed beak. The bird hissed, barked and cackled at him and Jabari hurried away.

On his way out of the garden he should have encountered the herbarium, but in its stead stood a high-rise blinker steepling into the heavens. Jabari's knees gave, but he was unwilling to sit on the new bouncy enviro-cushies in jacaranda, framboise and tuberose colours that had replaced plain army-green park benches. He walked briskly out of the gardens through the discomfiting auto-sensor monoliths, and attempted his normal coffee stop before work.

But there was nothing normal about the coffee or the stop. Every day the sign read: *Stories So Far*. Today it read: *Stories About Us*.

He was glad to see the board was still there: *Specialty coffee, bar and bottle shop*.

What surprised him was that the café was in the exact location it should be, but it now stood next to a carpark he'd never seen. He tried not to question it. Not far was a metro hub, an industry training centre he'd also never seen. Jabari figured what the hub was from the signage, and the students spilling out of it. His normal café was supposed to be ensconced in an apartment building, an arched doorway leading to it. It held a homely tightness about it, and you could get a real liquored – not flavoured – affogato. You could ask for premium tea or coconut milk. Its wall rack was craftily arrayed with vintage wine. He hadn't bought the shiraz, but had taken a loaf of rye, raisin, orange and fennel sourdough bread, and a bottle of pure sparkling water from the little black fridge. Today, there was no fridge in sight. The barista used almond milk for his fresh chai latte – Jabari took one sip of it and spat. Who used fucking almond milk in a chai latte? He marched outside, chucked the lot and instead ordered (and paid again for) a hot chocolate for himself and a skinny latte for his co-producer, Moha.

Moha was clarified butter, and Jabari was hopelessly in love. He did this all the time: wrap his heart around a beautiful, soulful thing that didn't exist because people could never love him back. He created things that were perfect in his head, but that kind of perfection did not exist. Already he had been abandoned in childhood by his own *mother*, and all his life he carried this deep and terrible fear of abandonment to such extent that his life was vanilla. Everybody loved vanilla. Mint was a risk. Buttered pecan was a risk. Cookie dough was a risk. But who the fuck didn't like vanilla? He liked to imagine Moha as the exquisite Madagascan kind, subtly floral and indulgently creamy.

He walked out of the spacious, not homely tight, café holding
Moha's coffee in a Styrofoam cup. He contemplated his anomalous
morning, baffled at the deforming and distorting all around him,
and looked back to the night before…

•  •  •

Jabari had first watched the news – a shooting in a suburb and all
that shit – as he ate a burger with the lot. He watched a sitcom on TV,
and liked how Doreen, his fave on the cast, talked:

"We here…"

"They tooks…"

Doreen looked a bit like Moha with her smooth cheekbones,
sophisticated, intimate eyes and blonde-tinted braids. He imagined
going to a *doof doof* with Doreen (or Moha), somewhere with a
smooth-wand DJ zinging top cunt-mixers like a wizard. He saw
himself sipping highball cocktails of shaken rum, sugar, lime and
mint.

But the last time he'd tried a night out, it was at a club called
District, patrons constantly vaping and smoking darts. A bunch of
tossers acting butch, but they were all pussies, didn't like his face
and were too soaked in booze to be subtle about it. He reckoned
that if he got any of them solo, they'd cave. Jabari left and went to
a pub where he played pool, until some drunk idiot with missing
front teeth and swearing "Fahkin' hell" began causing trouble and
calling Jabari a dog cunt. It wasn't just a vibe. It lost Jabari the sweet
on night outs, and that was that. Still, it was the most excitement
he'd ever had.

He switched to the sports channel, watched a bit of the Sydney-
to-Hobart sailing race, looked at different boats and how they were
named *Scallywag, Gunn Runner, Fruit Gambo, Joyride*… He wanted to give
himself a joyride without having to become a skipper on a 15m sail.

Jabari switched channels again and was watching cricket – Aussies trouncing the Poms – when first the TV then the house wobbled.

• • •

Now Jabari walked towards the studio, finishing his hot chocolate. The morning was white and sunny. A crisp, cooling breeze touched the nape of his neck just so. Studio 59 was a ground-level building near a crossing. It was embossed with a Jupiter symbol, a hieroglyph of an eagle: a curled letter Z with a line drawn through it. It stood next to a bank ATM. A black-framed glass wall allowed you to look inside – well-lit and furnished in accent chairs and charcoal pillows.

Jabari peered inside. Cellar pendant chandeliers interspersed with smoked-glass chandeliers splashed their light onto a mid-century fireplace, all Romeo. He looked at his watch – 8 a.m. sharp. He swiped his staff card on the reader.

The door swung open, and he entered.

• • •

**Scene 1.**

**INT. PRODUCTION STUDIO—EARLY MORNING**

No Trackie Dacks in Here

*The studio interior is in classic neutral colours – modern, inviting. A lit sign says:* THE WEEKLY SET. *Another red flasher says:* ON AIR.

There's a poster of a movie actress standing in pose against a sportscar. She is holding a cigar, a wisp of smoke wafting from her Monroe kissy-mouth in photographic freeze.

*Centre stage is transitional furniture – suited for a home office and includes a koala sofa set in greys and creams. It's the kind you look at its comfort and want to touch your head on it.*

The cameraman, BOYLE, *is behind a pedestal. A flood of lights is angled towards the koala sofa facing a teleprompter. The soundman* LAMB's *headphones are dangled across his neck.*

The producer, MOHA, *is restless and holding a clipboard. She looks up as* JABARI *enters.*

JABARI: (*Smiling shyly at* MOHA) I brought you a skinny latte. (*Offering her the coffee*)

MOHA: (*Tossing her braids, snapping the coffee from his hands*) This is going to be a ripper. (*Eyeing him up and down, frowning at his tracksuit and runners*) You well know you're darn late. A fucking latte won't get me happy! And what the blitz are you wearing?

JABARI: (*Puzzled*) I don't know what's all the fuss for a radi—

MOHA: (*Turning to the costume girl*) New wardrobe, Gigi!

*Heavily mascaraed* GIGI *is wearing her short crop dyed cyan. Wordlessly, she leads* JABARI *out of the set and into a room labelled:* MAKE-UP.

## Scene 2.

### INT. PRODUCTION STUDIO

Where the Fuck Is Radio?

JABARI *emerges from the make-up room dressed in a sky-coloured suit, double-breasted and made of textured wool.*

GIGI *is arranging the collar of his sleek coral button-down shirt of Egyptian cotton, all tucked in. She straightens a lavish platinum tie in silk twill.*

*He looks at his watch and is surprised that the time is still on 8 a.m., although the second hand is still ticking.*

JABARI: (*Entering the studio set*) The runners—

MOHA: No one will be looking at your goddamn feet.

JABARI *sits on the high stool centre stage.*

GIGI *dabs more powder on his nose.*

*There's a large screen on the far side of the room. JABARI sees himself on it, a ticker with ads running at the bottom of the screen.*

JABARI: (*Surprised*) Why? It's TV—

MOHA: (*Rolling her eyes*) Seriously?

JABARI: (*Raising his palms in a sign of peace*) Can I have some water?

GIGI *hands him a filled glass.*

BOYLE *winks and repositions the camera.*

LAMB *puts on the headphones, gives a thumbs up.*

*Lights come up.*

MOHA: (*Raising the clipboard*) And action!

*(Techno music playing)*

JABARI: (*Puzzled*) That's not Jamilla's "My Country".

MOHA: (*Lowering the clipboard*) And cut! (*Glaring at JABARI*). The hell!

JABARI: I emailed the song order…

MOHA: We don't do song orders. The theme song for *The Set* is always "Street Ace".

JABARI: (*Frowning*) I don't know about "Street Ace". It sounds like yowling cats and farting alpacas.

MOHA: Gee, thanks.

JABARI: I don't question much, but if you didn't like what I sent earlier…

MOHA: Jesus Christ!

JABARI: (*Shrugging*) Oh, never mind. (*Straightens his posture and looks at the camera*)

MOHA: (*Raising the clipboard*) And action!

*(Techno music playing)*

JABARI: (*Reading from his cue cards*) Welcome to *The Set*. We're live from Melbourne. It's another record day—

MOHA: (*Lowering the clipboard*) And cut! (*Looking angrily at JABARI*). The fuck are you doing?

JABARI: The usual?

MOHA: (*Angrily snatching* JABARI*'s cue cards, drops them on the floor*) Look straight ahead and read the fucken teleprompter. (*Raising the clipboard*) And action!

(*Techno music playing*)

JABARI: (*Reading the teleprompter*) The crypto bank has announced a rollout of new loans for first-time homebuyers... The world is in a state, with a new strain of the mutant virus body-jumping and causing premature conception in women, mostly quadruplet babies, even in sterilised people. (*Briefly glances in puzzlement at* MOHA, *but continues to read*) There is major concern that the virus is especially targeting women on contraception, triggering panic across the globe. The US is no longer accepting flights to or from South Africa, where scientists first discovered the new virus strain that is contagious by human touch, skin to skin...

JABARI *scratches his head at how unreal this all sounds. He casts a beseeching look at* MOHA, *who gives him a stone face.*

JABARI: (*Continues reading the teleprompter*) Pharmaceuticals companies globally are scrambling to develop a vaccine to curb the baby pandemic in an already crowded world. Airline passengers are hurting with a soaring number of cancelled flights, following an increase in positive cases among crew. Testing centres are struggling to cope with the surge as women scramble for testing. In other news, anti-vaxxers are still protesting worldwide. Let's take a look...

*The large monitor shows a congregation of angry people chanting and roaring, "Stop the fib!" They are swaying placards saying, VACCINE GUMBO, MANDEMIC PANDEMIC... The scene repeats with crowds in London, Sydney, Nairobi, Luxemburg, Dodoma, Lagos, Delhi, Paris...*

MOHA: (*Lowering the clipboard*) And cut!

JABARI *is relieved to leave the set and find a toilet. He frowns as*

*he discovers the men's is not at its usual place, two doors left, but*
*rather down the corridor where the fire-exit door normally stands.*
*He hurries out of the toilet and blinks in surprise that he's suddenly*
*barefoot and wearing torn trousers and no shirt. He steps through a*
*door and...*

**Scene 3.**
**INT. PRODUCTION STUDIO**

It's a Bloody Comedy

*... JABARI steps onto a new stage now decorated to resemble a desert*
*island: fake palm trees and a beach.*

*(Crow squawking)*

*(Monkeys jabbering in the distance)*

*To the side is a door that leads to the stage with a live audience.*

*A large clock on the wall behind the live audience says it's 8 a.m.*

GIGI *dabs more powder on* JABARI*'s nose. She opens a make-up kit.*

JABARI: (*Quickly*) No mascara, thanks.

BOYLE *winks and repositions the camera.*

LAMB *wearing the headphones, gives a thumbs up.*

JABARI *opens the side door and lights fade on.*

MOHA *approaches him, wearing a sisal skirt and stringed coconut*
*husks covering her breasts.*

MOHA: Thank Fonz you're here!

JABARI: (*Surprised*) Wow.

*(Live audience laughing)*

JABARI: I've always loved this show. Ever wondered who the heck this
Fonz is that they keep thanking? I never for a minute imagined I'd
find myself in one of their skits.

MOHA: (*Fourth-wall performance*) Babe, we're on set. (*Speaking*
*loudly, pointedly*) THANK FONZ YOU'RE HERE!

*(Live audience laughing)*

JABARI *gets into character, tilts his chin in a flirty way.*

JABARI: I like to arrive the way cats do.

MOHA: (*Coyly*) Purring, rubbing and swaying your tail?

JABARI: (*Smiling*) Bet it ties your tongue, hey.

MOHA: It does, but don't mind me – I'm just a fragment.

JABARI: I don't know what the heck that means, but I likey. A lot.
(*Winking at live audience*)

(*Live audience laughing*)

JABARI: (*Sniffing in* MOHA*'s direction*) Your perfume...

MOHA: Wild rose – I bet it's confounding.

JABARI: Makes my bones ache... the inner sea... this is disaster.
(*Grabs* MOHA*'s hand*) But you, darling, make it all better when you—
(*Approaching drumbeats*)

(*Tarzan howl that grows loud, louder*)

JABARI: Babe, what the hell is that?

MOHA: The musicality of fiction that will set you free. Which reminds
me – come! (*Tugging him towards the edge of the setting*)

JABARI: Oooh, but where—

MOHA: In your absence, as you were gallivanting to god-knows-where,
leaving me ALL ALONE, (*Dramatic pause*) I discovered a circumcision
tree!

JABARI: (*Dragging his feet*) A what?! (*Pulling away from her grip*)

(*They vanish from view, but the live audience can still hear them*)

JABARI: There's no anaesthetic!

MOHA: (*Firmly*) Just dip that dongle in the calming water. That's what
the Bantu men in East Africa do. Ice-cold water for anaesthetic.

JABARI: This here is not ice-cold – it's fucking tropical!

MOHA: Yes, and it's salty. Now, sweetheart, drop those pants.

JABARI: (*Gut-wrenching man howl*)

(*Live audience laughing*)

MOHA: Shhhh! You'll wake the big fat crocs, and with all that blood...

Let's dip into the salty water, shall we? Healing properties, and all.

(Sound of MOHA and JABARI entering the water)

JABARI: (Gut-wrenching banshee howl)

(Live audience laughing)

(Clapping)

MOHA: (Offset, to the production crew) And cut!

MOHA and JABARI return on stage, JABARI hobbling with a large patch of fake blood on his crotch. They hold hands and take their bows as the live audience claps and whoops.

JABARI approaches MOHA outside the set.

JABARI: (Grinning wide) That was fun! I can't believe I was just on Thank Fonz You're Here.

MOHA: (Frowning) Fuck's wrong with you? (Turning away from him)

JABARI wonders woefully what is happening. Where is his normal life? The set is suddenly too claustrophobic, and JABARI wants to be back in the dirt. He walks quickly out of the studio and...

## Scene 4.

### EXT. EXOTIC BEACH

A Friggin' Love Paradise

(Cheery islander drumbeats)

JABARI steps out of a beach hut and onto a private islet all tropical and near the sea. He blinks in astonishment at the real outside world, no longer on set at the studio. He's barefoot and wearing fire-wave swim shorts in tangerine and black.

He looks at the golden sand and beach huts all around, lights up when he sees GIGI and MOHA.

Heavily mascaraed GIGI is dipping her toes by the side of a turquoise pool in a sweeping curl around palm-tree islands. She's tits out, wearing cyan-dyed hair and only a dive bikini bottom in a red and white passion blend, string ties on the side. She is holding a fizzy *drink in a champagne flute garnished with a sliced berry.*

MOHA *is sprawled on a swaying hammock. She is wearing a neon bikini outside a magnificently tanned body.*

*(Splashing water on a fountain near the pool)*

*(Cockatiel whistling, smooth and sweet)*

BOYLE *winks and repositions the camera from a distance.*

LAMB *puts on the headphones, gives a thumbs up.*

JABARI *approaches the girls, wondering how he got onto a* Love Island *skit.*

GIGI: (*Sarcastic, from a distance, to* MOHA) Here comes your *boyfriend*. He's all yours. Sorry for dumping him on you.

MOHA: (*Sarcastic laugh*) Really? Wow.

GIGI: Yeah. Give him your rose at the ceremony tonight, 'cos he's not getting mine.

MOHA: Like, why not? You worked so hard to pull that dick move last night. How do you think that made me feel?

JABARI: I don't know what you're talking about. Where are you getting this dick move shit from? (*To* GIGI) Nothing happened between us! (*To* MOHA) Honest.

MOHA: Like I care.

JABARI: (*Glaring at* GIGI, *then softly, to* MOHA) Don't listen to her, babe. She's bat-shit crazy.

GIGI: (*To* MOHA) He leaves you on read every day. I can show you the text messages he's been sending me.

MOHA: That's so fucked up.

GIGI: Him, or you? What's more fucked is if you get pregnant with a cheater. He'll do everything in his power to make sure that baby never gets born.

MOHA: (*Yelling angrily*) I am not pregnant! And he loves me!

GIGI: (*Eyeing* JABARI *in disdain*) Last night didn't seem like it. I think he's ditched you like a sack of bricks.

MOHA: (*Crying*)

JABARI: (*Putting his arms around* MOHA) I didn't ditch you! I love you!

MOHA: (*Shrugging off his touch, continues crying*)

*It dawns on* JABARI *that this is reality TV, not a skit, and the emotions are real. He'd craved for adventure, but this? This?*

JABARI: (*Looking angrily at* GIGI) Happy with yourself now? (*Down on his knees and wrapping his arms around* MOHA) Babe—

MOHA: (*Muffled*) Fuck off, yeah. Don't act so angry. You've kinda become a dick.

GIGI: (*Shouting at* JABARI) And I meant every word! You're not getting a fucking rose from me tonight.

JABARI *walks away, glum.*

*He enters his cabin, sits on the bed. He rubs his temples, lies down and closes his eyes.*

JABARI: (*Uncharacteristic shouting at the ceiling*) It's meant to be a fucking radio show!

(*Wobbling sound*)

JABARI *sits up, startled, as the bed humps and wobbles. The cabin begins to shake violently as if a griffin is having at it. The beach hut suddenly topples.*

(JABARI *screeching*)

JABARI *clutches about wildly as he slides downwards and slams his head against a topsy-turvy roof or a wall. He crawls to what might be a window, bashes it open with his feet and...*

## Scene 5.

### EXT. TROPICAL JUNGLE—MORNING

Effin' Jungle Survivor Shit

... JABARI *rolls out of a tilted shipwreck and plunges headfirst into a thick jungle, eerie with wilderness.*

*(Tiger growling)*

*(The cry of a howler monkey)*

*A black eagle soars overhead.* JABARI *sees a tiger loping down a tree out yonder. He cries out in alarm and jumps at a rustle.*

*(Deer honking in the distance)*

JABARI *turns towards the rustling sound and sees to his left a python wrapping itself around a forest antelope.*

*Up on a hill from a distance,* JABARI *makes out two shapes watching, perhaps filming.*

*He sees* MOHA *and* GIGI *up on a fat oak in what seems to be a treehouse. They are dressed in combat gear matching what he's wearing.*

GIGI*'s face is covered in war paint. She is sharpening a tomahawk against a stone.* MOHA *is holding a machine gun.*

JABARI *plods across mud and shrubbery in army boots and clambers up the tree.* MOHA *offers him a helping hand. A dog-like gruff-gruff of a hornbill echoes through the jungle.*

GIGI: (*Scornful*) What's with the poo face?

JABARI: Yeah. I was born with it, like seriously.

MOHA: (*Glaring at* GIGI) That's just being a dick, mate. We need to be united.

JABARI: The fuck is this place?

MOHA: (*Pointing at a weapons cache spilling with machine guns, katanas, throwing axes, pistols, rifles, sabres and grenades*) The right question is the fuck can you use these?

JABARI: The hell! I mean, adventure and all, I'd take monochrome any time. Not this! Can someone just delete this scene?

GIGI: Better try at least one weapon, 'cos I don't see you at any moment doing praying-mantis-kick-type shit if it came to hand-to-hand.

*(High-pitched cry of a tapir, like the sound of a car braking)*

*(Growling, close now)*

*The three of them look in alarm in the direction of the jungle.*

MOHA: (*Pointing the machine gun*) I guess we're all going to die, but we might as well die fighting.

HORNBILL: Rrro-rrho!

GIGI: (*Grinning maniacally*) 'Cos, like, why not?

JABARI: I'm getting outta here! War is not – is never my thing! And not with a goddamn jungle!

GIGI: Sure thing, pussy.

JABARI *grabs the nearest pistol and leaps down into the jungle. He starts running like mad towards the capsized ship in a murky river.*

(*Snake hissing*)

JABARI *screams as he catches sight of an anaconda slipping into the water. He fires wildly, a few nothing shots – he's not good with guns.*

HORNBILL: Rrraaa!

MOHA: (*Shouting to JABARI*) Wait for me, I'm coming!

MOHA *leaps down from the treehouse into the jungle and starts running through the water to join JABARI as he tries to climb back into the shipwreck.*

GIGI: Fucking jungle is a hive mind. (*Warning shout to MOHA*) It's comin' at ya!

(*Machine gun rattling*)

MOHA: (*Screaming*) Shit! Shit! It's the fucking anaconda! (*Beating at the anaconda with the butt of her gun*) Help!

JABARI *aims and fires another nothing shot.*

(*GIGI's war cry*)

GIGI *is striking air with her tomahawk, facing off with a crouching tiger up on the treehouse.*

(*MOHA's ear-piercing scream*)

JABARI *turns to see the anaconda wrapping itself around MOHA. The tiger leaps and topples GIGI under its weight.*

(*GIGI grunting*)

JABARI *turns and flees. All his life he's been abandoned. Now it's him doing the abandoning. He has a choice between saving* GIGI *or* MOHA, *and once upon a day he might have picked* MOHA. *But today he's choosing himself. The last thing he sees before he falls into the shipwreck is the tiger wrapping its jaws around* GIGI*'s head.*

*(Crunching sound)*

## Scene 6.
### INT. INSIDE THE SHIPWRECK

A Bloody Hole

*(Sound of sobbing)*

JABARI *huddles inside the shipwreck, arms around himself.*

*(Thump)*

*(Thump)*

*(Thump)*

*He cries out. Something big and keen wants to get in from the jungle and eat him alive.*

*(Rumbling sound)*

*The shipwreck wobbles.* JABARI *sees a hole for him to crawl in. It's not a hole; it's a cave. He sees the mouth of the cave and crawls out...*

## Scene 7.
### EXT. OUTSIDE THE STUDIO—EVENING

The Hell?!

*... * JABARI *rises to his feet and blinks at the onset of dusk outside the studio where it all began. He looks at his watch: it says 8 p.m. With a gulp, he breaks into a run.*

*He doesn't know where he's running to, just away from the goddamn studio, and...*

•••

He raced past his usual café, Stories So Far, with its sign that said: *Specialty coffee, bar and bottle shop* – not the fake Stories About Us near a metro hub. He turned into the botanical garden and was glad to see it back to normal with arcs and sweeps, nothing angled, and gates that were once again spear-head wrought-iron, no stupid platinum monoliths with auto-sensors.

But he couldn't trust its grass lawns, though they were real. He laughed out loud as he raced past a woman walking a dog, a man pushing a stroller. They both turned, looked at him as if he were mad. He didn't care, and waved, laughing louder now because the sign to the Visitor Centre was pointing the right way. And there, right there, was the herb garden, and the visitors' café with its wombat-butt latte. And bins! He stopped to touch a yellow one for recycling, held himself from kissing it in delirious relief. He nearly cried at the sight of the lofty banksias and fat oaks, oh, and all those eucalypti! He flopped onto an army-green park bench near the herbarium and hugged its back with his elbows.

He seriously questioned this godawful day and wondered what had happened to him. He considered if it was brain fade. He pondered if he'd gobbled some hallucinatory drugs overnight and had simply forgotten about them… He wondered if, when he got home, he'd find a copy of himself sleeping on his bed, oblivious to all that had happened, and perhaps he'd have a new friend who was his own self. But how would they coexist? The more he thought and thought, the less and less understanding came to him. So he altogether gave up trying to make sense of anything, or figuring it out.

He sat on the bench a long time, emptying his mind until he calmed.

He strolled out of the gardens… The street leading to his house was nowhere in sight. There were no streets. Just one long, empty road in the middle of nowhere.

"No, no!" he cried. If this was his life getting interesting, he didn't want it!

What he wanted was his old self that watched Doreen on sitcoms, caught up on sailing, trounced the Poms in cricket. He wanted his life back, to be the Jabari who worked in friggin' radio.

"No!" he cried one more time, and started running...

• • •

**Scene 8.**

**EXT. DESERTED TARMAC ROAD—NIGHT**

The Set

*... (Staccato pounding of running feet on gravel)*

*The zoom starts in his mind. First on a ticking clock in his head, and its hand is on 8 p.m. Suddenly he can see as if he's the man behind the camera. He zooms in on running feet, his, pound, pound, pound on an endless tarmac road. It zooms out to reveal*

*ankles, knees, torso*

*finally, the whole*

*of him furiously running*

*pound, pound, pound.*

*His expression brightens as the lens zooms away from him, locks in on a building in the distance. He knows the need. He runs faster, poundpoundpound. He's hoping, seriously hoping, that he's found the norm. He's hoping that it's home. He is the usual suspect, a part of something bigger – he just doesn't know what. But all he wants is to find a bed that's decent, to sleep and forget the nonsense that's just happened. He wants to watch cricket on a green wicket that's doing something. To see batsmen punchy on game, swinging balls both ways to four runs, four runs and a boundary.*

*To see bowlers drawing blood.*

*Good hands on the field...*

*He needs to know.*

*Poundpoundpound!*

*He tastes the salt of labour, a rewarding sweat, but his relief turns to dismay. He's circled right back to the studio, yet not. This one is a towered office complex near a bank ATM. It's embossed with Neptune's symbol, a trident of hidden depths. It stands next to an acoustic centre selling guitars in classics, electrics, even preowned vintages that beckon with accessories and guides. Unlike the real studio, the one he knows, the one with a black-framed glass wall*

*one can peer through*

*this studio is walled*

*he can't see*

*a damn thing.*

*Despite his loss, he now thinks that he doesn't have a staff card to swipe on the reader. But the studio anticipates him. It wobbles. Suddenly he can see through its walls, fading out from brick, fading into black-framed glass. He doesn't know if this is progress or rollback, if someone might cry: Cut! There's a poster, not of a movie actress with kissy lips blowing smoke from a cigar. It's an enlarged photo labelled: In Memoriam. MOHA and GIGI, each holding a champagne flute garnished with a strawberry, smiling at someone behind a camera at some event. MOHA – braids, smooth cheekbones, sophisticated, intimate eyes. GIGI – mascara-gobbled eyes, a short crop dyed cyan. JABARI is outside looking in.*

Chandelier light in the studio winks.

*(Creaking sound)*

The door s-w-i-n-g-s

O

P

E

N

# THERE IS A HOLE, THERE IS A STAR

## JEFFREY THOMAS

**Punktown was** an old city, so old that no one really referred to it by its actual name, Paxton, anymore except in an official context. So old that no one alive had lived in the town that had preceded Paxton, that had been overlaid and subsumed by it. That town had been inhabited only by the people indigenous to this world, the Choom, before the coming of the Earth colonists and thereafter by sentient races from many other planets. Today, not even the Choom use the name of the original, digested settlement. If you asked a kid in the street that town's name, whether the descendant of an Earth colonist or even a Choom, they might not be able to tell you. Would their own children one day have trouble summoning the name Paxton? And by what future appellation might Punktown be known?

The Choom town had been impressive in size by precolonial standards, but was so much smaller than present-day Punktown, and only quaint remnants of it existed in its original state, mostly concentrated toward Punktown's center. Here, red brick buildings of only a few stories huddled in the shadows of glassy titans, and occasional cobblestone lanes where vehicle traffic was prohibited so as to preserve them.

Just at the periphery of this red brick nucleus was the apartment building Nahool lived in, which had formerly been a Choom factory. Some of these historied structures had been renovated and commanded high rents, but if they were pearls in Punktown's tissues, Nahool's apartment building was more a gallstone. Its exterior walls were more grimy black than red, this layered with the graffiti of multiple generations in something like geological strata, the most recent graffiti being holographic and hovering inches from the brick, sometimes even traveling around and around the building at various rates of speed in a kind of orbit.

Generally, Nahool didn't mind the building's degree of decrepitude without and within; rent was affordable, considering its proximity to the generally more upscale historically preserved area, and she could easily walk to her job at one of the little clothing shops in the Salem Arcade mini-mall, instead of relying on public transit.

Still, there had been unpleasant incidents since she had moved into this neighborhood, but wouldn't there have been in any neighborhood of the city, no matter how exclusive? This was, after all, Punktown.

One evening, after stopping at a corner market for a few things on her walk home from work, a mutant high on purple vortex— its head faintly glowing red, the flesh looking like a loose bundle of towels—had accosted her in a demand for money, had tried to block her way to the front door, even grasping her arm. She had managed to jerk away, used her wrist comp's key feature to unlock the apartment building's front door, fled into the vestibule where the beggar-turned-mugger couldn't follow, but she had dropped her groceries in the scuffle.

Another time, right outside her apartment door as she was about to unlock it, again utilizing her wrist comp, a man she had noted only peripherally, whom she had thought meant only to walk along the hallway, lunged and seized her from behind, intending to rush her inside her own flat once the door slid aside. He was premature, however, and together they banged into the closed door, and they struggled and Nahool screamed. Her screaming and resistance drew out her neighbor across the way. She had never spoken with this woman before, except to exchange a hello when they passed each other in the hallway or in the basement laundry. Whereas Nahool was a Choom—who were nearly identical to the descendants of the Earth colonists, except for the wide mouths that extended almost to their ears, their jaws full of multiple rows of molars evolved for the mastication of their generally tough vegetable diet—her neighbor was an Earther, and a good-sized Earther at that, and she set upon Nahool's attacker and drove him off, bleeding from his nose. They never did learn how this man had gotten into the building; he apparently wasn't one of the tenants.

Nahool had tearfully and profusely thanked her neighbor. Despite that, however, they didn't so much as learn each other's name during their exchange, and thereafter simply returned to their habit of shy, quick greetings when their paths happened to cross.

• • •

When the event occurred, the news outlets asked, "Where were you when the Hole appeared?" A year later citizens would still be asking this of each other, comparing notes, the phrase having been imprinted in their minds, but right now it had less to do with spurring reminiscence and more to do with ascertaining the Hole's effects on people, and on structures, in regard to their proximity to the anomaly when it manifested.

In the days that followed, Nahool listened to news reports on VT and net sites, listened in on exchanges between fellow employees and customers at the Salem Arcade, and to conversations she overheard when buying a coffee or visiting that corner market.

She heard people relate where they had been when the Hole had appeared, and what effect it had had on them—or that they imagined it had had on them, at least. One man said his wife had left him the day after, without warning, without there having been any problems in their relationship. One woman said her cat had disappeared from her apartment, though she did admit there was an air duct in her flat that her pet had got into before, but this time the cat had not come back. Another person said they had discovered a fallen-away section of wall at the back of the cabinet under the kitchen sink, that they had never noticed before.

One of her coworkers asked her plainly, "What about you, Nah?" That was her coworkers' nickname for her, because she'd once happened to mention that Nah had been the nickname given to her by her former boyfriend, Myke, an Earther. Hearing herself called that was like a scab peeled off a deep red puncture, and she regretted having opened up about him at all, now.

Several pairs of eyes, some belonging to customers browsing garments on racks, swiveled to her then, and she quietly answered, "Oh, I just… I just had a nightmare that night. I don't usually have nightmares; or at least, I don't really remember them."

"What was it about?" her coworker persisted.

"Well… uh, I still don't remember much. People were walking around in the streets, crying, calling out for each other, like they were lost… or looking for loved ones who were lost. Everyone was naked. Me included."

"Nice," joked one of her other coworkers, Rhay.

She ignored him and went on. The more she related the dream, the more she saw it open up before her, like a film playing on a holographic screen that obscured her audience and thus made her less self-conscious. "Everything was dark, but not like night-dark. When I looked up, I saw an eclipse. These long beams of light shot out from behind the black moon or whatever it was that covered the sun." To express what she pictured, she raised one hand and spread her five fingers wide. "Down in the streets it was all foggy, too… or maybe it was smoke. People looked like ghosts unless you saw them up close. There were no lights on in the city; all the buildings were dark… like they were made of solid stone with no windows or doors. I was lost, too, and calling for someone, but… I don't know who I was calling for, if it was anyone in particular."

"Yeah," said Rhay, his tone more serious now. "Sounds like the wave from the Hole went through you, too. I heard other people had these weird nightmares where they were all disoriented and afraid."

"And lonely," said one of the customers, a Tikkihotto woman. Like the Choom, the Tikkihotto were one of the most Earth-like of sentient races, descendants of colonists like the Earthers, but rather than globular eyes, their skull sockets housed restless bunches of translucent ocular tendrils, and consequently their sense of sight was unrivaled, except for the similarly equipped animal life on their world.

The others all looked from Nahool to the Tikkihotto female now, with her agitated writhing eye tendrils and her bristly-short, violet-dyed haircut. The attention her impulsive comment had won her no doubt unsettled the Tikkihotto, because without another word she turned from the rack she'd been browsing through and left the clothing shop, with a few stray tendrils angled backwards to peek nervously at the others as she departed.

• • •

Not long after the appearance of the Hole, Nahool had gone with Myke to a birthday party for an old college friend of his, and she had been shyly taking in the conversation between some of the other partygoers, whom she had only met tonight, while Myke chatted heartily and drunkenly with a few men at the far end of the living room. In the gulf between them were intermittent tables laden with transportive substances, intermittent clusters of sweating young bodies. Nahool had glanced over at Myke, wanting to join him but afraid to disrupt that knot of men, and seen that he had set his bottle of Zub beer down on a side table and was bending over it as if to take the bottle neck deeply into his mouth, while hooking his fingers into the corners of his mouth to pull the ends back as far as they would go. He bobbed his head a few times. As he straightened up and unhooked his mouth, his friends convulsed with laughter, Myke shot a look her way and met her eyes, and his already small Earther's grin faded away altogether. Nahool had jerked her gaze away, her face flushed hot, returning to the conversation she had been listening in on before, without herself participating.

"How do we know that bubble or whatever it is will really hold the thing?" one young woman was saying to another, her eyes wide with alarm and alcohol. "*Right?* How do we know it won't get any bigger?"

"You don't think this thing is a black hole?" slurred a Choom male holding a little metal bulb of anodyne gas. He opened his great mouth wide to jet another spray against the back of his throat. The exaggerated wideness of his mouth made Nahool conscious of her own, though her jaws were presently clenched tight, too tight.

"Definitely not that," said someone else. "No, no, no. If that was a black hole, even if it's only the size of a… what did they say?"

"A human head."

"The second it opened up there'd be this burst of radiation that would've already killed us all, and… and… oh, no way. Even a black hole with the mass of only one blasting *millimeter* would have a mass about equal to a tenth of this planet! In no time this whole planet would be sucked up its own ass and *gone*, wanker!" A laugh that ejected spittle flavored with vodka. "We'd *already* be gone! We wouldn't *be* here! This conversation never *happened!*"

"It's a terrorist attack," someone else said gravely. "Red Jihad, man."

"Oh, come on with that Red Jihad dung," another partygoer scoffed. "They're long gone."

"Well someone else, then!"

"Wouldn't there be far easier ways to level Punktown without having to expend the energy to create a black hole?"

"It is *not* a blasting black hole!"

"It's purely an accidental thing, that maybe we're not meant to know," said a delicate-looking Earther man, with ghostly white flesh over seemingly glass-like bones, weaving on his feet with eyes half-focused. He had the holographic tattoo of a water lily floating just above his forehead, with a human eye nested at its center. The eye blinked occasionally, followed the movements of others. These others had whispered about him mockingly tonight: "Oh, how *precious!*"

They spun to him now. They were all getting animated, from the uncertainty and anxiety and from their respective ingested substances. They had all been on edge ever since the coming of the Hole, and before that, since having graduated from college, and having to formulate new lives for themselves that involved solid plans and commitments.

"An act of *God?*" someone said, misunderstanding the man with the lily-pad tattoo and thinking to deride him. "Or is that what they have under a dome? A trapped god?"

Defensively, the frail-looking young man retorted, "There isn't any God. But there are things we'll never understand, and this could be one of them, and that's fine by me."

"*Oooh!*" said Myke, wiggling the fingers of both hands in the air spookily. He had approached Nahool unseen, and embraced her from the side unexpectedly, sliding his hand along the midriff exposed by her shirt, and he nuzzled her neck through tight dark curls.

Nevertheless, Nahool had broken up with him the next day, and to be honest, Myke hadn't seemed all that upset about it… which in turn only upset *her* all the more.

• • •

The apartments in the old factory tended to be small. The flats in Nahool's section of the building had once been individual offices set along carpeted hallways. In other former departments, on the ground floor like hers or upstairs, some flats were little more than one-time office cubicles now fully enclosed for privacy, while some of the actual factory machinery had been left in place and converted into living spaces for other tenants to nestle inside. Due to the smallness of all these varied flats, therefore, as far as Nahool knew no one had a laundry machine in their own unit and everyone used the communal machines in the basement.

She had taken the big clunky freight elevator that communicated between all the floors, and was pleased to find no one else in the basement; no one wanting to make empty small talk, no one to steal furtive looks at her body. The bricks of the walls down here had once been painted yellow but were now mottled black with mildew. Sooty webs festooned exposed pipes and power cables overhead. Articles of clothing and a few home decorations, toys, and other odds and ends had been laid out on one of the tables used for folding clothes. These were a combination of lost-and-found articles and used items people had left for anyone who might want them, but Nahool never knew which status was which for any given article. She had left a few of Myke's overlooked belongings there and she was weirdly relieved to see the last of them were gone.

She actually liked the damp, subterranean smell down here, overlaid with the smell of warm air wafting laundry detergent. She liked the humming quiet that she had all to herself right now. It was like an externalized comfortable headspace.

Having loaded her clothing into one of the laundry units, she leaned her bottom against the edge of another folding table to read news stories on her wrist comp, reluctant as always to leave her clothing unattended lest some items be stolen, as had happened in the past. Of course, she didn't have to scroll far through the stories to see they were still talking about the Hole. A picture of it accompanied the article.

In this dramatic shot, which Nahool opened up into a three-dimensional hologram that floated above her forearm, two uniformed guards cradling big assault engines stood watch over the clear dome that housed the Hole, one to either side. She had read that an energy barrier to house the anomaly had been considered but dismissed, as no one was sure if the Hole might interact in an undesirable way with a force field. The Hole itself… well, once again Nahool could see why some had suggested it was a black hole. Within that clear vessel, about a foot off the base, hovered motionless a perfect oval, matte black, two-dimensional and with sharply defined edges. An oval about the size of a human head.

No instrument could see into it. Several Tikkihottos had even been summoned to try to peer into it, without success. But objects could be inserted: several drones had been introduced into the oval, and had vanished and not returned and no communication could be established with them.

The Hole had simply appeared one day, and what this particular image didn't show in its narrow field of focus was *where* it had materialized: in a basement used for storage under a pizza shop on Forma Street. The pizza shop employee who had discovered the Hole, upon descending to see what had caused a tremendous bang down there—like a hovercar collision, as he later described it—ended up losing his arm just below the elbow for being too curious. He was interviewed in the hospital later but spoke calmly, as he swore he had felt no pain at the severance, or disintegration, of his appendage, and still didn't. He insisted, though, he could feel his lost arm *somewhere* else, grasping at empty air, though it was suggested this was merely the phantom limb effect.

There had been an earthquake in the city, with the pizza shop at the epicenter, that much could be agreed upon, but nothing like the great earthquake that had caused so much damage to Punktown some decades back. Only 4.0 in magnitude, so how seriously could one take some of the reports that came in from all over the city (without regard for what should have been a diminishing area of effect, radiating from that epicenter), claiming all manner of damage, from cracks in walls to people thrown out of bed to sinkholes opening in a number of people's apartments? And then there were the subsequent crippling headaches, the attacks of anxiety if not outright panic; reports of strange behavior in pets, even alleged poltergeist activity. Claims of birds spotted flying backwards, dogs barking-blurting a word or two in English, and the nightmares. Chilling nightmares, of feeling displaced somehow, adrift on an icy ocean or lost in a titanic maze or misty prehistoric forest.

Nightmares. That much Nahool could attest to. Just the one, but it had shaken her.

She sucked the hologram back into the wrist comp, scrolled to another story, something less confounding. An ugly chunk of celebrity gossip. She hated this celebrity, so she took some satisfaction in reading about their romantic woes. It was while she was skimming this article that something in her peripheral vision drew her complete attention.

Behind the laundry unit into which she had loaded her clothing was an open area in the yellow bricks, low to the floor. One might have thought this was to facilitate the passage of water pipes or power cables or such into the back of the machine, except that these connectors passed up the wall beside the gap in the bricks, to join an overhead network to which all the machines were linked. The edges of this opening were erratic, as if not only full bricks had been removed but half bricks, all of it smashed out, no doubt, though no rubble appeared to have gathered either on this side of the opening or in that dark space behind the wall. It had apparently been cleared away. Someone had had a reason for breaking open this section of wall, back there, but that reason wasn't apparent to her.

Strangely, she thought of the intruder who had tried forcing her into her own flat that time, before her neighbor came to her aid. She wondered how long this opening had been here, masked behind the laundry unit, visible to her for the first time only because of where she had propped herself. Did it even date back to when this building had been a factory, prior to the coming of the colonists? Or was it something more recent?

As she stared down at the gap in the wall, what looked like the tips of several fingers—as purple-black as those of a corpse—curled slowly around the severed end of one of the bricks.

Nahool drew in a deep intake of breath, removed her bottom from the edge of the table and put a backwards step between herself and the laundry unit, but as she continued staring, an animal laboriously pulled the rest of its body into view, emerging fully from the wall. It left a glistening, silvery trail of slime behind it, and Nahool realized there were a few streaks of this slime already across the mildewed yellow bricks behind the machine. The creature, when completely in view, proved itself to be a mollusk with five tapered arms, about the size of a child's hand, like a dark purplish starfish. But a land-dwelling starfish? Then

Nahool realized the thing was familiar. It reminded her very much of a kind of indigenous slug she had learned about in school as a child, when she had been very much interested in biology and particularly paleontology. In fact, she had dreamed back then of becoming a paleontologist.

She leaned in close to the slug-thing, less wary of it now, and took a picture of it using her wrist comp.

Having inserted a detergent pod into the machine and started its initial cycle, Nahool moved to a plastic chair by one of the other folding tables. While her clothes were washed and then dried in the same humming unit, she ran a net search on the animal she had stolen a picture of.

It didn't take long for a match and report. The report identified the purplish, five-armed slug as an invertebrate that had been considered extinct for over two hundred million years.

"No way," Nahool said, looking up, but from this angle she couldn't see the creature where it inched itself along the wall behind the running laundry unit. The artist's rendering in the report was a perfect match. Logically, or in denial, Nahool might have suggested to herself that this animal must be from another world, either brought here as some race's food source, or as a pet, or as a stowaway in a teleported freight shipment. Her intuition told her, however, that none of these were the case; that the slug's appearance was connected to—another direct consequence of— the appearance of the Hole.

It was more than an intuition. It was, to her, a certainty. Another sign, however humble, that change had come to her city.

She read about the prehistoric slug for a while, then drifted to articles about other creatures she had enjoyed reading about as a child. She used to fantasize about time traveling to ancient cycad forests, to study long-extinct fauna in person. Her youthful imagination had been so strong that, staring raptly into artwork meant to represent such scenes, it had almost felt like she truly had transported herself.

The gentle beeping of the laundry unit woke her from her reverie. Her clothing was finished. She got up from the chair, went to the machine, began pulling out and folding her warm laundry on the table where she had propped herself before. She craned her neck to look behind the machine for the slug, but saw only its gooey trail. It had disappeared back behind the wall.

Nahool placed the last articles of clothing onto the pile in her basket, took it by its handles, and turned toward the freight elevator… which had been called upstairs a little while ago by someone on one of the other floors. She set her basket down near her feet and rang to call for it, and just as she lowered her finger from the button she heard a gunshot above her.

Handguns could easily enough be made to fire silently, whether what came out of their barrel was a bolt of energy or a solid projectile, but some people *chose* to use guns that made a loud bang. It was part of the threat, part of the experience, for them. A lot of gangs stole weapons and modified them for maximum noise, or even 3D printed their own.

Nahool froze. The boom was so loud, her first thought was that it was the Hole again. She remembered that pizza worker saying he heard what sounded like the impact of two hovercars colliding. In its basement across the city, had the Hole suddenly grown bigger, bursting its encasing shell? Or had a second Hole opened… perhaps somewhere just above her, the sound carrying down the brick-lined elevator shaft?

But following the boom she heard a man screaming in a high-pitched voice upstairs, and another man's voice, too, muffled but shouting, angry… then a second bang. Nahool understood then that it was an attack, and it had to be in the area of the building's rear door, on the ground floor, where there had once been loading docks. That was where the freight elevator was.

Its buzzer started ringing, then. Long, frantic buzzes. She had called the elevator to descend for her, but now someone else was in need of it. Apparently, desperate need.

More high-pitched screams, and two more booms echoing down the elevator shaft in a cascade of sound. The screams were abruptly cut off, but she could hear the elevator rattling as it continued ponderously descending, most likely from the uppermost level.

Intruders, muggers... this was Punktown. Gang members, gangsters, violent mutants. She had read that crime, already of legendary proportions in this city, had seemed to increase since the appearance of the Hole.

Nahool left the basket where it lay, looked around wildly for a place to hide. The victim, dead or dying, might have made it into the elevator, might be lying in there bleeding. It was still slowly descending. The shooter might come following after, via the stairs instead, to make certain his victim was dead. Or, in pursuit, the shooter might have jumped into the elevator with him already.

The elevator began to settle into place at the bottom of the shaft. In seconds, its safety cage and double metal doors would slide open.

Nahool sprang toward the still-warm machine where she had cleaned her clothing. She squeezed herself behind it, sank down, and crawled into the rough opening there just as she heard the doors clatter open. Trying not to make any sound, she didn't stop crawling even when the whole of her body had passed through the wall. There was a low, dark passage here, maybe an old air duct—maybe the wall had been broken away here to get at it—and she continued along it on hands and knees, ignoring the veils of spiderwebs that she butted her head and shoulders through, and which clung to her in tatters.

Something soft, sticky, squished under her right palm. Oh God, it must have been that slug. She felt badly but didn't look to find out, only wiped her hand once across her pants leg and kept scurrying. What little light came into the passage from the basement was almost lost behind her now.

She didn't hear any further sound from the basement after the elevator doors had clanged all the way open. No dying moans, no assassin's footsteps. Her guess, then, was that the victim hadn't made it into the elevator, after all; it had responded first to her earlier call, descended right on past him. Still, she wasn't going to come out until she was sure. She would steal even deeper inside the unlit brick passage, to minimize the risk of being heard when she finally stopped to call the authorities on her wrist comp.

Was she deep enough into the passage, at least, to turn on her wrist comp's flashlight feature, if only to a dim setting, so she could see? She almost preferred not to see; to not see the webs she was tearing through, and the weavers no doubt poised within them. Still, she thought it might be a good idea, as long as she kept the beam facing forward instead of back toward the opening. Nahool stopped advancing, found she could rise up on her knees without bumping her head, and activated her wrist comp's light.

A subdued glow illuminated her surroundings, and Nahool discovered she had entered a small circular chamber, still lined in brick, though it wasn't painted yellow in here. It couldn't be called a room, really; the ceiling was still too low to permit standing fully upright, and there were no furnishings. It was more a nexus point, because rounded openings ringed the little chamber. There were five of these openings, including the one she had just passed through without realizing it. But she took in all of these details only in a flash of awareness, because what commanded her attention most profoundly was the face her wrist comp's glow revealed. The light glittered in wary eyes fixed on her own.

"Oh my God!" Nahool gasped.

"Shh," said the solidly built Earther woman who sat on the floor of the nexus chamber, her back propped against the space between two of the black openings. "I thought I heard shooting out there."

They had recognized each other. The woman who had been sitting here in pitch darkness was Nahool's neighbor from across the hallway.

"The shooting's upstairs," Nahool whispered. "I didn't see you come in here. Did you crawl in before me?"

"You came in from the basement?" the neighbor asked. "I came in through there." She pointed to an opening to the left of the one Nahool had emerged from.

"Yes," said Nahool. She settled into a seated position, too, pulling in her legs and leaning her back against the space between the opening she had crawled through and the one her neighbor said she had come through. Then, glancing about, she spotted another figure, smaller than her neighbor, lying curled on its side in a fetal position on the floor in another space between the openings. "Oh!" she hissed.

"Don't worry... it's harmless. It's always in here. I think it lives down here."

Was it an animal, or a sentient being? Granted, there were many sentient races in Punktown and more coming all the time, but Nahool couldn't recall ever seeing this one about on the streets before. She could only ascertain that the dozing life form was lizard-like, covered in dusty grey scales, with a blunt snout. Its three black eyes glistened, lidless. Maybe it wasn't sleeping? Maybe it was just calmly lying there listening to them?

"It doesn't talk… just smiles all the time," the neighbor went on.

Nahool returned her attention to the woman, whispered, "So are you hiding from the shooting, too?"

"No," said the neighbor, nudging her own wrist comp awake to glance at the time. "I've been down here almost an hour."

"Why?" asked Nahool.

The neighbor seemed to hesitate, searching for the right thing to say, but finally all she said was, "It's quiet. It's peaceful. This whole city gets to be… you know."

Nahool nodded. "Yeah. I know."

"I just like it in here. I come in here every day now, since I found it."

"I'm sorry to bother you, then. I was just afraid… about that shooting."

"It's okay. You can stay here, too."

"I should really call the forcers about that shooting, though," Nahool said.

"Go ahead. Just don't tell them where you are. I'd rather they not know about this place."

"Okay, sure. There's no reason for them to know where I am."

In a hushed voice, Nahool called the emergency number for Punktown's law enforcement, and reported the gunfire and screaming she had heard in her apartment building, but didn't reveal where she was hiding. She exited the call as quickly as she could. As she was lowering her arm, she saw a figure crawling into the nexus chamber from one of the openings opposite and again gasped.

"Hello," said the newcomer, looking up to nod in greeting to Nahool's neighbor. Then the newcomer assumed a sitting position, crossing his legs in his lap. He was a fragile-looking young man, with a lily-pad holographic tattoo floating at his forehead, a seemingly aware human eye blinking at its center. He noticed Nahool and nodded to her also. "Ah! Hello."

"I know you," she said.

"Oh?"

"We were at a party together, a few weeks ago."

"Really? I'm sorry if I don't remember," the newcomer said quietly. Did he know about the shooting, or did one automatically become hushed, as if in reverence, when they entered this chamber? "Let's just say I'm usually not in a perfectly clear state of mind at social gatherings. A bad habit… but I'm working on it. Coming in here helps."

"I see," Nahool said.

The lizard-thing stirred a little (in its sleep, or to listen in on their conversation better?). Nahool could see what her neighbor meant about it always smiling. Its long lipless mouth seemed perpetually held in a good-natured smile. She had the sense now that its three tiny eyes were indeed consciously and placidly studying her.

"What is this place?" she asked the two Earthers.

The cross-legged man shrugged. "Just some little pocket in the city. I first found it a couple weeks ago."

"I found a hole in the back of my closet, behind some boxes," the neighbor explained. "It wasn't there when I moved in. That's how I found my way here."

"I think the earthquake from the Hole opened up this place," said the man.

"I think the Hole might have *made* this place," said the woman.

"It's either very old, or very new," the man concluded.

Scuttling sounds could be heard in the throat of one of the other off-branching low tunnels. They all turned their heads to see a fifth being entering the chamber. This person, who also settled into a sitting position against the circular wall, was a Tikkihotto woman, with spiky violet-dyed hair, her eye tendrils stirring warily. "Who's this?" she asked the others, most of her ocular tendrils pointing toward Nahool.

"She's okay," said the woman from across the hall. "She's my neighbor."

"Oh," said the Tikkihotto woman. "Okay."

"Nice to meet you," Nahool said, to reassure her. This woman seemed familiar to her, too, but one saw so many faces, belonging to so many races, in such a massive city.

"This is a safe place," said the Tikkihotto, as if she anticipated some question from Nahool. A question about why she had just crawled in here, despite the webs and grime and dank smell, especially given how nicely she was dressed, in the neat suit of a businesswoman.

The Earther man with the hologram tattoo had tilted back his head and closed his eyes, apparently to meditate. Even the holographic eye closed dreamily, and Nahool saw REM movements beneath the lid.

She asked her neighbor, "How long do you people tend to stay in here?"

The woman shrugged. "That's up to you."

"Is it always around this time?"

The Earther woman looked to the Tikkihotto woman. "Yeah… I guess it is. More or less." She looked back to Nahool. "Do you think you'll be coming back here tomorrow?"

Oddly, Nahool didn't need to think about her answer. "Yes. I guess I'd like to."

The Earther woman smiled. The lizard seemed always smiling. The Tikkihotto woman said, "That would be nice."

Since her anxiety about finding others down here had passed, and since everyone had fallen comfortably silent, Nahool now had time to look above her and focus on something that had pretty much remained only a background detail for her before.

Stuck to the ceiling of the circular nexus chamber, with its five off-branching spokes, were a good number of those dark purplish, prehistoric slugs. The starfish-like creatures inched along in their slow, moist way, crawling blissfully over each other's bodies. They accidentally created enigmatic, intersecting patterns with the silvery ink of their trails, like indecipherable messages. Nahool smiled broadly up at them, not self-conscious about her great Choom grin, not down here. She felt the wonderment of a child, gazing up at them. The creatures had no place else to be, no predators here; they existed with each other in equanimity.

They were beautiful, and Nahool's eyes filled with grateful tears. They were a living constellation.

# THERE WAS A TIME

## BY CLIVE BARKER

There was a time
when all the world,
and sky and stars
and the dark between the stars
was called holy,
and shown its simple due.
The shore and sea were deities
and every rock and shrub
and scrap of earth blessed
and blessings both;
honoured with prayer or dance
or a bowl of the morning's milk.
And those that gave
the prayer, the dance, the milk
saw their devotion given back
by those powers
who turned the moon,
and coaxed the corn from seed.

If the Great Form of the Universe
is indeed enshrined in the unfurling fern
and in the scalp that rounds
above this thought,
what Doctor,
or Prince or Pope
can claim to better comprehend
the vital work between us
and all things that are
not us,
than those who called the tide
by its secret name
and saw the silver shoals
rise to fill their nets
when they had thanked
the sea with song?

# ACKNOWLEDGEMENTS

**Out of** all possible worlds, I'm grateful to inhabit one where I can work with the best writers, publishers, and editors in the field. Once again, thank you to George Sandison and the team at Titan – your commitment to expanding the genre and publishing quality work never ceases to astound and inspire. A debt of gratitude also goes out to the following, without whom this book wouldn't exist (in this particular timeline): Alastair Reynolds; Clive Barker; Phil and Sarah Stokes; Michael Moorcock; Donald and Kari Grassmann, for their tolerance and tireless support; and Yoshika Nagata, for the spirit and artistic vision that always inspires. This one is dedicated to the memory of my mother, with love.

# ABOUT THE AUTHORS

**CHARLIE JANE ANDERS** is the author of *Dreams Bigger Than Heartbreak*, the second book in a new young-adult trilogy. She's also the author of the short story collection *Even Greater Mistakes*, and *Never Say You Can't Survive* (August, 2021), a book about how to use creative writing to get through hard times. Her other books include *The City in the Middle of the Night* and *All the Birds in the Sky*. She's won Hugo, Nebula, Sturgeon, Lambda Literary, Crawford, and Locus awards. Her fiction and journalism have appeared in the *New York Times*, the *Washington Post*, *Slate*, McSweeney's, *Mother Jones*, the *Boston Review*, Tor.com, Tin House, *Teen Vogue*, *Conjunctions*, *Wired* magazine, and other places. Her TED talk "Go ahead, dream about the future" received 700,000 views in its first week. With Annalee Newitz, she co-hosts the podcast *Our Opinions Are Correct*.

**EUGEN BACON** is African Australian, a computer graduate mentally re-engineered into creative writing. She studied at Maritime Campus, less than two minutes' walk from the Royal Observatory of the Greenwich Meridian. Her books *Ivory's Story*, *Danged Black Thing*, and *Saving Shadows* were finalists at the British Science Fiction Association Awards. Eugen was announced in the honor list of the

2022 Otherwise Fellowships. She has won or been longlisted for or commended in international awards including the Foreword Indies Awards, Bridport Prize, Copyright Agency Prize, Horror Writers Association Diversity Grant, Otherwise, Rhysling, Australian Shadows, Ditmar Awards and Nommo Awards for Speculative Fiction by Africans. Eugen's creative work has appeared in literary and speculative-fiction publications worldwide, including *Award Winning Australian Writing*, the BSFA's *Fission*, *Fantasy Magazine*, *Fantasy & Science Fiction*, Bloomsbury and *The Year's Best African Speculative Fiction*.

A visionary, fantasist, poet, and painter, **CLIVE BARKER** has expanded the reaches of human imagination as a novelist, director, screenwriter, and dramatist. Barker's literary works include such best-selling fantasies as *Weaveworld*, *Imajica*, and *Everville*, the children's novel *The Thief of Always*, *Sacrament*, *Galilee* and *Coldheart Canyon*. The first of his quintet of children's books, *Abarat*, was published in October 2002 to resounding critical acclaim, followed by *Abarat II: Days of Magic, Nights of War* and *Abarat III: Absolute Midnight*; Barker is currently completing the fourth in the series. As an artist, Barker frequently turns to the canvas to fuel his imagination with hugely successful exhibitions across America. His neo-expressionist paintings have been showcased in an eight-volume series, *Imaginer*. Forthcoming are a book of poetry, a short-story collection, and the horror novel *Deep Hill*.

**PAUL DI FILIPPO** sold his first story at the tender age of twenty-three. Since then, he's sold over 200 more, afterwards collected, along with his many novels, into nearly fifty books. He lives in Providence, Rhode Island, in the shadow of H.P. Lovecraft, with his partner Deborah Newton and a cocker spaniel named Moxie. His most recent novel is *The Summer Thieves: A Novel of the Quinary*, a picaresque science-fiction adventure story evoking the styles of Gene Wolfe and Jack Vance.

**PRESTON GRASSMANN** is a Shirley Jackson Award finalist. He began working for *Locus* in 1998, returning as a contributing editor after a hiatus in Egypt and the UK. His most recent work has been published by *Nature*, *Strange Horizons*, *Shoreline of Infinity* and *Futures 2* (Tor). He is the editor of *Out of the Ruins*, published by Titan in 2021. His forthcoming titles include *War in the Linear Heavens* with Paul di Filippo and *The Mad Butterfly's Ball* (co-edited with Chris Kelso for PS Publishing). He currently lives in Japan, where he is working on a book of illustrated stories with Yoshika Nagata.

A former academic and adjunct, **ALIX E. HARROW** is a NYT-bestselling and Hugo Award-winning writer living in Virginia with her husband and their two semi-feral kids. She is the author of *The Ten Thousand Doors of January*, *The Once and Future Witches*, and various short fiction.

**RUMI KANEKO** is a pseudonym for a well-known film director and freelance scenarist for TV shows in Japan. Aside from her work in film and TV, she has also written screenplays and has completed a novel called *Good Morning Jupiter*, which is currently being translated by Preston Grassmann. Her recent translated work has appeared in *The Unquiet Dreamer: A Tribute to Harlan Ellison* (PS Publishing) and *Out of the Ruins* (Titan), and is forthcoming from various publications in the US.

**KEN LIU** is an award-winning American author of speculative fiction. His collection *The Paper Menagerie and Other Stories* has been published in more than a dozen languages. Liu's other works include *The Grace of Kings*, *The Wall of Storms*, *The Veiled Throne*, and a second collection, *The Hidden Girl and Other Stories*. He has been involved in multiple media adaptations of his work including the short story "Good Hunting," adapted as an episode in Netflix's animated series *Love, Death + Robots*; and AMC's *Pantheon*, adapted from an interconnected series of short stories. "The Hidden Girl," "The Message," and "The Cleaners" have also been optioned for development. Liu previously worked as a software engineer, corporate lawyer, and litigation consultant. He frequently speaks at conferences and universities on topics including futurism, cryptocurrency, the history of technology, and the value of storytelling. Liu lives with his family near Boston, Massachusetts.

**IAN MCDONALD** is a writer of the fantastic living just outside Belfast in Northern Ireland. His first novel, *Desolation Road*, was published in 1988. It won the Locus Award for Best First Novel. He's been nominated for every major SFF award and won a few. His most recent novels are *Moon Rising*, the third part of his Luna trilogy, and *Hopeland*.

**ANNALEE NEWITZ** writes science fiction and nonfiction. They are the author of the book *Four Lost Cities: A Secret History of the Urban Age* and the novels *The Future of Another Timeline* and the Lambda Literary Award-winning *Autonomous*. As a science journalist, they are a writer for the *New York Times* and elsewhere, and have a monthly column in *New Scientist*. They have published in the *Washington Post, Slate, Popular Science, Ars Technica, The New Yorker,* and *The Atlantic,* among others. They are also the co-host of the Hugo Award-winning podcast *Our Opinions Are Correct*. Previously, they were the founder of io9.com, and served as the editor-in-chief of Gizmodo.

**YUKIMI OGAWA** lives in a small town in Tokyo, Japan, where she writes in English but never speaks the language. Her fiction can be found in such places as *Clarkesworld, The Magazine of Fantasy & Science Fiction, Strange Horizons,* and more. In 2021, she was finally translated into Japanese.

**CHANA PORTER**, writes the *New York Times,* "uses incongruity and exaggeration to suggest some midnight-dark truths about human life and endeavor." She is an emerging playwright, speculative novelist, and education activist. Their plays have been developed or produced at New Georges, Playwrights Horizons, The Catastrophic Theatre, La MaMa, Rattlestick Playwrights Theatre, Cherry Lane, The Invisible Dog, and Movement Research. The *Houston Press* writes, "Porter's type of risky storytelling is, well…. like a lion's roar in an all too often timid jungle." She is a MacDowell Fellow, a New Georges Audrey Resident, a Target Margin Artist-in-Residence, and the recipient of an Honorable Mention for the Relentless Prize. She is currently writer-in-residence at the Catastrophic Theatre in Houston. Chana is a co-founder of the Octavia Project, a free summer writing and STEM program for Brooklyn teenage girls and non-binary youth. She has taught her embodied creativity course, "Writing from the Body," at the University of Houston, Fordham University, Hampshire College, Goddard College, Weber State University, and with Sarah Lawrence's Global Classroom. Their debut novel, *The Seep,* is out from Soho Press and Brilliance Audio, with starred reviews from *Publishers Weekly, Booklist, Library Journal,* and *Foreword Reviews. The Seep* is an ABA Indie Next Pick for February 2020. Chana is a queer Jewish genderfluid alien grateful to be embodied in human form.

**ALASTAIR REYNOLDS** was born in Barry, South Wales, in 1966. He studied at Newcastle and St Andrews universities and has a PhD in astronomy. He stopped working as an astrophysicist for the European Space Agency to become a full-time writer. *Revelation Space* and *Pushing Ice* were shortlisted for Arthur C. Clarke Awards; *Revelation Space*, *Absolution Gap*, *Diamond Dogs*, *Turquoise Days*, and *Century Rain* were shortlisted for British Science Fiction Awards; and *Chasm City* won the British Science Fiction Award for Best Novel.

**JAYAPRAKASH SATYAMURTHY** is a writer and musician based in Bangalore, India. His previous publications include the novella *Strength of Water*, the short-story collection *Come Tomorrow*, and *Broken Cup*, a volume of collected poetry. He plays bass guitar for the doom-metal band Djinn and Miskatonic, and lives with his wife in a house full of books, records, and rescued cats and dogs.

**D.R.G. SUGAWARA** has been published widely throughout Japan, writing science fiction for various markets until his semi-retirement in the late '90s. He is often regarded as The Box Man of Ueno Station, named after a character in a novel by Kobo Abe. But unlike the eponymous character from that story, he doesn't wander the streets of Ueno with a box over his head. Instead, he lives surrounded by books and magazines from every era of the genre. His most recent poem, "Live Inside Your Own Sky" (PS Publishing), was highlighted in a recent issue of *Sci Fi Magazine* and "The Box Man's Dream" appeared in *Out of the Ruins* (Titan, 2021). He is currently working on a book of poetry.

**JEFFREY THOMAS** is the author of such novels as *Deadstock* (Solaris Books), *Blue War* (Solaris Books), and *The American* (JournalStone), and his short-story collections include *Punktown* (Prime Books), *The Unnamed Country* (Word Horde), and *Carrion Men* (Plutonian Press). His stories have been reprinted in *The Year's Best Horror Stories XXII* (editor: Karl Edward Wagner), *The Year's Best Fantasy* *and Horror* #14 (editors: Ellen Datlow and Terri Windling), and *Year's Best Weird Fiction* #1 (editors: Laird Barron and Michael Kelly). Thomas lives in Massachusetts.

**LAVIE TIDHAR** is the author of the World Fantasy Award-winning *Osama* (2011), the Seiun award-nominated *The Violent Century* (2013), the Jerwood Fiction Uncovered Prize-winning *A Man Lies Dreaming* (2014), the Campbell Award- and Neukom Prize-winning *Central Station* (2016), the Prix Planète SF award-winning and Locus and Campbell award-nominated *Unholy Land* (2018), the British Fantasy Award-nominated *By Force Alone* (2021), *The Hood* (2021), and *Escapement* (2021). He is also the author of middle-grade novel *Candy* (2018 UK; as *The Candy Mafia*, 2020 US), created the comics mini-series *Adler* (#1–5, 2020), and edited *The Best of World SF: Volume 1* (2021) and *Volume 2* (2022).

**ALVARO ZINOS-AMARO** is a Hugo and Locus Award finalist who has published fifty stories, as well as over a hundred essays, reviews, and interviews, in a variety of professional magazines and anthologies. These venues include *Analog, Apex, Lightspeed, Beneath Ceaseless Skies, Galaxy's Edge, Nature,* the *Los Angeles Review of Books, Locus,* Tor.com, *Strange Horizons, Clarkesworld, The Year's Best Science Fiction & Fantasy, Cyber World, This Way to the End Times, The Unquiet Dreamer, It Came from the Multiplex, Shadow Atlas,* and many others.

# INFINITE STARS: DARK FRONTIERS

## EDITED BY BRYAN THOMAS SCHMIDT

The definitive collection of explorers and soldiers, charting the dark frontiers of our expanding universe. Amongst the infinite stars we find epic sagas of wars, tales of innermost humanity, and the most powerful of desires – our need to create a better world.

*Infinite Stars: Dark Frontiers* continues the acclaimed anthology series featuring today's finest SF authors writing new stories set in their most famous worlds. Authors include David Weber, Becky Chambers, Curtis C. Chen, Orson Scott Card, and Susan R. Matthews. The unparalleled collection also offers masterpieces by famous legends including Arthur C. Clarke, E.E. "Doc" Smith, and Robert Heinlein.

For more fantastic fiction, author events,
exclusive excerpts, competitions, limited editions and more

VISIT OUR WEBSITE
**titanbooks.com**

LIKE US ON FACEBOOK
**facebook.com/titanbooks**

FOLLOW US ON TWITTER AND INSTAGRAM
**@TitanBooks**

EMAIL US
**readerfeedback@titanemail.com**